MOTHER, REBEL, MISFIT, SLEUTH

LISA NICHOLAS

BLOODHOUND
BOOKS

www.bloodhoundbooks.com

Print ISBN: 978-1-917449-8-85

For Mum and Dad,
thank you for everything.

11 December 2023

Hey Wanda, I'm finally writing a journal. It must be ten years since you gave it to me, so the dates are all wrong, but I've crossed them out and I'll write my own in. See, I'm using my initiative at last. You told me you pinched it from the stationery cupboard at work and I knew, even then when I was just a stupid, angry kid, you were only saying it to prove something to me – to get me to trust you, to like you – at the time I wouldn't have understood why anyone would have cared what I thought. "I'm not all about rules", you'd say, as you filled out another form, the social services logo staring at me from every page. I'm sorry I was such a pain. You never stopped trying, though, did you? Next time you check in on me I'll tell you I've started the journal – and I'll tell you why – because it's big news, Wanda, and it's going to change everything. I'm going to record every moment of this, so, here goes...

ONE

FEBRUARY 2025

Mayor Susannah Wilson adjusts her chains and fixes her best smile, newly whitened teeth on show for the cameras. The skies above the Town Hall steps are starting to darken and she is worried the shot won't be cheerful enough. They need to get a move on but, of course, Mila Kiss is not where she ought to be.

'Where *is* she?' Susannah hisses in Lord Fabien Knutsworth's ear. Fabien shrugs, resigned to his constant inability to locate his girlfriend, trusting she'll show up when she's ready. 'Fabien, that's not good enough,' Susannah scolds. 'Look – it's Chris-Whatsit from BBC Radio Lancashire! He's not quite as dashing as his voice suggests, *that* I'll concede, but he's still very important.' Susannah smooths down her swishy blonde bob, making sure that any fly-away strands are in place. 'Oh my good giddy aunt, what is she wearing?' Susannah says, elbowing Fabien, who looks up to see Mila walking up the steps, a black corset over an old Iron Maiden T-shirt, skinny black jeans adorned with metal chains, her enormous rock boots giving her extra height. 'Fabien!' Susannah hisses behind clenched teeth. 'They have cameras! Didn't we tell her to wear something smart? Something *on brand?*'

'To be fair, I think that corset was quite expensive,' Fabien replies, his amusement not well hidden.

'Corsets are supposed to be worn beneath clothing, Fabien.'

'Hello,' Mila says as she reaches the podium erected specially for their big moment, 'ready?'

Susannah tuts – not even an apology, let alone an explanation.

Fabien kisses her and squeezes her hand, but Mila doesn't seem to notice.

As Susannah taps the microphone in front of her, waves to the gathered press, and unfolds her pre-prepared and well-rehearsed speech, Mila begins. 'I am Mila Kiss, and this is Fabien Knutsworth.'

'*Lord* Fabien Knutsworth,' Susannah corrects. After all, they have microphones and notepads and her first big press opportunity as mayor will set the tone for her entire reign. Susannah isn't sure if reign is quite the right word and makes a mental note to Google it later. She tells herself not to refer to herself as reigning today, in case they report her as having airs and graces, which, of course, she doesn't. 'And I'm Mayor Susannah Wilson.'

Oblivious to Susannah's plans to use this opportunity to solidify her role as mayor, community stalwart, and generally central to Mila's success story of war refugee turned community charity leader, Mila continues. 'Together, Fabien and I run the Last Chance Cooperative.' Standing tall and proud, shoulders back, head up and facing the audience, Mila doesn't notice, even out of the corner of her eye, Susannah's face going almost purple with restrained indignation. 'Our charity provides legal, technical, financial, and practical support to individuals and groups who have been let down by the system, and–'

'And as the newly elected mayor, I have selected the Last Chance Cooperative as my chosen charity for my twelve-month rei – er, *stint*, as... well... mayor.' *Stint?* Susannah can't believe she said that, or that she almost said reign. Mila has completely thrown her off. Behind her she can hear voices. She specifically asked Security Stu to keep the steps and entrance totally clear. It won't do to have background noise on the BBC, even just the local programme. She turns to see a greasy-haired woman arguing with another woman she recognises from the Town Hall corridors.

Mila takes her chance to resume her own speech. 'The Last Chance Cooperative will fight tirelessly for justice,' she reiterates to the press, as Fabien nods along, 'catching those who slip through the net.'

'And what do the likes of the Knutsworths know about justice?' a voice in the crowd shouts.

Chris-Whatsit from BBC Radio Lancashire suddenly looks a bit less bored. Susannah looks aghast, and Mila looks furious.

'After all, wasn't Lord Knutsworth embroiled in a financial scandal last year, and that just disappeared, eh?' They locate the speaker, a spotty young man, notepad in hand, other hand waving about in the air holding a chewed-up biro. 'Gareth Davies, *Farlington Gazette.*'

'That was all cleared up,' Fabien says, clearing his throat.

But the young reporter hasn't finished with them yet. 'And we reported Mila as a main suspect in the murder of your father, the Late Lord Knutsworth, just last July? Yet here you are, wandering around free, owning castles.'

'Steady on, my father was proven to have died of natural causes. And we don't live in a castle,' Fabien says.

'It's a *hall*,' Susannah adds, 'and neither of these nice young people did anything wrong.'

'That is, in fact, why we are here today, Gareth Davies,' Mila tells him, calmly and slowly, as if speaking to a particularly stupid child. 'We have personal experience of injustice and hope to help others in the same position.'

'Not many people are in the same position though, are they, love? Living in *halls* as lord and lady of the manor?'

'To be fair, Mila arrived last year as a war refugee, and there are quite a few of those,' Fabien says, wondering how to change the subject before Mila decides to punch Gareth in the face for calling her "love".

Young Gareth Davies opens his mouth to speak again, but Chris-Whatsit from the BBC gets in first. 'This is Town Hall charity PR, not investigative journalism. How about we let them say their piece, eh, son? Try for your in-depth interview another day?'

Gareth Davies looks like he may argue and then most likely thinks better of getting on the wrong side of the nearest thing they have to a local journalistic celebrity. Susannah decides Chris-Whatsit from the BBC might be more dashing than he first appeared. 'Thank you Chris, er, from the BBC,' she says, smoothing down the fly-away hair once more.

Fabien begins to reel off their grand plans, forthcoming fundraising events and website address, but the arguing in the background is getting louder. Everyone on the steps has turned around to see what is going on, the small gathered crowd of media types looking over them and past the podium to see if the growing fracas might be something worth recording. Mila starts to walk towards the quarrelling women, but Fabien gently pulls her back. She allows him to, but Fabien can feel her tense, ready to pounce if someone needs her help, regardless of whether they want it.

The greasy-haired woman clutches her head in her hands. 'I didn't do it! Just please, believe me!'

Susannah suddenly places the other woman, hair somehow too long and wild for her age, a flowing velvet skirt, bangles that clink and clatter as she moves, and a soft, sing-song voice. Susannah recalls the woman is a social worker, known for organising bake sales and looking earnest. Too earnest, someone once told Susannah at the water cooler as they kept their heads down, avoiding her calls for sponsorship. Always getting attached to her clients, apparently. Susannah can't quite remember her name... Willow, Wendy...

'Wanda! I need her; you can't take her from me!' shouts the woman with the greasy hair. Ah – Wanda, Susannah thinks. She looks around and, thank God, sees Security Stu heading their way. Still though, it's all a bit messy, not at all the neat event she had so carefully orchestrated. The social worker sends Stu away with a sort of "I've got this" gesture, which seems entirely misplaced to Susannah. The situation is out of control so she tries to grab Stu's attention, but he's gone back in already, which Susannah decides is very unprofessional, given the potential threat the altercation could pose.

The social worker reaches out to the woman who is now sobbing, saying something in a quiet voice, but she pushes her away. 'Screw you!' she shouts and starts to storm down the steps. 'You promised! And now I've got nothing and it's *your* fault!'

Susannah hopes the various local news outlets and journalists have stopped recording, as this really isn't a typical scene in their community and it's not at all the impression she would like to give.

The woman, face streaming with tears now, pushes past Susannah, Mila, and Fabien, and barges through the gaggle of reporters. A few manage to capture the moment; a skirmish can always evolve into a story on a slow news day.

'Jo! Come back, let's talk in my office!' calls the social worker.

But the woman doesn't look back this time. Instead, she picks up her pace, running across the road to the town square, almost colliding with a motorcyclist while cars around her beep. She disappears around a corner.

'I do hope that doesn't turn out to be the main story they run,' says Susannah to Fabien and Mila. 'We should probably take some final questions, end on a good note?'

Mila sighs, and slips Fabien's hand, chasing down the steps, causing another set of honks and beeps and *watch outs* as she takes the same corner at speed, just in time to see the woman collapse onto a wooden bench underneath a pretty oak tree. She slows her run to a gentle walk and quietly sits next to the woman on the bench. 'Jo, is it?' she asks. 'I'm Mila.'

TWO

'What's the matter?' Fabien asks his mother, seated at the breakfast table in Farlington Hall, as Lady Lydia Knutsworth fans herself dramatically with the newspaper.

She takes an audible intake of breath, mouth agape before being quickly covered by a wrinkled yet delicate hand. 'Susannah isn't going to be happy, that I can assure you.' She passes the paper to Fabien, and he puts down his piece of toast.

'Oh dear,' says Fabien.

'What's up?' Mila asks as she enters the room, dropping her car keys on the side, children safely deposited at school. 'Morning, Lydia.'

'You've created quite the stir, I believe, giving chase to that unhinged girl.'

Mila peers over Fabien's shoulder, her own face staring back at her, though at least this time she isn't the *missing war refugee wanted for questioning*. How times change.

'She isn't unhinged. She was upset.'

'And you both had a job to do. As patron of this charity, I must remind you that you need to remain professional at all times. It wasn't easy obtaining official charity status and getting the trustees on board.' In fact, it had been very easy indeed, as Lydia has spent her whole life swanning around doing charity work, which usually consists of hosting luncheons and balls and utilising her great wisdom to provide unsolicited advice. Her telephone book is chock-full of potential trustees and donors and influential types who had gladly helped with PR and fundraising.

The Last Chance Cooperative is a project Lydia is keen to support – the kind of positive contribution that's appropriate for the Knutsworths to make to society. It is supposed to keep Fabien and his quite unmanageable girlfriend out of trouble and out of the papers for the wrong reasons. There have already been countless disagreements about the sort of projects their charity should support. Mila favours ambitious and complex cases involving difficult, unsavoury characters who are apparently *marginalised*, which Lydia suspects is just a polite way of saying down and out. Lydia feels local, contained issues should be their focus. Small wins, minimum controversy, good headlines and attractive pictures in the paper.

'You really must be mindful of our reputation, and the reputations of everyone else involved,' she says.

'Now look here,' Fabien says, pointing to the title, 'it's that dreadful boy, Davies, the young reporter? He had it in for us from the outset. And, by the way, Mother, when did you start subscribing to the local rag? What happened to *The Telegraph*?'

'I don't think your little drama would have made *The Telegraph*, dear – thank goodness.' Lydia shoots a look at the two young people, who made it into the nationals far too many times last year. This is supposed to be a fresh start. Lydia sighs and takes the paper back, flicking through the pages.

'So, why the sudden interest in the *Farlington Gazette*?' Fabien asks.

'I put an advertisement in about the auditions for the Easter show at the church, and I needed to check that they got it right this time,' replies Lydia.

'And did they?' Mila asks, eyebrow arched in mock concern as she takes a big bite of an apple. Juice dribbles down her chin, and forgetting Lydia's feelings about using napkins, she wipes it away with the back of her hand.

'They made two spelling mistakes and one grammatical error; I don't know what they teach them at school these days.'

'Clearly nothing,' Mila replies. 'Karlie and Konstantine are both far stupider since they arrived in the UK, and they are only seven and nine. Just think how dumb they'll be by the time they leave school.'

Lydia bursts into laughter so suddenly that Fabien spills his tea. She is unsure if Mila is serious or not, but sometimes the girl's blunt observations tickle her. She believes in the importance of etiquette as much as the next person, and Mila is in dire need of training. However, her cutting remarks contain a freshness that can, in the right and proper context and definitely not in front of any cameras, liven up the dreariest of conversations and change the tone in seconds. 'Perhaps the children can get a job at the *Gazette* with their poor schooling, and then finally we can control the stories,' Lydia replies.

Now it's Mila's turn to laugh, losing some flecks of apple in the process. She, too, never knows if Lydia is serious or not – and terrifyingly, quite possibly, she is. Mila wouldn't put it past her to feel entitled to control the media. Yet, the old woman's self-belief rivals Mila's and that *is* something she can get on board with: a strong woman is always a good thing, aristocrat or otherwise. Plus, she can't deny Lydia's kindness in not only welcoming Mila, but also her young niece and nephew, who Mila became guardian to when her sister died. Since they arrived last summer, Lydia has surprised everyone with the gusto with which she has embraced her role as Granny.

'Listen,' says Fabien, reading aloud. 'Lord Knutsworth refused to answer questions about his own financial scandal, while Ms Kiss gave chase to a distressed and hysterical woman who had started a fight with officials on the Town Hall steps. Meanwhile, the mayor seemed anything but *"a calm hand for your community"* as her election slogan promised when she stood at the council's by-election last year.'

'Really, Mila, could you not have waited for the event to finish? And Susannah said you were very late, it was almost dark by the time you arrived,' Lydia reinvokes her disapproving tone, her brief amusement safely boxed away.

'I lost track of time,' Mila replies, not looking up. She hates all that PR media nonsense and can't deny the possibility her brain had quite possibly blocked out the time as she had snuggled by a roaring fire reading the poetry of Serhiy Zhadan. 'Oh, by the way, I had a meeting with the playground committee. I'm sorry Lydia, but not being able to afford new swings really doesn't fall under injustice or people being failed by the system.'

'Well, Mila, I really think you should reconsider. What about Konstantine and Karlie?' asks Lydia, who thinks raising money for playground equipment which the council claims it is unable to afford is precisely the type of work their charity should do. In her mind, local children denied a proper playground is absolutely an injustice.

'My niece and nephew have an entire wing and thirty-two acres to play in. I'll ask Danny to build them a rope swing.'

'Hmm, interesting,' Fabien says.

'What?' Mila demands.

'Well, isn't that a bit have versus have-not, darling? You'll ask the gardener to build them a rope swing? Never mind all the other local children.' Fabien bites his lip to hide his smile.

Mila seethes – a little at being caught out on one of her own principles, but mainly at one of her many hated pet-names – *darling* – just so *British*. Fabien only ever uses it to wind her up.

'So, let's open the gardens to everyone.' That'll teach them, Mila thinks, knowing that despite claiming they want to do good, they very much prefer to do it outside of their own gates and without getting too close to controversy. Rumour has it the old, late, Lord Knutsworth pretty much kicked the village out for carriages at ten at the annual ball, switching out lights in rooms full of partygoers, and once even changing into his dressing gown and yawning his way from room to room.

'Absolutely not,' Lydia tells her, and pours more tea. 'And don't look at me like that; you live here, and the children. It isn't as if we are selfish with our space.'

'I only meant the grounds,' Mila says quietly, still uncomfortable about living in their home. If it hadn't been for the children needing more than she was able to give them – being a surrogate mother to her sister's kids had not been part of her life plan – she'd have found a flat, told Fabien she needed to slow down. Now he was hinting about marriage, which was awkward, as that too had been conspicuously absent from her future aspirations. Mila knows what her sister would have said, urging her to jump at the chance of nabbing her Prince Charming – and a charmed life for her orphaned children to boot – but where had marriage got her sister? That's right, six feet under.

'And I need a new housekeeper, I really do. I miss Anna being around the house all the time,' Lydia says.

'Really?' asks Fabien. 'She only lives in the gatehouse down the drive and she and Elodie are always bloody here... and honestly, Mila, *that's* bad enough. I'm with Mother on this issue. Let's not open the grounds.'

'Fine. But Last Chance Cooperative is not for funding swing sets.' Mila didn't expect them to open the grounds, but she isn't wasting any more time on small-fry community projects that don't interest her in the slightest, and are mainly chosen to make the likes of Lydia and Susannah look good in the local paper. She has bigger plans. Jo, for one, whom she'd met the other day in such distress at the press event for the charity. That is a story that does interest her. But Jo had got up to leave as soon as Fabien found them sitting beneath the oak tree, and it was all she could do to quickly give Jo her number, and ask her to call. So far, nothing.

'What *is* the charity for, then?' Lydia asks. 'Come along, you keep telling me you're going to change the world, but we all must start somewhere, and I don't see why it can't be swings.'

It's for Jo, Mila thinks. And women like Jo. But she doesn't know enough to make her argument – yet. From previous attempts to take on other cases she has found that where she sees vulnerability and injustice, they often have a different perspective, veiled by cynicism, seeing only people who have made bad choices of their own volition. Not victims, but willing perpetrators of their own demise. Not charity cases, but people beyond saving. In Mila's view, no one is beyond saving. In the rest of the family's view a new swing set for some middle-class kids is pushing themselves far enough.

'We *did* start somewhere,' Fabien says, increasingly aware of being in the middle of something he probably can't sway, let alone win, but in this moment feeling that the silent Mila beside him, lost in her own thoughts, eyes narrowing involuntarily, poses the greater threat. 'We helped to campaign for the extra teaching assistants at the local primary school, so that children with additional needs didn't have to travel all the way to that special school.'

'And a very good job you did too,' Lydia replies, 'but what next? One must never rest on one's laurels, and you've got your name out there now, although the PR angle could do with some finessing.'

'What on earth do *you* know about PR?' a teasing female voice says, as Elodie wafts into the room, kaftan flowing over paint-splattered denim dungarees, followed dutifully, as always, by her little dog Offal.

'Sis!' Fabien says. 'Here to scrounge breakfast as usual? Would have thought Anna would have taught you to boil an egg by now.'

Mila throws Fabien a look, not appreciating the joke. Anna had been the housekeeper until she and Fabien's younger sister Elodie became an item. Anna and Mila bonded over their shared Eastern European heritage when Mila first arrived in Farlington, and Anna had stood up for Mila and supported her when she felt completely alone. Mila does not think that jokes about Anna's servitude are at all funny. Frankly, Mila finds jokes in general to be vastly overrated by the English.

Anna strolls in behind her girlfriend, and starts tidying up around Fabien and Lydia, until Mila throws her a look too and Anna stops what she is doing and takes a seat. She doesn't mind helping, but it seems to offend Mila enormously.

'Actually, *bro*,' Elodie says, rolling her eyes, 'we already ate a very healthy meal of home-made granola and yoghurt.'

'You made yoghurt?' says Mila. 'Why? They sell it in the shops. And granola.' In the hall she deals with people who expect everything to be done for them, and down the driveway, in Elodie and Anna's gatehouse-come-studio, they feel they have to make everything from scratch and toil the earth with bare hands. Last week they hosted a sound bath, and now Elodie is talking about forest bathing. Mila does not understand any of them.

'Um, no, just the granola. We bought the yoghurt. But it's organic.'

'So, you crushed up some nuts and raisins?' Fabien says, going back to his paper. 'There's bacon and eggs on the side if you're still hungry.'

Elodie ignores the sense of a smirk she gets from behind her buffoon brother's newspaper, and pours tea, swiping a piece of crispy bacon and dropping it into Offal's open mouth. His tail wags furiously as he messily crunches away, hoovering up the crumbs he leaves on the rug as he goes. 'We have an announcement, actually.'

'You're getting married!' Lydia says, quite desperate to have the first gay wedding in Farlington. She even organised a gay pride march in the village last year, and it was Lydia who started the campaign cumulating in Mila's arrival (although she's not sure *everyone* thanks her for that, these days). Despite her outward embodiment of the traditional British class system and insistence upon adherence to social etiquette, Lydia takes great pride in her woke credentials. Her children keep telling her it isn't actually "woke", it's just *normal* to treat people all the same, regardless of gender or sexuality or whatever. Lydia thinks her offspring are very under-appreciative of her efforts to embrace the modern world, given how much trouble she went to in order to learn all the jargon and lingo associated with being an up-to-date, liberal-minded person.

'No, Mother,' Elodie replies, 'we're having a baby!'

Everyone stops sipping and chewing and rustling papers, and stares.

'*Who* is having a baby?' Lydia asks. 'You? Or Anna?'

'We are both having a baby.'

'Two babies? One each?' asks Mila.

'Without wishing to lower the tone at breakfast, presumably there's at least one other person involved?' Fabien says, frowning a bit.

'There are a lot of other people involved, actually,' Elodie says, as her mother swallows a piece of toast down the wrong way, and coughs and splutters and knocks over the milk jug as she attempts to rectify the issue. 'Aren't there, Anna? Lots of men, and women, and *professionals*.'

Anna smiles. 'Elodie, don't tease. We're going to adopt, Lydia. We wanted you all to be the first to know, as we hope you'll all support us.'

Lydia is still finding it hard to swallow. First, her daughter takes up with the housekeeper, and then they shack up. Surely, she had thought, marriage would come next. Children, she hadn't got around to considering, although she'd already started a list of ancestral names for when Fabien and Mila provided the next heir. Maybe she isn't as right-on as she likes to think.

'Well?' Elodie says to the unnaturally quiet people assembled in the room, who by now should be on their feet declaring their best wishes and excitement.

Realising their mistake, everyone rises, Fabien bear-hugging the women, Mila holding each in turn by their upper arms and kissing them generously, wishing them luck. Lydia stands more slowly. 'Of course we support you, darling. Both of you. I just wasn't expecting you to say that, though of course now I think about it... Forgive me,' she says, and kisses her daughter and not-yet-daughter-in-law on both cheeks.

Will anyone in this family ever see fit to get married? Fabien and Mila had better not get any ideas about continuing this modern living arrangement for too long; it's one thing for the youngest daughter to be a bit mad, but quite another for the first son and lord to reject tradition. She must dig out a ring, perhaps Mila would like a darker stone rather than a diamond. Maybe she could offer another to Elodie, but would both women need rings? Lydia decides she needs to do some additional research into modern relationships, and feels suddenly quite tired, despite it not yet being half past nine in the morning.

'They don't just assess us,' Elodie explains, 'but the whole family living here at the hall, which means,' she looks meaningfully at her mother, then at Fabien, but lingers longest on Mila, 'no scandals, no involvement in barely legal, secretive *projects*. Just be normal, for once. I swear this so-called charity is just begging for trouble.'

THREE

Mila turns the hot tap and steaming water tops up the lukewarm bath, raising the temperature back to almost unbearable, just the way she likes it. She adds more bubbles, melts deeper, feeling her skin tingle. She closes her eyes and thinks about Jo.

In just five minutes it hadn't been possible to get much sense out of the distraught woman, raging with anger and repeating herself, concerned more with the unfairness of it all than what had actually happened. What Mila does know is that Jo's baby has been removed from her care, and a permanent adoption has been arranged. But, and this is where it becomes really interesting, Jo is convinced they have taken her baby illegally.

When they saw Fabien approach, Mila acted fast. 'Take my number. If you tell me your story, I'll help if I can.' Jo had looked surprised at first, and then her probably once pretty face, now too thin, a stretch of bad skin hiding her jutting cheekbones, contorted into disbelief; was this woman for real? Jo had told Mila she'd read about their charity online and, completely out of options, had turned up at the Town Hall not really believing anything would come of it. And then she'd spotted Wanda and seen red. 'I can't make any promises,' Mila had continued carefully, 'but if the system has let you down, call me. I'll look into it.' No longer frowning, as if even that was too much energy for this broken young woman, Jo handed Mila her phone and Mila tapped in her digits.

'Hey,' Fabien had said to Mila, 'There you are.' And then, noticing Jo, he had proffered his hand, 'Pleased to meet you,' but she just snatched her phone back, then turned and walked away.

Earlier today, as she'd shared her hopes that Jo would reach out to them, Fabien had accused Mila of irrationally assuming anyone with a sob story and a tough life was always in the right. Hadn't they listened for over an hour as Elodie and Anna explained everything they knew so far about the adoption process? How far social services go to keep children with birth parents, and how difficult it is to adopt? He suggested that maybe Jo's accusations of illegality and injustice stemmed more from self-pity than reality. He'd told Mila to face facts; Jo had probably lost her baby because she was unfit, and she wouldn't call, because deep down she most likely knew that.

Unfit. Mila ponders the word as she immerses her head beneath the bathwater and re-emerges, red faced, hair slick, the long, dark ends floating on the surface. She makes waves with her hands, the bubbles shifting shape around her, landing on her clavicle, swishing over her concave belly. In a rare moment of playfulness, she pops a few suds onto her nose with her index finder, and blows them into the air. She thinks of helping to bathe Karlie earlier, the mermaid toy rescuing the old Ken doll (she has taught her well), and wonders what makes her "fit" to mother these children traumatised by violence and war and the loss of their mother. And yet they seem to be thriving in a strange country in the oddest of homes, with the most eccentric of families. It's not what her sister had planned for them, but plans change.

What happened to Jo's plans? Mila asks herself. And are they really so changed that she is unfit? Mila hates that word.

'They stole her, my baby,' Jo had said. 'Sarah, she was called. After my sister. She died.'

Mila was visibly shaken. She knew what that felt like, the loss of a sister.

'When I was away,' Jo had explained, between sobs, 'They sent me away, you see, and they took her when I couldn't stop them. It can't be right, what they did, the whole thing – they planned it, they set me up to fail.'

Mila had tried to ask more about what Jo meant by all of this, but Jo had returned to ranting: about the social worker Wanda, who broke her promises, the parents who abandoned her, the boyfriend nobody liked. Then Fabien had turned up.

When she'd relayed the bits of Jo's story she had pieced together to Fabien, he'd simply shrugged as if that explained everything. 'She doesn't take any responsibility, Mila,' he had told her. 'You'd be wasting your time. *Our* time. Besides, she won't call. That would mean getting up and doing something for herself.'

At that, Mila had lost her patience and stormed off to run a bath. After all, Jo had come to the Town Hall in the first place and that was something. Were they seriously going to spend their funds on new swings, rather than helping a woman at rock bottom? Last month, she had read about a woman who had been jailed for life – no extenuating circumstances – for murdering her abusive husband, and they hadn't wanted to help her either. The family solicitor Harrop had even been dragged in to make Mila "see sense", despite her repeated reminders that she too was trained in law in her home country; human rights law in fact, which, she had explained slowly, includes the right not to be beaten by your husband. She had been outvoted and they'd secured the extra teaching assistants instead.

'Mila?' Fabien's voice tentatively floats through the closed bathroom door. 'You still in the bath?'

'Yeah,' she replies, although she has already pulled the plug. The water is draining and she is starting to break out in goosebumps.

'Can I come in?' Nearly all the keys to the internal doors' keyholes had been lost long ago, and nobody had bothered to replace them with bolts. But the family is all spread out so much that she, Fabien, and the children practically have their own house within the house.

'Okay.'

Mila is standing, shivering in the bath as he walks through the door, her knee raised as she readies herself to step out of the huge cast iron bath with brass feet, each in the shape of a lion's paw. He holds out his hand to assist, and then with his other hand he grabs the slightly threadbare but enormous old bath sheet from the towel rail, which is not heated as everything in Farlington Hall is ancient and more often than not, broken. He wraps her in it as though this fierce woman he loves is a delicate bird. Because standing there, skinny and pale, she looks like one to him.

Mila allows Fabien to first embrace her, then kiss her.

'I'm sorry, Mila,' he says, 'I was judgemental about that woman.'

'Jo.'

'Jo,' Fabien corrects himself, 'and if she calls, there is no harm in finding out more, in case we can help, but I do doubt it. I talked to Elodie, and she said if the baby has been permanently removed by the family courts, then that is irreversible. She said it takes a long time for that decision to be made, and they don't make it lightly. They've really done their research.'

Mila sighs, and thinks perhaps he is right. She knows nothing about Jo, except that the look of desperation, the love for her lost baby pouring out was genuine, evaporating in the cool evening air like hot breath. Mila silently concedes she may not be being entirely rational; her evidence is on the light side, more a hunch than anything. She is just so frustrated, so hemmed in. She needs a proper case.

'Are you coming? We have something to show you in the playroom.'

Mila grabs her dressing gown and follows Fabien down the draughty hallway, turning a corner towards the children's playroom. As she enters she sees Fabien has built the most magical den of all magical dens, adorning it with fairy lights and, it appears, using every spare bedsheet and cushion in their part of the house. Her niece and nephew shout from within, 'Surprise!'

She climbs inside and finds a space snuggled in the middle of Karlie, Konstantine, and Fabien, and they start to chatter away about how they constructed the masterpiece. Mila smiles, and for a moment at least, she lets go of the rage inside, and allows herself to feel lucky. 'I love you,' she says to all of them.

In the distance, a few rooms down, a phone rings, the familiar death metal ringtone of Mila's mobile playing tinnily with increasing volume, and the spell is broken.

22 January 2024

I meant to tell you today, when you came over to do the drugs test, that the baby is the size of a peach now. Isn't that nice, Wanda? I imagine a soft, pink little round thing covered in downy hair, and I try to see a face, but I can't, not yet. So in my head it's just my little furry peach-creature bobbing around in my belly. I love this baby so much that nothing else matters. I don't miss Rob – you were right about him. I just delete his texts. What was it you said – "Don't even dignify him with a response" – I like that. I'm never going back, cos I know if I do, they might take her away. That's what you said.

And, not only am I doing the whole writing down my thoughts thing, but I'm "letting go" too, just like you said I should. How about that? I should tell you all this face to face really, but I'm telling you here, where it's quiet and no one can laugh at me. Not that you would, I know that.

Even when they look down their noses at me in the clinic, I just do my breathing, in for four, out for four, like we practised. I don't get angry. Same when Mum and Dad make me feel like shit. They keep printing out articles about babies born addicted to drugs with hep C and stuff. I got off it, didn't I? Wasn't easy, but I did it. I did it for my baby. They say it's to keep me straight, but it makes me panic, Wanda, in case the baby is messed up. And then I do my breathing again, but it doesn't work when I start thinking like that, so I write in my journal instead and try and focus on the future, like you told me to.

I'm going to get a job, and find my own place. I'll buy one of those huge teddy bears for the nursery. I can't bear it here, my parents just looking down on me, wishing it was me who died, instead of Sarah. You know, I used to wish that too, remember I told you that? How I only started with the drugs to numb the pain of her being gone? But I don't feel that way anymore – numb. I'd do anything to bring my sister back, course I would, but now I've got my baby, I want to be alive. I want to be better.

If it's a girl, I'm going to name her Sarah. And she will have the prettiest nursery with the best toys, and we'll go to the park and I'll go back to college to make her proud. You said I'd make a good nurse once, that I had a caring disposition, whatever that means. But, Wanda, the main thing is, I'm actually doing it: I'm building a life and a family of my own.

FOUR

FEBRUARY 2025

'I still think we should both go, Mila. After all, it is *our* charity,' Fabien says, swinging the battered old Defender into the Royal Oak car park. The handbrake moans into place, and the car gives one final jolt of exertion. He still misses his unreliable yet beautiful old Jag, which he'd given up when he'd returned full time from the city to the country and started taking turns at the school run. In under a year he's gone from hedge fund glamour to running the old pile and co-parenting with beautiful, crazy Mila. Life has never – and, he imagines – *will* never be the same. He doesn't mind one bit.

'She won't trust you,' says Mila.

'Because I'm a man?'

'Of course because you're a man. And a posh one, too. Unrelatable.'

'You related to me just fine this morning.' Fabien winks, and Mila raises her eyebrows, shakes her head. Fabien can be such a *boy*.

Mila opens the car door before Fabien can get around to her side do it, mainly to annoy him, and says as she hops down, 'You should have seen her eyes darken when she said she was going to go back to her boyfriend's bedsit. There's something going on there.'

Fabien was surprised when Jo called, and faintly irritated; he hadn't imagined she would be the type to follow through. He might not have been so gung-ho in his support of a hypothetical meeting if he'd believed for one moment the woman would actually get in touch. Clearly, there is nothing they can do for her, no matter how tragic they all agreed that it might be. He is all too aware of Lydia's preoccupation with reputation, and, like Mila, finds it frustrating at times, but Fabien has to admit that he too is keen to get the charity working properly and put some real distance between their present work and the stresses and disasters of the previous year. They can't waste resources or the little goodwill they have started to garner on people Mila feels sorry for, but who ultimately are way outside of their remit.

'She sounded strange on the phone, like she didn't want anyone to hear. She's frightened. I need her to open up.'

'And if it turns out she had her baby taken away for perfectly legal reasons, you'll let it go? You won't try and steal it back or something?'

Mila laughs. 'As if, stupid.'

Fabien laughs too, but feels a bit anxious still.

They pull their collars up against the wind as they quickly stride towards the orange glow seeping out from the little windows of the pub. Mila used to hate this place when she first arrived in Farlington; all the curious eyes appearing from dark corners. She has started to embrace their Friday night tradition since things have settled down: the familiar stench of old ale, the inexplicable room temperature white wine despite being homed in a fridge behind the narrow bar, the warm welcome from friends.

'It's busy tonight,' Fabien remarks, same as he does every Friday. But then he adds, 'What the hell is she doing now?'

Despite half the village of Farlington already squeezed for personal space, Elodie is taking up a large part of one corner with an enormous home-made banner, decorated beautifully – after all, art is Elodie's trade despite her family's protestations that it should really be no more than a hobby. A perfect rainbow forms the backdrop, with a quite realistic portrait of a man Fabien half recognises but can't place. Over his face is a prohibition red circle, its diagonal line cutting his face in two. The banner reads: *WOMEN AGAINST TRADITION*. Next to her is Anna, with Offal, huddled close to her chest, lest he be trodden on.

'That's a pretty good likeness,' comments Mila. 'Here, I got you a beer.' She hands it to Fabien and some spills as he barely looks at it, squinting to try and work out who the man in the picture is, and what his sister is up to. He doesn't have to wait long.

'Frederick Fawcett is homophobic, transphobic, misogynistic!' Elodie shouts to the crowd, which starts to pay some attention, 'but most of all, he's people-phobic!'

'What is she banging on about?' Fabien asks Mila, 'And why is she having a protest in the pub?'

Mila shrugs, smiling. She has seen this guy Fawcett in the paper, and she doesn't like him at all – a born and bred Lancashire man, leveraging his "man of the people" status to gain influence for his agenda, which is anything but normal. Though the Royal Oak in Farlington isn't the obvious choice to host this particular protest. After all, there easily could be a few supporters of his traditionalist agenda in here. Women in the home, married only to men, responsible only for children and housework. 'He runs some weird organisation – a think tank, he calls it. Basically, it's an excuse to lobby his bigoted agenda in a way that looks vaguely official.'

Elodie is mid-speech now, but after hearing the initial

headlines and realising they don't know who or what she is protesting against, the locals' loud chatter soon drowns her out. Fabien muscles through the standing drinkers, muttering apologies, hellos, and, 'How's that lame heifer doing, Harry?' until he reaches the makeshift stage and asks his sister to please sit down and have a drink before Mike, the landlord, ejects her.

'He wouldn't do that!'

'He probably wants to, though, Elodie,' says Fabien. 'Look, you've broken the spring in that old chair, and Harry and his nephews are complaining you're in their spot.'

He points over to Harry and his nephews. They're local farmers, tenants on the Knutsworth's land, and generally the kind of people you want in your corner. Last year Harry sprayed a group of journalists who'd been sniffing around for dirt on Fabien with some real muck.

'Okay, fair enough,' Elodie says, rolling up the banner and, with Anna and Offal, following Fabien back to where Mila is perched on a corner bar stool. 'Two G and Ts please, Mike,' she says, 'and sorry about the chair.'

'So why the pub protest, darling sister?' Fabien asks.

'Oh, we meant to go into Manchester, but the train was cancelled. We protested on the green for a bit, and when it got dark we came here to warm up.'

'And continue the protest,' Fabien clarifies.

'One must never miss a chance to make a difference,' Elodie says, taking a sip of her drink. 'Am I right, Mila?'

'Oh, here comes trouble,' Anna says, nudging Elodie, slurping past the ice with a straw. She passes Offal to her. 'Take him, for protection.'

The women are still giggling mischievously as Fabien and Mila turn back to see what they're talking about. Mayor Susannah Wilson is making a beeline for them.

'Martin told me you were here,' Susannah says sternly, without prior greeting as she reaches the bar.

'Boo, Martin!' Elodie calls back over her shoulder at the mayor's husband, who is looking deep into his lager.

'I've had a number of complaints, Elodie,' says Susannah, 'and I really don't want to escalate this to your mother.'

'I'm twenty-four,' says Elodie.

'Then you should know better, and she,' Susannah gestures to Anna, 'is much older.'

'Charming,' mutters Anna.

'It's just a protest for equal rights,' says Elodie.

'Jenny Beard left a very fraught message on my answering machine that suggested you were shouting quite crudely about the perks of lesbianism as well as chanting statistics on the failures of the traditional family.'

'Yes. And?'

'Well, you need permission to have an event on the green. And not all marriages fail. Martin and I have been married for twenty-seven years this coming May.'

'We are very sorry, Susannah,' Anna says, nudging Elodie once more, 'aren't we?'

'Yes,' says Elodie. 'It's forty-two per cent,' she adds.

'Pardon?'

'That's how many marriages end in–'

Before Elodie can rile Susannah any further, Fabien interrupts. 'May I get you a drink to apologise for my sister's spontaneous rebellion, Lord Mayor?' A cheeky mime of a doffed hat from the actual lord makes Susannah blush, and instantly soften.

'How kind,' she demurs, 'but no thank you, the wine in here is always a funny temperature. The red is cold, the white lukewarm, always been a mystery.'

'What's your take on Frederick Fawcett, then?' Mila asks

Susannah, before she has a chance to escape without a grilling, having dished out her disapprovals.

'Oh, I really don't know,' she replies. 'I only came because my phone hasn't stopped ringing all day, with parishioners upset by the hullaballoo, some of the language and, er, sensitive topics. Then, just when I can reassure people the green is clear, I hear the commotion is continuing in here, while hard-working people try to enjoy a quiet drink.'

'You think homosexuality is a sensitive topic, or that women *should* be kept in the home? How would that work, practically, with you as mayor?' says Mila, smiling.

'Oh no, no, of course not. I mean, I think *some* people like the idea of the return of *some* old-fashioned values, the ones that keep society ticking along nicely. Not all of them, of course.'

'Which ones?' Mila probes.

'Sorry?'

'Which old-fashioned values should we return to?' Mila says.

'Well, for example, a child should have two parents, a mother and a father.' Susannah hears the collective intake of breath. 'Or a mother and a mother, or a father and a father. Two parents, that was the main thing, I think. Except, of course, some single mothers do wonderfully. Just look at Fergie. Her daughters have turned out exceptionally well.' Susannah is looking flustered again; it doesn't seem to take much.

Fabien wonders again if her *"Calm Hand for your Community"* slogan was a poor choice. Still, he takes his role in the village seriously these days, or tries to – how he wishes he could tease and mock and say whatever he liked to whomever he liked – and so he gives Mila a look, half warning, half pleading. 'Balance in all things,' he says.

Martin suddenly appears, and shuffles into the small space the altercation is unfolding within. 'Evening,' he says, nodding to all. 'Shall we get off, love?' he says to his wife, who smiles gratefully.

Recovering her composure, she waves goodbye. 'Have wonderful weekends, everyone, and don't forget the parish council meeting on Monday night. You know we always want to hear your views.'

As soon as the door swings closed behind Susannah and Martin, Fabien, Mila, Elodie, and Anna let the laughter burst out of them, and don't stop for some minutes.

'And don't forget *our* meeting on Monday too,' says Elodie, 'where we absolutely do not want to hear your views, and instead wish you to be on your absolute best behaviour.'

'Ah, the first social worker visit,' Fabien recalls. 'You'll be back in time, Mila? From your meeting with Jo?'

'Of course,' replies Mila, glad to see Fabien has given up trying to attend, and trusts her to make her own, rational judgements about Jo's story.

4 March 2024

She's a girl, Wanda! And she's healthy and has all her proper body parts in the right place, so far as they can tell from the funny little picture. I'm starting to believe it might be okay, you know? When she's born. What was it you said to do? "Manifest my dreams and they will come true." Well, to be honest, I'm still not sure what you mean by that, but she is all I dream of – imagining her when she's born: my healthy baby, her little chest going up and down in time with those gurgling little breaths they do while blowing bubbles, her tiny fingers curling around mine. Breastfeeding her, cos I can as I'm totally clean and healthy, and all the reports say so too.

Normally the hospital appointments have been horrible because I know they're judging me while they prod and poke, waiting to tell me I've messed her up, but the twenty-one-week scan was actually the best day of my life. I feel like I met my baby. My Sarah. They were probably expecting she'd have no arms or something, but she was perfect, and now they have to be nice to me. Well, they don't, but this one nurse actually was. I think I'd like to be a midwife, and I'd never make anyone feel crap. She said the baby is the size of a banana now and so I keep picturing this banana with a cartoon face doing somersaults in my tummy.

Even my mum couldn't spoil the moment when she said it was more than I deserved and she hoped I'd remember that and stay straight. But I was really jealous of the other women, with their partners holding their hands in the waiting room, looking at the baby magazines together, arguing about what colour to paint the nursery walls and whether to get a white plastic cot that wipes clean or a wooden one that looks the part.

Rob said he's totally sober now, and he's got a job. He wants to be part of the baby's life. I wish we could be a proper family, but he's made promises before, hasn't he? So I've got to stay strong, stay by myself, focus on me and the baby, like you said. You told me that a leopard doesn't change his spots, but I changed mine, didn't I? So I'm wondering, maybe, Wanda, if it's not you who is getting things mixed up for once.

Don't worry, though; I'm not going back. I got a job at the Spar, and I'm saving for my own place. Dad said I should forget about college, cos who's going to mind the baby if I'm working and at college? But I can't work at Spar forever, can I? I've got ambition now, just like you said I should have.

I keep staring at my copy of the picture. I can't wait to show you when you're back from your yoga retreat.

11 March 2024

Wish you could hurry up and come back to reality, Wanda. Enough with your downward dogs and weird chanting already. Mum and Dad are driving me insane. Planning everything for the birth, making the box room into a nursery. They didn't even ask me about the wallpaper I wanted, and I'm almost there with enough for a deposit for a bedsit but they just go mad every time I mention it, say I need to be with family, but what they really mean is they need to control everything and I can't be trusted. I just want to be normal. And I'm lonely. How lame does that sound? Like some sad old lady and I'm only twenty-two. All I ever wanted was to have a normal family, like when it was four of us, before my big sister, my best friend in the world, died and everything went to shit.

Rob came into the Spar the other day, all clean-shaven,

33

and in his work uniform. He looked just as good as any of the dads in the clinic waiting room. I'm scared to ask you what you think, cos I know what you'll say. You reckon you're all full of light and love and forgiveness, but are you, Wanda, really?

FIVE

FEBRUARY 2025

Very little time has passed since PC Hoppy Atkins believed Mila to be guilty of a long list of crimes including faking her identity (true, but she had her reasons), and two murders (both false, though you could understand how it might have looked that way). In fact, it has only been a matter of months. But Hoppy had ultimately been able to play the part of the hero, so Fabien thinks the young police officer might be open to providing a small favour.

It's Saturday, and although Fabien doubts that Hoppy will have any social plans on his day off, he still texts ahead to ensure he isn't covering the weekend shift. Fabien doesn't want to call Hoppy while he is in uniform or at the station, in case he gets even more professional, ethical, and annoying than usual. Or in case the boss, DI Cora Payne, is still keeping a very close eye on him, following his off-the-record antics the previous year.

'Hoppy, old pal!' Fabien bellows into the phone when Hoppy answers after a single ring.

'Lord Knutsworth?'

'Call me Fabien,' Fabien says. 'We're friends, aren't we?'

'Um, yes? Yes, please,' replies Hoppy.

'How are you?' Fabien asks.

There's a silent pause, then some hushed whispering in the distance down the line. 'I'm very well, thank you – *shush, Mother!* – I'm very well, thank you, Lord Knutsworth, and may I enquire as to how you are?'

'Hoppy, are you quite all right?'

'Yes, I'm just–'

'Anyway, I was wondering, can you still access your computer for police stuff from home? Assuming you can, expect you practically run Hipton station these days, after all your heroics with Mila's case?'

'Oh, I don't know about that...' Fabien can hear Hoppy redden.

'There's a girl, you see...'

Hoppy audibly gulps.

'No, nothing like that, old boy!'

Hoppy sighs with relief.

'I was simply hoping you could look into her for me. Criminal record, that sort of thing?'

'Lord Knutsworth, I'm afraid–'

'Fabien, please.'

'Um, Lord Fabien, it isn't possible, you see. I couldn't share the information. The thing is, you understand...' Hoppy pauses, and Fabien hears the faint ping of a device waking up. One or two moments later, Hoppy continues, his reading voice even more affected than his voice reserved for speaking to the aristocracy on the telephone while wearing his pyjamas. '"The processing of personal data relating to criminal convictions and offences or related security measures based on Article six – in brackets, one – shall be carried out only under the control of official authority or when the processing is authorised by domestic law providing for appropriate safeguards for the rights and freedoms of data subjects."'

'Eh?'

'It's against the law,' Hoppy clarifies, 'data protection.'

'I'm worried about Mila. She's going to meet this woman alone and I suspect she isn't all she says she is.' Fabien has no idea who Jo is, or what she may or may not have done, but he does know that Mila is pretty good at keeping secrets when it suits her. 'I know, after everything, you wouldn't want to put Mila in danger. Again.'

Hoppy is trying to work out what's happening. He struggles with reading people at the best of times, and the telephone is his personal Everest.

'Look, I'm not trying to manipulate you into doing anything unlawful. I'm just trying to find a way to ensure Mila's safety.' And to ensure Mila isn't able to make a case for taking on a hopeless client with no real injustice to fight. He needs facts, and as he's not allowed to attend the meeting, this seems his best bet. There's a slight churn in Fabien's belly as he feels Hoppy's resolve weaken, which he puts down to this morning's sausages being a little past their best.

Hoppy feels a little abated. He's been told off for being manipulated before and he thinks he's got better at swerving those tricks. 'Perhaps if you mentioned her name? If she's local I may know something offhand, off the record, not on the computer?'

Mila ignores the chime of the WhatsApp messages chorusing through her pocket as she makes her way past the Monday lunchtime workers queueing for takeaway sandwiches. She waves at Jo, already sitting at a table right at the back, refillable bottles of ketchup and brown sauce obscuring her face. Jo seems distracted, looking at her phone then up and around and over her shoulder. She doesn't look up when the door tinkles to announce Mila's arrival, nor does she see her take the whole length of the café in three long, purposeful strides, deftly manoeuvring through the clutter of plastic tables and chairs, almost all occupied, customers jostling for space.

'Hi,' Mila says, scraping back a chair opposite Jo.

Jo actually jumps as Mila sits, and drops her phone on the tiled floor with a crack that doesn't sound good. 'Shit,' she says, retrieving it, inspecting the device for damage. She fingers a chink in the corner. Jo eyes Mila suspiciously. 'I can't stay long.'

'I'm glad you called.'

'I don't know why I did,' says Jo, checking her phone for damage. 'What's done is done.'

'Pardon?' Mila leans forwards, struggling to hear Jo's words over the babble of the busy café and the clatter of the cutlery.

'What's. Done. Is. Done,' Jo repeats, pointedly louder, staccato.

'So, why turn up at the Town Hall?' Mila leans back, irritated, although she can appreciate what it's like to not feel grateful when you are apparently supposed to.

'I got a letter from the family court. It all seemed so final. I didn't know what else to do, then, well, I just lost it. Wanda promised me I wouldn't lose her, said I'd get her back.'

'Your baby?'

'Of course my sodding baby,' Jo spits.

'Right,' Mila says, unmoved, and wonders if Fabien could be right for once. But she's not quite ready to give up. 'You want something?'

'I'd love a tea. And some chips,' Jo says, still frowning.

Mila raises her eyebrows, and smiles. Jo, surprised, smiles back. Mila gets up and goes to the counter. Her phone, on silent now, vibrates, but she continues to ignore it. She told Fabien she'd be back in a couple of hours; he needs to let go.

'Sugar's on the table, spoons on the side,' the woman behind the counter – who doesn't *do* espresso – calls after Mila, as she carries the tray balancing a mug of insipid tea and an instant coffee back to the table.

'You said your baby–'

'Sarah. She's called Sarah.'

'Named after your sister.'

Jo nods.

'You said Sarah had been taken unlawfully. Can you tell me more?'

'*Unlawfully?* I think I said they *stole* her. What are you – some kind of lawyer?'

Mila hesitates.

'You are, aren't you? I don't have any money. I don't even know you. What can you do, what difference does it make?' Jo stands up to leave. 'I knew it would be another scam, like those PPI calls, those ambulance chasers, those ones who ring up and say, "No win, no fee." Well there's no bloody winning here, so forget it.'

'Wait,' Mila says, firmly, but quietly. 'I was a lawyer. Now I run a charity. I don't want your money. Sit down.'

Jo obeys, which those who know her would be surprised about, but Mila doesn't know Jo, and she is rarely surprised when people do as she asks.

'I try to fix stuff. My charity, Last Chance Cooperative, helps people who have run out of official channels.'

'Channels?' Jo interrupts, foot tapping either impatiently or anxiously, or both. She looks at her phone again.

Mila shakes her head at herself, she was turning into a British person, full of jargon and metaphor. 'People who have run out of luck. Who nobody else will help. People who might have been misjudged.'

'Well that's me all right,' Jo sits a little straighter.

'Tell me.'

'One chips?' The young waitress says, banging down the plate haphazardly in front of Jo when she points to the space in front of her. Two chips slide onto the table with the impact. Jo picks them up together and stuffs them in her mouth. Mila notices that she is very thin.

'Okay,' Jo says, finishing her first mouthful. She shuffles her chair closer to the table, and brushes her fringe away from her face with greasy fingers, revealing a scabbed-over cut across her forehead. It looks pretty fresh.

'What happened to your face?'

'I fell.'

Mila says nothing. She's seen that look before.

'So, what happened is that Sarah had to go and live with foster parents when she was born, but that was a misunderstanding.'

'A misunderstanding?'

'Yes!' Jo shouts. 'It's complicated, okay? But that's not the main thing; the *main* thing is they were supposed to give her back, after I'd proved myself. And I did, and Wanda said it was all fine and that she'd be home in weeks. I bought a cot. I had a flat. On my own, away from him.'

'Your... boyfriend?'

'Yeah. Rob.'

'So what happened?' Mila asks gently.

'Rob,' Jo repeats.

'Yes, I heard that, but what happened?'

'No,' Jo hisses, bending down, turning to the wall, her arm hiding her face. 'Rob. Rob is here. He must have followed me. I said I was going to the doctor. He doesn't like me going places.'

Mila turns to look through the front window, largely covered in painted signage. 'That him? Red puffa jacket?' The man who could be Rob looks far from relaxed. Face scrunched, and movements jerky and agitated. He's searching for something, someone. He looks at his phone and his stare springs upwards towards the café. A smile breaks onto his furrowed face.

'Find my phone,' Mila says, 'he's tracked you.'

Jo has already started to grab her things, but Mila knows she cannot get past him unnoticed. Unless... 'Here,' Mila grabs her car key out of her jacket pocket, 'Red Lion Street, round the corner, then first right, old white VW.' As she reels off the reg, she tells Jo, 'Wait a few seconds. I'll distract him. Then run, and I'll meet you there. And turn your phone off!' Mila hopes Jo and her car are still there by the time she gets there.

Mila gets up and runs straight into Rob as he walks through the door, pushing him backwards out of the café and onto the pavement, landing square on top of him. 'I'm so sorry,' she starts to say, as he roughly pushes her to one side, so Mila shouts, 'Owwww, my ankle!' and a small crowd gathers close enough for Rob to have to help her up. She sees Jo disappear around the corner. 'Oh actually it's fine, sorry, bye.'

'Watch where you're going next time!' Rob shouts after Mila, as she quickly follows the streets back to her car, not looking back.

Up ahead, her little car is still parked where she left it, engine off. Mila decides she had better warn Fabien, as obviously Jo can't go home, not now Mila has seen so clearly that it isn't safe for her. She can stay at the hall while Mila extracts the full story. And even if it turns out there is nothing they can do to get baby Sarah back, they can keep Jo out of danger, at least for now, and help her make a plan to escape the clutches of this Rob bloke. After Mila's sister suffered at the hands of her husband for so long, unable to find a way out, Mila had vowed never again. Mila does not break her promises.

'Fabien,' she says when he picks up.

'Mila! Finally! I've been texting you all afternoon. There's something you need to know about that woman.'

Mila squeezes the steering wheel tighter as she swallows her urge to remind Fabien "that woman" has a name.

'She's a criminal. She's only just been released. Mila, she's playing us.'

SIX

Mila is quiet on the drive back to Farlington Hall.

'Are you sure it's okay for me to stay with you tonight?' Jo asks.

'Yes.'

'How come I have to hide under these old coats in the back then?'

'The situation requires delicacy,' Mila says, parroting one of Lady Lydia's favourite diplomatic responses. She can't tell Jo that Fabien has heard she has been in prison, amongst other things, and now fears she is some rural Lancashire mafia don. Has he even seen this scrappy woman, afraid of her own shadow, and broken? The law isn't always right, and Mila should know. She will not be satisfied until she hears the whole truth from Jo and she has helped her find a safe place away from Rob. Everything else is secondary.

Mila may have felt bad about lying to Fabien and sneaking Jo into his family pile if it wasn't for the fact that he'd gone behind her back, snooping, desperate to prove her wrong.

At the press of a button on Mila's keyring, the wrought-iron gates open even more slowly than usual. 'Keep low,' she says, as she drives through, the gatehouse on her left, bare trees lining the way forward.

'Bleeding hell, you live *here*?'

Mila nods, looking around. Danny, the gardener, handyman, and long-time fixture of Farlington Hall, is driving fence posts into the ground. He drops the rammer onto the ground heavily, and waves, wandering over towards the car. Mila has no choice but to stop and wind down the window. She is about to shout one of those polite, "Hello-goodbye-got-to-dash" things she is trying to get the hang of, when Elodie and Anna emerge from their front door with another woman.

Crap, Mila thinks, the social worker meeting.

'Danny! You must meet our lovely social worker,' Elodie calls, causing Danny to swerve towards her, still waving. 'Mila, you too!'

'Is that...?' Jo starts to whisper.

'Keep down,' Mila whispers in response.

'It is, though, it's her,' Jo says. 'What the hell is going on?'

'This is Danny,' the introductions begin. 'And that's Mila – Mila! Are you coming over to say hi, or will you just meet us at two in the main house with the others?'

'Yes, main house,' says Mila, revving the engine, and speeding off up the driveway, gravel and dust flying up behind her.

'She's not from here,' she catches Elodie explaining apologetically, 'she doesn't mean to be rude.'

Mila pulls up around the side of the house, where the cars don't cause what Lydia refers to as an eyesore. It's already ten to two, so Mila knows Fabien and Lydia will be sitting in the drawing room, a platter of cakes and pots of tea laid out on the coffee table, already irritated by her lateness, despite the fact she is not yet late at all. That means the entrance will be clear, but they need to be fast.

'Hurry,' she tells Jo, as she attempts to close the heavy doors to the entrance hall silently. 'This way. Quick.'

Jo has to run to keep up with Mila's pace, down one corridor, then another, and another. Through doors, unlocked but stiff, along lit walkways, dimming with each corner. From plush runner rugs and oil paintings, to decreasing decoration and increasing dust. They finally stop at a door, which Mila opens. 'This way,' she says, closing the door behind her, 'nobody comes in here.'

Mila pulls the dust sheets, draped over almost every item of furniture, off a large Chesterfield sofa. 'Want to sit?'

Jo remains standing, arms folded. 'That woman,' she says through gritted teeth, 'helped them steal my baby. And now you've suddenly turned up and brought me here, where *she* is. What the hell is going on?'

'I could ask you the same thing,' Mila replies.

'What's that supposed to mean?'

'What haven't you told me?' Mila asks.

Jo laughs. 'Done your homework, have you? Then why even ask? Why bring me here?'

'To help you.'

'Why is Wanda here?'

'Wanda?'

'My social worker. And now, weirdly, here *I* am... You need to tell me what's going on right now.' Jo's scowl and angry tone doesn't hide her frightened confusion. She scratches at her arms.

'You came to find me, remember? And I didn't know who their social worker was. It's the first meeting. They're adopting.'

Jo releases an ugly snort. 'Well isn't that nice for them? So, Wanda does adoptions now? She used to do the other bit, you know, with us *"birth mothers"*. So she didn't just give up on me, she gave up on the whole horrible messy side and went to work for the perfect people with the nice houses and good jobs.

Maybe that should make me feel better, that she just doesn't care at all. That it isn't personal...'

'Look, I know you went to prison, Jo. How is that your social worker's fault?'

'It wasn't exactly, but she didn't believe me – she didn't fight for me. And it was her fault my baby was taken away as soon as she was born. Her damned paperwork, reporting every little thing, knowing what would happen. '

'So you didn't lose Sarah because you went to prison? You'd already lost her by then?'

'It was only supposed to be temporary. I was about to get her back. I'd bought a cot and this huge teddy bear, bigger than her. With a yellow bow tie.'

Mila's phone rages death metal in her pocket. Fabien. 'Hey,' she answers before he can speak. 'Two minutes, be right with you.' She ends the call.

'I did everything right. Almost. And, you know, Wanda said I was exemplary. Exemplary! That means totally perfect. And then, I had to stay with Rob, I didn't have anywhere else to go, and suddenly Wanda's boss is all like, "She's unsafe, the baby has to go to Foster to Adopt when she's born until she can provide a secure home", and Wanda knew I was off the drugs, had been for ages, that I'd protect my baby, but she still went along with it all. She said it was only temporary! She promised, and I did everything I could, and there was no way the courts could argue. Wanda said it was in the bag, and then someone set me up. I tried to tell them, but who'd believe me? Nobody believes me.'

'Set you up?' Mila's phone starts to ring again, and she silences it.

'Nobody believed me, or cared – they all thought Sarah was better off without me. Your mates down at the little house at the gate will think that too, I'd bet. That whoever's kids they adopt will be better here, in your fancy castle with all your money. But nobody could love Sarah as much as me, and isn't that what matters most? I love her so much it hurts. I ache for her, in my belly, right here.' Jo jabs at her own stomach. 'Every morning I wake up and I'm dreaming of her crying and needing me, and she's not there.'

'I don't think I understand, Jo; you're going to have to walk me through it.' Mila's phone rings again. 'Shit.'

'Go. Ask her. Ask Wanda about her processes and assessments and rules and their blasted baby-centric approach – adopter-centric, more like – people like me never stand a chance. Then come back here and I'll tell you how it really works.'

'I won't be long,' Mila says, as she starts to turn towards the door.

'Is that a shotgun on the wall?' Jo asks. 'You people...'

24 April 2024

I wish I could make you see, Wanda. He has changed. He never meant to hurt me – that was the booze, the drugs, making him different, and he's totally sober now, like me. I knew my parents wouldn't understand, that's why I didn't tell them, but I thought you were different – I thought you'd support me, like you promised. She followed me, you know, my mum, when I went to meet Rob, and I'm fuming she called you. What even was that, a sodding intervention? It's not like I'm moving back in with him. I told him there's no room in the bedsit, and you'd only turn up and take one look and tell us we weren't fit. He said he'll find somewhere proper. You know he's off the drugs, so why are you so mad? I can't believe you took their side. Three against one. Or is it? Cos me, Rob, and the baby are a three now too, aren't we? If you'd have stopped lecturing me for one minute I would have told you that Sarah has opened her eyes and learned to blink now. Shame all she has to look at is my insides. I can't wait to show her the world. And the world is going to love her, and she's going to be good at being in it, unlike her mum. I just want to be a good mum to her. If you'd just listened, Wanda, I would have told you everything is going to be okay. I know what I'm doing and I'm not taking any risks when it comes to my little girl, my Sarah. I love her so much.

13 May 2024

Where are you, Wanda? I called and called. Mum and Dad kicked me out today. I know you said don't get back involved with him – I've too much to lose – but what would you have done? He's been so nice, so supportive – not that they'd know, seeing as we have to sneak around. But doesn't that change things, like whether I can live with him again, so we can be a proper family? I haven't got enough for my own place yet, and fat chance my parents are going to help now. Surely it makes more sense for us to have one place, and then we'll have more money for baby stuff? And he's looking for somewhere bigger with two bedrooms, and we'll have the money soon. He's promised we'll be in the new place before she's born so none of your lot will be able to find fault with anything. And, I am thinking logically, whatever you said last time. It's not my hormones, not at all. I only want what's best for Sarah, and that's definitely not my parents hating her before she's even born cos she's just a reminder of everything I've done wrong. She's the one thing I'm going to get right.

Rob said he'd get her the best pram they have – there's a stall down the market that does one he said is the same one that Stacey Solomon had. I mean, if he wasn't a changed man, how would he even know that? He must have looked it up. I hope you call me back soon. Sarah's the size of a cabbage now, and she can suck her thumb – like a real-life Cabbage Patch Kid. My sister and I loved those funny little dolls so much.

16 June 2024

I never had you down for histrionics, Wanda. Seriously, you'd think I'd moved into a war zone, the way you were going on earlier. Maybe you need to meditate or journal or something, because, Wanda, surely you can see we're doing okay. Wasn't the flat clean and tidy? And there's space for a cot and a changing table. Rob's going to get them this week. You know how much I love baby Sarah – that I wouldn't have done this if I wasn't sure things were different now. I mean, you can't class it as unsafe just because of how things were back then. Don't you have to write your report based on now? He'd only had a couple of beers, and that was cos the football was on – everyone has a few when the footie's on. And that stuff – that wasn't even his, I told you his mate left it there.

You said you'd do your best for us, Wanda, but that I wasn't helping myself. The only person I want to help is Sarah, and why shouldn't she have a proper home with her mummy and daddy who buys her things that celebrity babies have? She's the size of a honeydew melon and they had those in the Spar, so I bought one to show Rob and then we ate it, which seemed a bit weird seeing as we were imagining it was our baby. You know her eyes can focus now? She's getting ready to see the world, Wanda, and I'm going to make her world as perfect as she is. I promise, you'll see. You're going to be proud of us, Wanda. I'm going to prove you wrong.

28 June 2024

I'm so angry I'm shaking, Wanda. I can hardly write in a straight line. You did this. You say you didn't, that it was your horrible new boss, that the evidence looked bad on paper, like my life is just one big sodding assessment. You kept saying you tried your best, but I don't believe you. I told you Rob isn't always like that – he is trying, and maybe you don't know what it's like to be scared, in your perfect life with that perfect gold ring too tight on your stupid fat fingers. I can't do this on my own and big surprise, my mum and dad didn't need much of an excuse to do what they've wished they could do for years and wash their hands of me. But you know I'd look after her. <u>YOU KNOW ME!</u> So just cos the bedsit had some junk lying *around, just cos Rob turned up half pissed and had a go that one time – he's just stressed about the baby, about money. He didn't mean to grab me like that. He didn't mean for me to fall. It was an accident, and the baby is fine. You didn't need to write all that down, Wanda. There's still loads of time to get the cot and the table and the pram. And I just hated that look on your face – I don't need your pity.*

I don't even understand what you were saying – all that official shit and "Oh I'm So Sorry Jo, but the Director of Children's Social Care is Zero Tolerance," BLAH BLAH BULLSHIT. You're taking her when she's born, "until I get back on my feet", you said? I'm on my fucking feet, Wanda, and all I want to do is kick and scream and punch. I want to hurt you, Wanda, like you've hurt me. She's got hair and fingernails, now, did you know that? She's real, and you're really going to take her away...

SEVEN

FEBRUARY 2025

Mila starts to make her excuses quickly as the meeting with Elodie and Anna's social worker draws to a close, promising she will fill Fabien in on the meeting with Jo later. Wanda seems so nice, not at all like the sort of woman who would let down someone in the way that Jo has implied. She must have repeated her message five times or more: they do everything they can to keep children with birth families unless there is no other choice. Elodie and Anna had started to look a bit disheartened at one point – the journey ahead to find their family was clearly not going to be fast or straightforward. And Lady Lydia had lost all the colour from her face as Wanda explained how much the family history would be assessed.

'But, Mila,' Fabien says, following her out of the drawing room, his voice laced with frustration, 'did you not get my message?'

'Who told you that stuff?' She swivels suddenly, almost causing a collision with Fabien, and puts her hands on her hips. 'You bullied Hoppy into it, didn't you?' One look at Fabien's sheepish face tells Mila everything. 'Why can't you trust me to even interview a woman over a coffee?'

'Did she tell you?'

Mila folds her arms in response.

'Well then.' Fabien's triumph is fleeting.

'We were interrupted. I'm sure she was about to tell me everything.'

'Interrupted by whom?'

'Rob.'

'The boyfriend you're convinced she's frightened of? Who may be dangerous? Mila! This is exactly what I'm always so afraid of! This is why I should have come with you.'

'I can handle myself. And this is *exactly* why we need to help her.'

'Help her do what, Mila? Her baby was adopted because she was in prison on drug charges. You can't do anything to help her, and if you ask me, she needs to start helping herself.'

'We can keep her safe from Rob. While she gets back on her feet. She isn't thinking straight, and she doesn't seem to know how to get away.'

'How can we do that...? Oh no, no, Mila, you can't mean–'

'Look, I just think–'

'How did you handle it, exactly? When Rob showed up?' Fabien interjects.

'Huh?'

'How did you get Jo safely away from her hooligan boyfriend?'

'Look, it's just for a couple of weeks,' Mila begins.

'Where is she?'

As Mila leads the way, Fabien muttering and huffing behind her, she tells him not to frighten Jo. 'Let me go in first,' she instructs.

'Oh, I'm going to frighten the drug kingpin?' Fabien says, as they continue through the darker, dustier corridors, to the rarely used wing Mila has chosen for Jo's concealment. 'Don't be

53

ridiculous, let's just hear her side of the story, okay? And maybe you're right, and we can't do anything about the baby–'

'You heard the social worker, Mila, they don't make these decisions lightly – I expect she has a long history, and quite reasonably, prison was the final straw. And once the adoption order is signed, and the adopters become the legal parents, there is no going back. Can you even imagine if Elodie adopted a child and they tried to take it back because the birth mother spun a tale? Don't you think any child would be better off with Elodie and Anna here with us, than with an ex-con with addiction issues?'

'Fabien. Do you seriously want me to send her back to a boyfriend who doesn't let her out, who tracks her, who clearly caused a nasty cut on her face? After what happened to my sister?' Mila's sister, dead at the hands of her husband, is not something to be countered, so Fabien stays quiet. 'We just need to listen to her; she's in a mess. Maybe we can find her somewhere safe to stay, somewhere she can start to get herself together. She's lost her child, Fabien.'

Fabien sighs. 'I'll listen, and of course, we can't send her back somewhere unsafe.' Fabien fiddles with his thumbs and takes a galvanising breath. 'But aren't there refuges and whatnot?'

'Shut up and wait here.'

Mila walks into the room and sees that Jo is having a meltdown. Her hands are pulling at her tangled hair, and mascara smears her cheeks. She rocks back and forth on the floor, surrounded by dozens of pieces of crumpled paper, handwritten scrawl smudged by tears.

Mila runs over, grabbing Jo's hands, but she pushes her away. 'It's no use, I just want Sarah, I can't, I can't!' Jo wails, and Mila thinks even in this disused corner of the house, they could be discovered and Jo would be swiftly ejected before they have a chance to help her.

'Fabien!' Mila calls, but he's already through the door and as it slams behind him, Jo looks up and pauses in her struggle long enough for Mila to embrace her in a hug. The suddenly spent woman cannot fight. Mila allows her to sob.

'This is Fabien, he's going to let you stay here.'

'For God's sake,' Fabien says on a sharp inward breath, mostly to himself, taking in the mess around the room, and the woman who looks like she belongs in a padded room in a second-rate horror movie.

'We are going to listen to your story, Jo, and then we can decide if we can help.' Jo gradually quietens, as Fabien starts to pick up the pieces of paper. 'What *is* this?' he asks.

'It *was* my journal,' Jo replies. 'I carry it everywhere. Wanda told me to write it.'

'The social worker?' Fabien asks.

'Yeah, she said she'd help me, was there when I was a kid, always checked in. I thought she cared, you know?'

'Small world,' Fabien says, shaking his head, wondering when life took this bizarre turn, and thinking it was almost certainly the moment Mila entered it.

'But she let them set me up; she gave up on me, like everyone else.'

'You keep saying that, Jo,' Mila says, gently, 'that you were set up. Can you explain?'

'Someone was following me, they must have planted those drugs on me. I'd been clean for ages, soon as I found out about my baby. I had a job, my own place. I was getting her back. He must have set me up.'

'Who?' asks Mila.

'Rob!'

'But why?' Fabien asks, incredulous.

'I don't expect *you* to believe me,' Jo spits at Fabien, then deflates again, closing her eyes, pulling away from Mila's embrace. 'I'm going to go.'

'Why do you think Rob set you up, Jo?' Mila asks, raising a calming hand.

'To keep me down, to make me need him. Inside, the counsellor said they did that, these types, that they'd want you to fail so you'd think you couldn't manage on your own.'

'But you're still with him?' Mila says.

'I thought I could get proof... Stupid, right? Got him to visit me inside. I had a plan. He didn't budge an inch, and every time I thought I could get something out of him I'd just make him angry. When I saw Wanda that day at the Town Hall, I tried to explain again, told her I needed help to prove what happened, but she *still* didn't believe me – she just kept on with all that bollocks about the process, and the investigation, and the guilty verdict. She said I should move on... That's when I lost it. I will *never* move on from losing my baby, not like this. I was framed, I know it – I've worked it all out. But it doesn't matter because no one will believe me, and who can blame them? I've not always been all that honest.' Jo smiles sadly.

'You've worked it all out?' prompts Mila, gently.

'I wrote everything down that happened since I got pregnant, right up to pretty much now. I've had a lot of time to think. It's all in the journal.'

'The journal you just tore up?' Fabien asks.

'They called me a fantasist in court, paranoid. I showed it to the police, but they didn't care either. They said I probably had long term issues from using in the past. Wanda did nothing. *Nothing*! I showed her what I wrote before I was arrested – about Rob having someone follow me – but she wouldn't listen.

I don't know why I kept writing, why I kept the stupid thing. All it does is remind me I had a baby once, I had hope. And I've just realised, being here, seeing you lot, that people like me don't ever win. I've been *so* stupid.'

'Did you write down exactly when and where you were being followed?' Mila asks.

Fabien sighs loudly. Who cares? The woman clearly *is* a fantasist.

'I always wrote the dates on the top of the page. It started as a nice thing, to remember Sarah getting bigger inside me, making plans for her for when she arrived.'

'Why would Rob want you to lose your baby? His baby, too, I guess?' Mila asks.

'Yeah. His. But I couldn't be with Rob if I wanted to keep her. It was one of the main conditions of what they call *reunification*.'

'So, he'd rather the baby was taken than lose you?' Fabien says, more disbelieving than is polite.

Jo stares at him, and her mouth hangs open. She starts to form an unsavoury response, but Mila's raised hand silences her.

'A woman is accusing a man of stalking her and planting drugs on her. A man who is still stalking her, and hurting her. These serious allegations have been dismissed by the police and by social care. Regardless of your prejudice, I think the very least we can do is take a closer look,' Mila says, glaring at Fabien. 'Well?' she demands. 'Isn't this precisely what the Last Chance Cooperative is for: people failed by the justice system?'

'Well, yes, but–' Fabien begins, thinking that if the police and social care have already concluded that Jo's story is little more than desperate paranoid delusions of an ill woman then perhaps they have a point. Though he doesn't dare say so, because both he and Mila know the police have got it very wrong before, and Mila is still pretty sore about that. In this matter, however, Fabien imagines they're most likely on the money. 'But–'

'Fabien, can you get some Sellotape, please?' Mila turns to him. 'We have a journal to repair.'

15 July 2024

At least you didn't actually say I told you so, Wanda. And maybe I should have said thank you, but to be honest, I never thought I'd be in a women's refuge the week before I'm due to have my baby. And you're still taking her, aren't you? When she's born. But I'll get her back, right? Definitely? Cos I never went back on booze or drugs and I've not taken a single day off work since I started. I've not even had mayonnaise on my sandwiches. Didn't have any raw fish either, but why would I? Sounds disgusting. It was on the website, what not to eat, and I was surprised that anyone would in the first place, but as my grandad used to say, "Nowt stranger than folk".

I know they don't believe I won't go straight back to Rob again. I won't though, not this time. The doctor said I was lucky, the way I landed when he pushed me. Her heartbeat is still strong; she's a survivor. But she won't have to put up with that shit again, not ever. I'm going to bring her up to have self-esteem, like you said I need. And I'm digging deep, like you told me to, and I'm going to find mine too.

I hope you're right, that I might be able to get jumped up on the waiting list for a flat, then I'll get it all sorted and ready for Sarah. Reunification, you called it. I call it coming home.

23 July 2024

Sarah was born yesterday at 2.15pm, and she weighs 7lbs 2 oz. She's healthy! She's perfect. I took a million photos with my phone, but I can't put any online in case it gets back to Rob, like, where I am, what she looks like. Don't worry, Wanda, I'm *not taking any risks this time. Maybe I'm finally learning, hey? I feel stupid, but you said it isn't stupid to want to believe the best of people, for wanting to be a family.*

You came to take her to her foster parents at teatime today. I could hardly watch as you walked away, Sarah was still wearing the pink hat with ducks on I bought her. I bet they'll take it off when they're outside and put on something they bought.

You said we'd go visit her next week, and every week after that, and then you'll fill out all the forms, and I'll get my flat, and the family courts will give her back. I have to believe you, Wanda. There's nothing else I can do, except picture her peachy pink screwed-up face, her flash of dark hair. Those lashes.

You said they're just fostering her, just for a while, cos of Rob and the junk and the history and the past. Most of all, you said, they worry about the risk of me returning to an "unsafe environment". Don't they make it sound so clinical? I know last time you got me in the refuge I went back to him, but things are different now. You know that. And why call it Foster to Adopt, if it's only for a bit? In case I screw it up, right? Like everyone thinks I will. And then they'll get to keep her.

Wanda, I won't screw it up – not this time. I promise. I've already told Spar I'll be back full-time next week. You don't need maternity leave when your baby's been taken away.

I'm saving for a cot, and a huge teddy bear – that one in the window with a yellow bow tie.

EIGHT

FEBRUARY 2025

'Do you know what I wish, Susannah?' says Lady Lydia Knutsworth, taking a delicate bite of her tiny triangular-shaped salmon sandwich. 'That one day I will be able to open the newspaper and not see one of my offspring named and shamed.'

'I did see, I'm afraid, Lydia. That awful news reporter really doesn't seem to like our little community, does he?' Mayor Susannah Wilson lifts the china saucer and takes a sip of her Earl Grey tea.

'Gareth Davies. No, he does not, and he seems to bear our family a particular grudge. He called Elodie an "upper-class hypocrite". It said – hold on,' Lydia says, retrieving the newspaper from the stand next to her armchair, and leafing through to the already well-thumbed spread of yesterday's protest in Manchester, and begins to read, '"The privileged young lady is happy to benefit from years of the patriarchal tradition, not ever having held a job in her charmed life as an aristocratic heir, but she feels entitled to assault a man who is fast becoming one of the most influential lobbyists in the country for having the gall to speak up for the everyman and his right to uphold traditional family values."'

Susannah tuts in sympathy. 'Awfully kind of you to have me, given the shock of the article this morning. I wouldn't have minded had you postponed.'

'Well, that's the thing, you see; these days nothing they ever do shocks me. If Gregory were still alive he'd be having another heart attack, God rest his soul. But it's the inaccuracy that really irks. Elodie isn't an heir to anything, and she does sell the odd painting, which I'm sure counts as a job of sorts. I'm not sure it was assault, either. Seems a tad melodramatic, in my view.'

'Did they actually arrest her?' Susannah asks, trying not to sound too delighted at the scandal. 'I believe it was the same chap that was on her banner the other day?'

'She does seem to have a real bee in her bonnet about this Frederick Fawcett,' Lydia says, 'but apparently she wasn't arrested, just removed from the protest.'

'Eggs, wasn't it? That she threw at him?'

'Yes, and she shouted something obscene to do with ovaries. I don't know where she gets it from. I'm sure we met this Fawcett fellow once at a charity dinner in Lancaster. He really didn't seem so bad – a bit old-fashioned, maybe. But one must be tolerant, I always say. Isn't that what the wokes say?'

'Quite, Lydia, quite.' Susannah isn't quite sure what a woke is, but Lydia has been mentioning the movement for some months now, and it feels too late to ask for clarification.

'This Gareth chap called Fawcett a man's man, and of course Elodie doesn't like that at all.'

'Is that a bad thing now?' Susannah asks, thinking most men were what she would call "men's men," with the exception of her daughter's boyfriend, who works in computer coding.

Lady Knutsworth ignores the question. 'Apparently he's become a bit of a hero to some, speaking up for all the rights they've ostensibly lost to women. Of course, I don't pay attention to such things – it sounds like a petty squabble to me.

Men and women never did see eye to eye, but in *our* day we just quietly manoeuvred them to our will without causing a fuss. I don't recall Gregory ever making a decision in his life, nor did he ever knowingly acquiesce to mine. That's the way to do it: *peacefully*. Of course, when I said this to Elodie, her rage could have removed the roof. She's particularly cross about his stance on women in the workplace.'

'Oh, yes, she mentioned that in the pub.'

'And when you think that Elodie has always refused to work outside of the home, it seems a bit funny to get so upset about it. Besides, I think he said *mothers* were best placed to serve society in the home, rather than suggesting a blanket ban on women working. They will exaggerate, our young ones – always looking for someone to cancel.'

Susannah shakes her head in solidarity. She has read about cancel culture in the *Daily Mail* and it sounds ghastly. You can't say *any*thing these days.

'I must say Gregory and I, although both mostly performing our duties from the home, always took a more hands-off approach to the business of child-rearing. The nannies were wonderful though, very thorough.'

The telephone on the little table next to Lydia's favourite armchair rings and she apologises to Susannah, lifting the receiver. 'Ah, speak of the devil. Elodie, what can I do for you? Perhaps you're in jail now, and need bail?' Lydia smiles and winks at her friend. 'What?' she says as the smile vanishes. 'Oh, for goodness' sake!' She reaches to the bottom shelf of the large coffee table where the television remote control is kept, and fumbles with it, the telephone in the crook of her neck, as she tries to remember the order of buttons to turn normal terrestrial channels on, finding ITV playing the local lunchtime news.

On the screen is a protest outside the Midland Hotel in Manchester, where the Conservative Party Conference is being held. The camera is zoomed in on her daughter's face, as she is dragged away by two police officers, shouting imperceptible things eclipsed by beeps. She mutters into the telephone, 'This is no way to behave if you expect to be a mother, and on *ITV* of all places, too – the shame!' She replaces the handset sharply.

The camera pans to the centre of the scrum, where Frederick Fawcett stands his ground, egg yolk on his expensive suit as he wipes more of the same from his eye. 'I was invited today to speak to the Conservative Party delegation about my bold strategic plans to help any future government prevent the further demise of this country by fostering traditional Christian family values, in which all members of society may prosper in the roles that allow them, as individuals, to thrive. As you can see from the behaviour of many young people today, we have quite the mission on our hands.' A small laugh ripples through the crowd, and peters out as he continues. 'My organisation will fund schemes to build hope, provide moral education, and allow our children to grow up in safe, loving environments cultivating the best possible futures for them.' Questions are thrown at Fawcett, some clap, others boo, and the camera returns to the reporter.

'We understand that the woman throwing the eggs was Lady Elodie Knutsworth, sister of the current Lord of Farlington, Lord Fabien Knutsworth, who made headlines last year when he was accused of financial misconduct. Although he was eventually cleared, it has been a tumultuous year for the Knutsworth family. Lady Elodie Knutsworth was one of a small group of protesters without links to any official organisation, although the Knutsworths run a charity – the Last Chance Cooperative – whose slogan was on one of the group's banners. Frederick Fawcett seems unperturbed by the disturbance, and despite his somewhat divisive rhetoric, he seems to be able to charm any crowd at the moment.'

The television goes black and Lydia drops the remote control onto the coffee table with a clatter. 'Susannah darling, do you still have Chris-Whatsit from the BBC's contact details after your event on the Town Hall steps? I think we may need to do a bit of our own PR.'

12 November 2024

Jesus, I knew you weren't keen on your new boss, Wanda, but you didn't tell me just how enormous the stick up her bum is! Julia is not cool. Why did you have to bring her just so she could turn her nose up at my place, my stuff? She didn't even smile when I showed her the enormous teddy bear with the yellow bow tie. She's dead inside, if you ask me. I know you said she just doesn't like to make promises, but she made it sound more like it could go either way at the hearing. Like maybe I wouldn't get my Sarah back, after all. I wish I had your confidence. You promised though, said the decision would be made on your recommendation, and what did you say it was? – "A glowing report" – ha! Not had one of those since before my sister went and died, and somehow none of that school stuff seemed to matter anymore. Probably shouldn't have started throwing stuff around classrooms, looking back. I'll admit that now, so there's a win for you – changing hearts and minds and all that. Go on – I'll give you another couple – I shouldn't have smoked weed in the library or shagged Wayne in the store cupboard during PE, or run away to Manchester to sleep on the streets for a week just to get away from Mum and Dad. It wasn't long after that you swooped in to rescue me. Sorry I wasn't easy to save, Wanda, but you know what? you got there in the end. We both did.

19 November 2024

Two weeks today, Wanda, and she'll be home! I can't believe it. I keep cleaning – "nesting", they call it online – normally do it when you're about to have your baby and bring her home, but for me, it's just bringing her home. I can't wait! I've even put a chain on the front door, screwed it on myself. Got to make this place safe. You know what this estate is like. Not that I'm complaining. I love having my own place – and I know I wouldn't have managed it without you. You're my guardian angel, Wanda. I don't often say it, but it's true.

20 November 2024

I know it sounds stupid, but I keep thinking someone is following me. I think it must be Rob, but when I look he's never there. But there is one guy I've noticed, it's hard to see his face underneath his massive hood, but I recognise his walk now cos it's been a few times. I almost started to tell you today – I hadn't said anything cos I thought I was being silly, like, obviously I'm going to see the same old dodgy guys in hoodies hanging about out on the benches – I used to buy from half of them. Something feels a bit not right though, so I thought maybe I should say something, just, you know, just to hear you say I am being daft, but I didn't cos I don't want any of that shit in my glowing report; they'll think I'm paranoid and mad like a druggie. And I know you have to be thorough, learned that the hard way. Not that I'm angry anymore, Wanda, I know you were only doing your job.

But I am going to write it down here, whenever I feel he's there. Just in case something does happen. Then you'll see this old journal you gave me all those years ago, and it'll be like a clue. Now I really do sound mental. Reckon I'm in some thriller, don't I? I need to watch less telly. Well, there'll be no time for that when Sarah gets home and she's keeping me run ragged like those women in the park who complain about it and don't know how lucky they are.

25 November 2024

I got a promotion! Assistant Shift Manager. On and up, as you always say! And I took your advice and called Mum. She and Dad came over and they even cried when they saw the teddy bear.

30 November 2024

Saw that guy again, outside the newsagents, and in the park. I'm sure he's following me.

1 December 2024

I put my Christmas tree up. Dad said it was too early, but Mum helped me decorate it and she gave me this bauble saying, "Sarah's First Christmas" that actually used to belong to my sister. It's really naff, but I cried so much I used a whole box of tissues blowing my nose. I've hung a stocking on the wall for my Sarah, and I'm pretty sure this Christmas is going to be the best one of my life.

25 December 2024

If you're expecting a thank you for the photo of Sarah with Father Christmas, you can piss right off, Wanda. Don't think I'll ever want to speak to you again. I hate you. You were the only one who said you believed in me. That says it all, doesn't it? When it came down to it you were happy to accept I'd got drugs again, fallen off the wagon just a week before the hearing, and got myself done. As if! You know I wouldn't have risked it. You saw how well I was doing, hadn't even thought about drugs since forever.

And so then I told you someone had been following me, I told them all, and just like I thought – they said I was paranoid, mental, a typical druggy. But I'll be out in a few weeks, Wanda, and I'm going to prove you all wrong. I'm going to get my little girl back, because I've worked it all out now, how Rob got me framed and arrested so I'd lose Sarah, so that I'd need him back, so I'd think I couldn't manage on my own without him. Well, I don't need him, and I don't need you. I only need my baby girl. My little Sarah.

NINE

FEBRUARY 2025

Mila is exhausted, but she is finally getting somewhere.

'Have you ever thought of becoming a criminal mastermind, rather than a justice fighter?' asks Fabien. 'Your capacity for subterfuge is actually quite alarming.'

'And this from you?' Mila responds, and for once they both have the decency to look a little sheepish, given that neither started out in this relationship with anything even close to honesty.

They have come a long way in a short time, they know that. Though Fabien thinks he may be the only one truly dedicated to building trust through truth, whereas Mila seems to see honesty more as a nice-to-have, depending how it might impact on her getting the desired outcome of whatever plan she's most recently hatched.

'And to think she was in the car, hiding in the back when you met our social worker on the driveway... Imagine how that might have looked, given what you've just told us,' says Elodie with a pout. 'We did say the whole household was being assessed to ensure we were suitable to adopt, and you swan past with a woman who was just released from prison and has been categorically confirmed unsuitable to care for her own child. I'm not sure it's very fair, you coming here asking for our help, when you've just jeopardised our future without a second thought. Isn't that right, Offal?' she says to the dog on her lap. He licks her face in return.

'Gross,' says Fabien.

'She doesn't mean it, Mila,' pipes up Anna, from where she sits on a beanbag in the corner of the gatehouse living room, a pile of books for her teaching training course beside her, closed, the current conversation being of far more interest. 'We want to help.'

'If Wanda ends up thinking we are mad and therefore unsuitable to adopt you won't be saying that,' Elodie tells her girlfriend, but her eyes give her away; smiling and full of warmth, despite her constant anxiety about the adoption process. Elodie doesn't want to be the one who pushes back on Mila's ongoing quest for justice. She genuinely believes that in some respects she and Mila are kindred spirits, both fighting against *The Man*.

Except, Mila thinks, to her the aristocracy is *The Man*, even when it comes dressed in a floaty kaftan with a few lofty left-wing principles. Still, she likes Elodie's rebellious drive, and like Elodie and Anna, she needs the whole family on board. Except Lydia. She doesn't need Lydia and she is pretty sure Lydia will not be adding "helping ex-cons" to her charitable to-do list, beneath campaigning for new swing sets and organising the flower-arranging rota for the church.

'It's just a few questions,' Anna says, level-headed as always, the very tonic for her flighty partner.

'And I'll be there to help,' says Mila.

'Absolutely, unquestionably not,' Elodie says, unintentionally raising her voice to a near-shout, scaring Offal to death, who isn't the bravest of little rescue dogs at the best of times. He jumps to the floor and slopes towards Anna, with her nice quiet voice and calming strokes. 'I said I *don't* want them to think we are mad. And that's final.'

Mila nods. It has been hard enough to get everyone to agree to help Jo in the first place, particularly as it involves keeping it from Lydia, which is less of a moral question for most of the group and more of a taking-your-life-into-your-own-hands concern for when she inevitably catches them out.

Jo's journal is heartbreaking to read. Her determination when she first discovered she was pregnant, the fallout with her parents over Rob, their relationship too damaged over the years to survive any dent in their trust of their surviving daughter, and then Jo's almost inevitable return to him as he manipulated and lied his way back into her heart – which has only ever craved love and normality, and a proper family. So much history, so much pain, never enough love. Jo's luck has been unfathomably bad, her parents too wrapped up in their own grief and lives – and frankly, Jo's natural disposition is not the kind to easily repel the calling of oblivion, rebellion, and anything else that takes her away from a reality she cannot stand.

The Foster to Adopt order could have broken Jo, but she had eventually seen Rob's true colours. She had dug deep to find a reservoir of resilience and over the first few months of her baby's life she had proven herself day after day. She worked hard, made her little flat homely, and painted the nursery a pretty pale pink, placing decorative wall stickers in the shape of elephants around the walls. She had never missed a visit with Sarah and had all her phone pictures of the two of them printed on little canvases that hung all across the flat.

Wanda had helped to organise the family court hearing, with a recommendation of reunification. A return to the birth family outcome had been expected. The foster parents, Jo had written in her journal, had been told to expect this too and, by all accounts, were resigned to it. They'd understood both the risks and the potential outcomes for their family when they had entered into the scheme. Adoptive parents signed up for Foster to Adopt on account of it being far more likely they would be able to adopt a young baby, particularly in cases where a baby had to be taken into care at birth for a whole plethora of reasons, but there was always still the hope that the birth family would be able to turn things around over the following months. The baby was fostered to facilitate a temporary care arrangement, whilst also allowing for the fact it might become permanent, which was often the case. In those instances, the baby would be adopted by the foster parents, and endure less upheaval than would be caused by being adopted by a new, different family.

Hope jumps from the pages, before the darkness creeps back in. Jo was stopped and searched and found to be in possession of a selection of baggies full of various highs and lows. Although not one item was officially enough for intent to supply, as a combination of products it was enough to fill a door-to-door salesman's display briefcase.

Nobody believed Jo when she said she had thought she was being followed for weeks, and especially not when she used it as an excuse for being arrested, on account of her long list of previous offences. Her chances with the law already long spent, she was sent to jail for five weeks for possession, which, on advice, she pleaded guilty to despite her protestations of innocence, in order to try to secure a community order rather than a prison sentence. But the prosecution successfully argued that she was planning on a new career in dealing, and that was that. The reports from social services were amended, and the outcome of the delayed family court hearing was not in Jo's favour. The pages that she scribbled from her cell had left deep marks, sometimes shredding the paper, showing the manifestation of anger as Jo realised what it all meant. For once, she had dared to believe in a happy ending, and now the world was teaching her a lesson. She had lost Sarah; she had lost everything.

Through those weeks in a prison cell, at first enduring and eventually embracing each group therapy session she had attended, Jo had discovered she still had a slither of hope left. *She* knew she wasn't lying; she hadn't bought the gear; she hadn't used drugs since she first saw the line on the test stick as she sat on the loo in Rob's bedsit. She had flushed it all away, and packed that little stick – a baton of hope – and a few items of clothing into a backpack before catching the bus back to her estranged parents. Ready to say sorry, to truly *be* sorry, and so very ready to be a mum.

From the bottom bunk in her cell, as the woman above her snored and cried out in her sleep, and women in cages down corridors shouted, doors clanged, and guards demanded silence, Jo lay awake night after night, staring into the dark. She vowed that she would prove her innocence, for Sarah – for her little family. She decided she could do it, she would show them all that it had been a miscarriage of justice. Lessons in prison on abusive partners, and the lengths that they might go to in order to exert coercive control, had reignited something in Jo. She had made a plan, and put it in place before she was even released, encouraging Rob to visit her in prison, giving him what he wanted.

Fabien isn't entirely convinced. The whole cloak and dagger story about being followed by an ex who wanted to frame her for a crime so that she would go back to him seems far-fetched at best. He's not sure this Rob bloke sounds smart enough for such an elaborate plan, and if he's honest he can't really see why he'd go to such lengths to win someone like Jo back, but he decides he probably should avoid saying these thoughts aloud. He still thinks Jo might be playing them, trying to prove a lie to get what she wants. And what then? He keeps asking Mila: what if we succeed, and it turns out she *is* a criminal, and the baby isn't safe with her?

'I still can't believe you're actually hiding her in the hall, though,' Elodie says, half amused by Mila's maverick approach and half hoping this isn't the wild goose chase her brother clearly thinks it is.

'Nobody goes in that wing, do they?' Mila asks.

'Not usually,' Elodie replies. 'I'm surprised you weren't attacked by moths or bats when you opened up those doors. Too expensive to heat, too much trouble to clean. A few dust sheets and forget about it is the family policy. Though Mother did mention she had stored some family heirlooms in there, out the way of visitors. You best make sure they don't get broken.'

Mila rolls her eyes, wondering why Jo would break some old vase, or whatever. She isn't five years old. Then she realises they're probably there in the first place because of her own niece and nephew, and she feels a little bad. 'I'll make sure she's careful.'

'I'll check what's in there. Some of the really valuable stuff from Mother's side looks like it belongs in a car boot sale,' Fabien tells her.

'So, do you buy Jo's theory, Mila?' Anna asks.

'About Rob? Well, it's clear he's violent and abusive, so he could have followed her, he could have wanted to hurt her, get her in trouble, make her vulnerable. Weirder things have happened with guys like that.'

'Plus, the texts he sent her were vile,' adds Anna, who has been listening very carefully as Mila replayed everything Jo had told them, believing that Anna and Elodie would keep their secret, hoping they would talk to their social worker to help either corroborate, *or not* – Mila reluctantly conceded – Jo's story.

'They certainly show that he thought it would be better if they allowed the baby to stay where she was, with the foster parents, and went back to being just the two of them,' says Fabien carefully, 'but they don't really prove anything else.'

'Other than he was happy to call her a bad mother, put her down, use disgusting language, and that he clearly didn't want her to succeed in getting the baby back,' Mila tells him, looking back at her notes. 'Listen to this: *"You're a druggy whore. The kid deserves better."* And: *"We were good together, babe. We ain't ready for a kid; let it go, and just be who you know you are."* Or this one: *"You're gonna lose her in the end; people like us always do. Just come home – don't make things worse."* It isn't hard evidence, but it explains why Jo would suspect him. He knew that she couldn't go back to him if she got Sarah back – that was a clear stipulation, and it gives him motive. Even if she is wrong about Rob framing her, I think it's definitely worth looking into the claims that she was being followed, which, unsurprisingly, the police decided not to bother doing, seeing as she's apparently not the sort of woman worth listening to.' Mila directs the last bit towards Fabien.

'I do think we should listen, Mila,' he begins. 'I just think we need to go in with an open mind too. She *also* has strong motive to lie. Proving her innocence on the drug charge is probably her only chance to get her baby back.'

'Even then, she might not...' says Anna, carefully. 'They'll have to decide if it is the right thing to do for the baby, especially given her long history of issues – whether the disruption is justified, given the adoption has been legally processed now.'

'Yes, Anna, I get that,' Mila says, trying to keep the exasperation from her voice, 'but if she was stalked, she deserves justice, some recognition for what she went through. And if she was framed as well, she could at least have her record cleaned up, which might help her build a better future.'

'That's still a big if, though,' Fabien mutters.

'We have work to do, I agree,' Mila says, Fabien's dissent beginning to get on her nerves, 'but it would be strange to lie to your own journal, wouldn't it? And she couldn't have fabricated the texts from Rob. We have the list of dates Jo thinks she was followed, and where she went, so we need to see if we can get access to any CCTV footage. Fabien, can you ask Hoppy for another favour?' She gives him a meaningful look, still annoyed that he went behind her back. 'If there's evidence of someone following her, surely that backs up at least some of Jo's claims, no matter how crazy they seem?'

'I can ask, Mila, but who is to say they even have it? Don't they erase it after so long? Besides, that DI Cora Payne has Hoppy on best behaviour after last year's shenanigans.'

'Shenanigans?' Mila says, laughing now. 'When he went rogue to prove that I killed your father, and in the process almost destroyed months of work to create a case against my sister's killer who was also a dangerous war criminal?'

'Those exact shenanigans,' replies Fabien. 'But it all came good in the end, didn't it, darling, with a little help from yours truly...?'

Ignoring him, Mila turns her attention to Elodie and Anna. 'At the next meeting, you just need to try and get Wanda to talk about what happened with Jo's baby. See if Jo's version of events matches up to hers.'

'Quite,' adds Fabien, who receives yet another look from Mila, which he decides to risk ignoring, 'as Jo could *actually* be a fantasist, as they said in court, and Wanda may confirm that her baby was removed for all the reasons babies are legitimately removed.'

'Yes, thank you, Fabien,' says Mila.

'I don't want to be negative, Mila,' says Anna, who really doesn't like upsetting her, 'but Wanda seems really straight. I'm not sure she'll risk her client confidentiality clause for a chat over a cuppa.'

'Probably not, but if you talk in generics to begin with, it could work – what-ifs, and example case studies – as if it is for your own information.'

Anna and Elodie look at each other, confused.

'And this is why I should be in the room,' says Mila.

'No!' shout Elodie and Anna together. Anna says, 'Mila we will do some digging, but you must leave us to it. We are being constantly assessed. You understand, don't you?'

Before Mila can argue, the intercom bell rings from the large front gates. 'Ah, that will be Chris-Whatsit from the BBC,' says Elodie, rolling her eyes. 'Yippee.'

'We best get over to the main house,' Mila says, jumping up.

'Since when have you been so keen on PR? I thought you hated that crap,' says Elodie.

'More deceit...' Fabien says, winking at his younger sister.

'It isn't a lie, it's a cover-up,' Mila explains. 'We have agreed to the playground project, otherwise everyone will wonder what the charity is doing. I'm going to talk this BBC guy through it, just like Lydia asked, that's all.'

'Basically, we need a distraction, as despite Mila's insistence that every underdog is a good dog, we don't actually know if Jo's legitimate... and right now, homing ex-cons with a view to having their legally adopted children returned to their care is not the look we're going for. Plus, you waving that banner with the charity's logo on it when you accosted that Fawcett bloke didn't help matters with our donors.' Fabien directs that last bit to his sister, resigned to the constant ludicrousness of his life these days.

'Let's get this over with then,' says Anna. 'Your mother will be spitting feathers if we mess this up.'

TEN

Lydia and Susannah have arranged the room perfectly. Fabien, Elodie, Anna, and Mila have miraculously all turned up on time. Fabien is predictably in his uniform of jeans, shirt and blazer, and Anna as always is quite the conformist. Elodie has managed to dig out something that isn't ripped or covered in paint, and although Mila is in her trademark black, she's held back on the chains and her T-shirt does not include a single depiction of Satanism.

As Danny leads their esteemed guests into the drawing room, Lydia thinks she really must get a new housekeeper, as having the gardener answering the door and showing her guests through is very odd indeed. Everyone stands to greet them, including Offal.

'Good afternoon and welcome, Mr–', Lydia begins, before realising she really ought to have checked Chris-Whatsit from the BBC's surname before he arrived, instead of reorganising the cushions. Why is his name so utterly forgettable?

'Chris, call me Chris,' Chris-Whatsit from the BBC finally says, drawing a close to the longer than ideal silence.

'Why thank you, Chris,' Lydia says, shaking his hand, and

making the introductions as Offal attempts to hump his ankle, before being quickly swept up by Elodie.

'And this is my producer Amy,' he says, as a solemn-looking, smartly dressed woman with thick black glasses and bright red lipstick offers a firm handshake and takes Lydia's usual armchair by mistake, leaving Lydia to perch on the end of the sofa with Fabien and Mila.

Lydia and Susannah know their pitch by heart and are rather proud of it, and Lydia is especially pleased with herself for becoming quite the expert in publicity in very little time at all. Until recently, the Knutsworths had never courted media attention, believing it to be the realm of the celebrity rather than the establishment, but Lydia has adapted somewhat this last year, on account of the numerous scandals that have befallen her family. These days she considers herself rather adroit.

Lydia has done her research, too. Chris-Whatsit may be something of a local celebrity, but rumour has it he has been hankering after a national slot for years, and he isn't getting any younger. He has done the odd television appearance, but most of those gigs were going to younger, slimmer, less red-faced people with more hair and a solid jawline. There is barely a jowl to be seen, these days, on the BBC, which Lydia thinks a great shame. She has to admit *Love Island* is rather a treat for the eyes, but in her opinion there's a reason Jeremy Clarkson keeps making it into the top ten sexiest men lists. Not that she pays any attention to such nonsense.

When she first started to think about organising some good spin (another new bit of lingo assimilated into the dowager's lexicon), all Lydia had really wanted was a lovely segment on the Last Chance Cooperative, and how it supported children in the community, first with the school project, and now with the new playground. The Mila angle, as she likes to call it, is the icing on the cake and will make them all look super. She's a war refugee making her home in Farlington, the little village with a big heart, who having benefitted from the kindness of the community is now proving all the sceptics wrong by giving so much back to the country that she has made her own.

However, as she lies awake at night, fantasising about her future television triumph, Lydia has realised that a set of swings for the village, although an excellent aspiration, might not fill an entire programme. If they are really serious about putting Farlington on the map, not to mention the Knutsworths – and what a noble, humble, and excellent family they are – the programme needs to be a little more in-depth.

'History is very *now*,' Lydia explains to Chris-Whatsit and his producer Amy, 'and those wretched people selling their grandfather's war medals are on all day long. Not that I watch daytime television.'

'What Lady Knutsworth means,' Susannah adds, hoping Chris-Whatsit isn't offended by Lydia's clear disdain for the very thing they are hoping to sell, 'is that we have noticed the trend in historical programmes... and where better to host a programme than right here, at Farlington Hall?'

When Lydia had told Susannah about her media plans, she had thought it would also be a fantastic vehicle for her own fledgling political career. Today local mayor, tomorrow, who knows? But she can absolutely see herself in a beautiful cape carrying a sword at the next coronation, not that she wishes the King any ill.

The meeting is going well, with lots of nodding all round.

'So, as you can see, the story is really quite bold. We are living proof of how the past and present can work in harmony, keeping traditional structures that serve the community whilst embracing modernity.' Lydia gestures to Mila and then Elodie, who both look perturbed at being the given examples of modern life. 'My daughter-in-law-to-be,' she continues, as Mila swallows a gulp the wrong way and tries to silence a coughing fit, 'is a refugee, and guardian to her niece and nephew... and my daughter Elodie is a lesbian! Aren't you, dear?'

'Um,' Elodie starts, but is swiftly interrupted.

'She and Anna, who, by the way, is Polish *and* used to be our housekeeper – are adopting a child. So, we are very *with it* here at Farlington Hall. Yet, we retain our titles and work tirelessly to serve our community. We are caretakers of this historic home, and all of its contents, and we would be honoured to share it with the world. Your documentary can chronicle the history of Farlington and trace the Knutsworth family line, as well as including a piece on the current work we do, demonstrating the continued relevance of the aristocracy. Here, I've drawn a storyboard.' Lydia gestures to Fabien, who duly distributes the photocopies of his mother's hand-drawn storyboard, another new skill acquired this week after googling how to pitch a television programme.

'It also includes a bit on village politics, and what it means to be a modern mayor,' Susannah adds.

Both Lydia and Susannah are very pleased they have remembered to hammer home the modernity themes. Chris-Whatsit announces he thinks it is all a wonderful idea, ignoring the look his producer Amy throws at him, as she interjects with cautions about having to pitch it to the commissioners first.

'But it could work?' Susannah asks.

'Actually,' Amy says with a smile, 'I think it could.' These people are bonkers, and this history-slash-antiques bore-off was already morphing into a BAFTA-winning reality show in her mind. Candid, fly-on-the-wall stuff.

'I'd be more than happy to help with the script, dear,' Lydia tells Amy, 'as I'm sure you're frightfully busy. And, of course, the story must be carefully orchestrated to ensure we keep our audience engaged.' Goodness, Lydia is even impressing herself, she sounds so professional, and she is starting to wonder if she could be a producer too.

Having waved Chris-Whatsit and Producer Amy off, Lydia congratulates everyone on being well-behaved for once. 'Though I do think that Amy was rather dismissive of my offer of help. Young people today think they know it all.'

ELEVEN

Jo is still holed up in the few rooms Mila has casually converted into a home for her, and is going a little stir-crazy, but she acknowledges it is much better than the alternative. She had overestimated her abilities, once again, and feels stupid for thinking someone like her could trick someone like Rob into a confession.

'I am sorry for hiding you,' Mila tells her again, 'but I'm not sure Lydia would understand.'

'I'm not sure your fella is that keen, either. He doesn't believe me. Do you, Mila?'

Mila is silent. She only likes to deal in facts. And the fact is that Jo has lost her baby after months of reform and hard work, and is in no fit state to find work or a safe place to live. Her journal documents her daily life, none of which suggests any drug use, but it does back up her suspicions that she was being followed. However, back then, Jo had clearly struggled to make enough money, she had been about to become Sarah's full-time guardian again, single and without much of an income. Could she have thought she could make some extra money through drugs? Or perhaps she just had a wobble, the impending hearing and everything that was to come tipping her over the edge. She certainly would have had the contacts to easily buy whatever she wanted.

And now, desperate to get her daughter back, might she say or do just about anything to overturn her conviction and try to reverse the adoption order?

From Elodie and Anna's reports of their discussion with Wanda, permanent adoption orders, once signed off, are set in stone. That's why social services go to great lengths to explain they didn't rush final decisions, and why the birth parents are given every chance to keep their children. In Foster to Adopt, birth parents remain in contact with their child until the order is signed, and if they are able to overcome their challenges and offer a safe and loving home, then the child is reunited with them.

'Isn't that hard on the foster parents?' Elodie had asked.

'Of course,' Wanda replied, ' but they understand the risks, and generally they want the best for the child, as we all do. They call them *concurrent carers*; even the language suggests that they are caring as foster parents, with a view to adopting if the child is in need of being adopted. But only *if*.'

'Wouldn't they try and make a case that they were better for the child?' Anna added.

'They can make a case in the family court, but ultimately, it is for the judge to decide. And the judge will favour keeping birth families together where possible,' Wanda had told them without reading from a pamphlet, despite sounding as though she might be.

Elodie and Anna had continued their gentle interrogation, taking turns to try and understand if there was something fishy going on, but as suspected, Wanda was squeaky clean. Though they did pick up on a poorly hidden dislike of the relatively new big cheese in Children's Social Care.

Wanda has been a social worker for more than twenty years, and has chosen to remain at her level, on the frontline. 'I didn't want to sit behind a desk all day,' she explained, 'though the new Director of Children's Social Care clearly doesn't want to either.'

'Interfering, is she?' Elodie probed.

'Oh, I wouldn't say that,' Wanda replied, looking a little red-faced. 'It's so very important for us to be thorough, for the sake of every child, and every parent.' She fanned herself with a beautiful fabric fan she'd taken from her bag and flicked open with a flourish, after a rather flustered fumble. She didn't want to appear unprofessional, or get herself into trouble. Julia had already offered quite a bit of constructive criticism on her being too attached to certain clients, especially after everything that happened with Jo. Apparently, she "let her emotions cloud her judgement".

'Do we need to get on her good side?' Anna asked.

'She's quite hands on, but very professional – and the process involves the whole team – us, your adoption team – who assesses and trains prospective adopters, and Children's Social Care, which is where I used to work until last year. Their remit is to safeguard the children's best interests and form relationships with the birth parents to establish if they can stay together or if foster care or adoption is necessary, and together with medical professionals and so on, decisions are finalised and matches are made.'

'Wow, so you kind of know the whole system?' Anna says. 'We're lucky to have you.'

'Thank you, Anna.'

Spotting an opportunity to win Mila-points, Elodie jumps in. 'How come you left your last job?'

'You know, I just wanted to see more happy endings, and help people to get them. People like you.'

'So you don't see as many happy endings with birth parents, like in the Foster to Adopt scheme?' Elodie pushed.

'I didn't think you were interested in becoming concurrent carers?' Wanda asked, referring to her notes, hoping she hadn't got it wrong. 'You're worried if you foster first that an adoption would be unlikely?'

'No, you're right, we weren't planning on it. We believe we can help a sibling group, maybe a little older than babies. Children who are already removed permanently from their birth families, and desperately need a loving home, right now,' Anna told her.

'We were just doing some research online, and we met a couple who recently adopted a baby girl,' Elodie said. 'They thought their baby was going to be returned to the birth mother, but at the last minute everything changed. The mother went to prison. Does it happen a lot, last minute changes like that? Must be very traumatic.'

Wanda had simply said, 'Yes, very.'

'Does it, though? Happen a lot?' Elodie nudged – this was what Mila wanted, to know if this was an everyday, common occurrence, or rare – rare enough to suggest foul play.

'It's very rare for such a huge change at the eleventh hour, or at least it used to be. Sadly, we've had more than usual of late. Sometimes, people who have lived very difficult lives, experienced trauma, addiction, and so on... They can be unpredictable, I'm afraid, and we can't save them all.' And with that, Wanda had taken out some leaflets and forms, and started her own gentle interrogation.

Mila looks at Jo, and says, 'According to Elodie and Anna, it seems that until recently, cases such as yours were rare. That suggests that firstly, something could have been wrong in the way your case was handled, and secondly, if there's been a surge in sudden reversals of plans, we could check out if the system has failed you in some way. You said everyone dismissed your claims and your evidence – if there is real evidence that you were being followed and set up and it was missed, we could have a case.' Mila doesn't usually need much convincing that a government-run system might be broken.

'*If* there is real evidence?'

'You have to understand, Jo, I need to see it for myself. Your journal isn't enough.'

'The judge said that too. I could have written anything, for any reason, at any time. Like, why, though? That's what they couldn't say, not that they cared. The adoptive parents' statements didn't help either. They kept contradicting me about stuff, said Sarah always came home unsettled and upset, that they'd heard from someone at the centre that I was unwashed, and looked unwell. I thought they sounded so nice, and they knew she was coming home to me, but then as soon as the opportunity came up to trash me in court, they did. I know they probably loved Sarah, that they'd do anything for her – and obviously they thought she was better off with them.'

'Same as you, then,' Mila replies.

'What?'

'You also would do anything for her, wouldn't you? And you think she's better off with you.'

'Why are you helping me if you think I'm making it up?' Jo asks.

'I don't think you're making it up, I just don't know for sure if you're telling the whole truth. But something doesn't add up. Maybe you were framed. Maybe not. If you're lying, I'll have wasted a few days and will never hear the end of it from Fabien. If you're telling the truth and I can prove it, then we could have a huge case on our hands, and you could have a small chance to get your baby back. From my perspective, it's a risk worth taking. The possibility of uncovering something as heinous as your theory outweighs the annoyance of Fabien possibly being right for once.'

'I'm just a way for you to prove that you're better than your boyfriend?'

'Of course not!' Mila starts, aghast.

'I'm a safe bet. Fabien's going to look so stupid. Go on, use that big brain of yours to find the evidence we need. I know it's there. It has to be.'

TWELVE

When PC Hoppy graduated from the academy the previous year he was one of the top students. Things only started to go off course for him when he met Mila Kiss and Lord Fabien Knutsworth, and although he had been heralded a hero for his part in Mila's exoneration and the rescue of her niece and nephew, he is beginning to wish he had never got involved. His vast knowledge of rules makes breaking them all the more uncomfortable.

He shifts on the bar stool, feeling like an undercover agent as Fabien takes a piece of paper from his inside jacket pocket and unfolds it. Around him, diners at the Royal Oak take advantage of the pensioners' lunchtime deal. Liver and mash with onion gravy. The smell fills the busy pub, and clings to his uniform. Nobody seems to care that this on-duty policeman is sitting at the bar with the local lord, who alongside his crazy girlfriend, is always up to his neck in something. Hoppy fears that if people really took note, they might think he's a bent copper. Fortunately, most people don't take much notice of anything. Unlike Hoppy, who likes to think of himself as an expert observer. He sips his orange juice, as Fabien takes a swig of his frothy local ale.

'See, Hoppy, what we're looking for is any CCTV footage from between Ashworth Drive on the Ladywell estate and the Spar on Main Street in Hipton, on 20th November, between nine and ten in the morning... on 30th November between the estate and Halton Road Chippy, between five and six in the afternoon, and...' Fabien continues reading through his list of over ten dates and times and start and end points, all taken from Jo's torn up diary. She had written in the journal almost every day since she discovered she was pregnant, and in the last couple of weeks before her arrest she had recorded each time she thought she was being followed. Fabien thinks the entries sound like the ramblings of a mad woman, but Mila thinks they sound like fear. Ultimately, if he can get Jo on CCTV and it shows she wasn't being followed, then all the other lies will be revealed.

'Is that all?' Hoppy asks, but sarcasm doesn't come naturally to him, so Fabien takes him at face value.

'Yes,' Fabien says, refolding the piece of paper. 'There's no need to go through it, we can do that.'

'Brilliant, thanks very much,' says Hoppy, still not pulling off the sarcastic tone.

'You're most welcome.'

'I need a reason to get hold of private CCTV.'

'With that uniform and your badge? Surely not. Don't people just do what they're told when a policeman asks?'

Hoppy wishes that were true. Even with a warrant and a truncheon, he largely fails to convert his instructions into action. Last week, a ten-year-old had nicked his KitKat. 'If your friend believes she is or was being stalked, she should file a complaint. Then I can look into it officially.'

'She doesn't want to make a fuss.'

Hoppy sighs. Why can't everyone just do things properly?

'Ah, come on, old chap. How about you see what you can do, unofficially, then I'll buy you a pint in the pub later, and we can go from there?' Fabien knows full well that there is no point trying to get the police to take Jo's complaint seriously. She has already made these claims in her court cases – both of them, the drugs charge and the family court hearing – and her theory was dismissed as the paranoia and lies of a criminal and addict. There is no reason for them to change their stance, and Hoppy isn't exactly influencer of the year down at the station.

'I'll need a few days; I do have other police work to be doing.' Hoppy realises he sounds petulant, which wasn't what he was going for.

Fabien makes him feel worse by lacing his response with a patronising tone. 'And very important work it is, too.'

Hoppy swipes open his to-do list. A stolen ride-on lawnmower, graffiti on the new park bench, and a noise complaint over at the Ladywell estate, actually on the Ashworth Drive, where the alleged stalking may or may not have taken place. Given the rather uninspiring nature of local crime, Hoppy decides a possible stalker might be worth investigating after all, though he gets the impression that Fabien is holding back something. As usual.

'Are you telling me the whole story?'

'Yup,' says Fabien, looking at his shoes.

'And it doesn't have anything to do with the girl you wanted background on last week?'

'Nope,' says Fabien, gazing at the ceiling. Mila suggested that they didn't alert Hoppy to Jo's identity in relation to the accusation of being stalked, in case he mentions it at the station and is told that he is once again investigating something that the likes of DI Cora Payne has shut down as nonsense already. Hoppy can't always be trusted to stand up for himself.

'Right,' says Hoppy, not believing Fabien for a moment, and deciding that he will, in fact, look at the CCTV himself. If he's being dragged into yet another of Fabien and Mila's schemes, he at least plans to do it on his terms. Besides, if they are onto something – and let's face it, they more than often are – he could find himself at the epicentre of a proper criminal investigation. First, they look into this woman's criminal past, and now they're investigating someone who might be stalking her. It is the stuff spy novels are made of. Could she be a spy, this Jo? Are Fabien and Mila working for MI5, and recruiting dangerous yet brilliant ex-criminals, like in *Bourne Identity*? Buoyed up by his fantasy, he downs his juice in one, coughing slightly as the acid burns his throat, and stands up, accidentally upending the bar stool. 'I'll be in touch,' he says, bumping into two elderly people as he rushes off in pursuit of crime and glory.

THIRTEEN

Mila softly closes the large hardback book of fairy tales. Both children are asleep, and she carefully tucks them in. She remains seated on the chair, between the two beds, and looks at Konstantine and Karlie. Her beautiful nephew and niece, with those dark eyebrows and long lashes, look just like their mother, Mila's sister, who she misses so fiercely it hurts.

And that is why she must help Jo.

Mila never wanted to be a mother, but she has become one to these children all the same, and loves them more than she knew was possible. 'I'm doing my best,' she whispers to her sister. 'I hope you would be proud.'

The night light glows beside her, and she places the book next to it, on Karlie's bedside table. Something has been bothering her, and she closes her eyes, trying to knit the loose strands of Jo's story into something tangible, meaningful, but the stitches keep dropping and coming undone. It's something Elodie said after talking to Wanda: that the number of sudden U-turns in family court hearings had increased recently, when it used to be pretty clear from day one whether the adoption order would go through or not.

The adoptive parents would have been told that Jo was on a positive pathway to being reunited with Sarah. They should have made their peace with that, and be happy that a young woman had turned her life around. So why does Jo claim that their evidence to the family courts suggested a different picture – a falsified one, at that – and that their decision to cast doubt over Jo's competency as a mother through their statements even contributed to the outcome? The simple answer is that Jo is lying about that too, just like Fabien says.

Jo says they must have fallen in love with Sarah, panicked, and gone to extreme lengths to keep her, not caring if their statements were what was best for Sarah. Perhaps, thinks Mila.

Jo is adamant she was framed by Rob and that her journal is concrete proof. Weirdly, it was ten years out of date when she began writing in it, but Jo had scribbled each date out and written a new one in, certain she had been careful to do so accurately. She was making memories, she had told Mila with a sigh, in the beginning. She had been planning to share the journal with Sarah one day.

Is anyone able to lie this fervently and persistently, and with such consistency? Well, Mila probably could, but she isn't sure Jo is logical enough – she frequently flies off the handle, and that volatility alone is often enough to make most people slip up. Jo has never seen Rob following her, but when challenged on that she had an answer ready: Rob must have paid someone else to do it. Fabien had scoffed at the notion of such complex stratagems, and Mila has to admit, the theory of someone other than Rob following her is far-fetched. But surely if you were going to lie, you'd come up with something more palatable, more believable?

Mila kisses Karlie's cheek, then Konstantine's, brushing his long hair from his face, accidentally tickling his nose. He sneezes, but doesn't wake. She tiptoes from the room, whispering, 'I love you, sweet dreams, see you in the morning light.'

Downstairs, Fabien and Lydia are in the television room watching the nine o'clock news.

'Not that awful man again!' Mila says as she takes a seat on the huge, plump sofa, covered in blankets and cushions. She plops her feet onto Fabien's lap and pulls a crocheted blanket over her legs. 'He's never off the TV.'

Frederick Fawcett is being interviewed outside Westminster. 'I have established an agenda to shake up a system that for too long has been corrupted by our tolerance of the intolerable. I will stand for strength, tradition, and proper British values. I will fight for your rights and I will fight against putting the rights of criminals above those of their law-abiding victims – above those of our children; our *future*.' He pauses for applause, given readily by a small group of people wearing the same purple rosette as Fawcett. 'I'm delighted to announce that I shall be standing as an independent member of parliament for my local constituency, the South Ribble Valley.'

'Good God,' Mila mutters, 'he'd be practically next door.'

'Your local geography is really coming on,' Fabien says, before receiving a playful kick to his thigh.

'I don't know why everyone seems to have it in for the poor chap,' Lydia comments. 'Yes, he's a tad old-school, but he's very charming, and not all traditions ought to be done away with at the earliest convenience.'

'He wants to revoke women's rights, Lydia!' Mila says, staring at her boyfriend's mother.

'Anyway,' Lydia continues, 'the Conservatives have held South Ribble since it became a seat in 1983 apart from a Lib

Dem blip in 1991, which was briefly troubling for all concerned, but soon rectified... so I very much doubt he will win as an independent candidate with an agenda he invented last week.'

'Seriously, he wants to revoke women's rights!' Mila demands a response with her eyebrows.

Lydia is very good at avoiding giving a straight answer when it suits her, and she is an expert in making whoever is questioning her and getting their knickers in a twist look quite unnecessarily hysterical. 'I don't think he said that, Mila,' she replies calmly. 'He simply purports the benefits of the traditional family unit. Besides, as I say, he's very unlikely to win. He's more of an agent provocateur, getting the debate going, which is always a good thing. Wouldn't you agree?'

Mila takes her phone from her pocket, and starts furiously tapping and scrolling. 'Ha, yes, here it is.' She starts to read from the screen. '"The stigma of single parenthood historically ensured that children were brought up by two parents in the sanctity of marriage within a loving home in which their needs could be met both financially and emotionally."' Mila looks up triumphantly. 'He wants to persecute single mothers!'

'Persecute? Don't exaggerate, dear. He used to be a vicar, you know? I believe he was renowned for his charity work in those days, particularly with children.'

'So?' says Mila, kicking Fabien harder this time, who is resolutely staring at the television screen although he's unable to hear a word over the argument being conducted over his head.

'Well, you must be tolerant, Mila. As a vicar, he'll be conditioned to believe in marriage, and really that is no bad thing. In fact, it's about time you–'

'Tea, anyone?' Fabien shouts, jumping up. 'I'll make us a pot,' he says, scampering out of the room at speed.

By the time he returns some ten minutes later, having

waited the usual age for the ancient stove kettle to whistle atop the range, Lydia has changed the channel to a rerun of *Fawlty Towers* and she and Mila are chuckling along quite merrily. Fabien suspects his mother was well aware that any foray into a discussion about whether Mila and Fabien ought to marry would stop Mila in her tracks, and have her immediately change the subject, which is quite insulting when he thinks about it. Being around the two of them together was very stressful, sometimes more so when the peace was kept, as you never knew when one of them would explode with outrage at something the other said or did. Sometimes, he wonders if they do it just to keep him on his toes. It certainly means he tends to stay fairly quiet.

As Fabien pours the tea, Basil Fawlty whacks Manuel across the head and Mila laughs, apparently okay with the subjugation of foreigners in service, so long as it is funny.

'Thank you, dear,' says Lydia as he hands her a cup and saucer, a slice of lemon on the side for her Earl Grey.

Mila takes her favourite mug full of milky, sugary tea – one of the few parts of British cuisine she has wholeheartedly embraced; that, and the local ale. Mostly, she finds British food and drink lacking. She sips, and then remembers she is supposed to say thank you every time anyone does anything for her. 'Thank you,' she says.

Fabien smiles, liking her occasional efforts at being what he might call normal. He loves her un-normalness, though. He squeezes her toes so that she knows. She does.

A little tune calls out from Fabien's phone, as it vibrates on the side table by the sofa. He picks it up and sees a WhatsApp message from Hoppy. As he reads the brief message, a little furrow appears in his brow.

'What is it?' asks Mila.

Fabien slides over to Mila, and shows her, taking care not to alert his mother of anything she might show an interest in. As John Cleese goosesteps through the hotel foyer and Lydia roars with laughter, Fabien quietly says into Mila's ear, 'It's Hoppy. It appears that Jo... ah... was telling the truth.'

FOURTEEN

Mila, Fabien, and Jo are sitting in a row on a bench in Hoppy's shed. Hoppy is perched opposite them on a small milking stool. Hoppy isn't the kind of man one would assume had his own shed, and indeed he did not buy or construct it. It was his father's, and the tools belonging to the long dead Navy captain are still taking up too much room. Hoppy uses the shed to paint his Games Workshop figurines at the weekend, and his latest pieces are proudly lined up on a shelf to dry.

Hoppy has managed to get hold of the CCTV footage Fabien requested, but has ignored Fabien's insistence that he need not look at the contents and should hand it straight over. Hoppy may be a pushover, but he isn't an idiot. His curiosity is his drive, and it is what will eventually ensure he passes the detective exam. He has saved a number of shortened clips on his desktop, and brings the first one up as a still, not yet pressing play.

'The first thing I suspected was that this request was related to your earlier appeal to find out background on a Miss Joanna Button. It didn't take long for me to find her. She's in every clip.'

Hoppy is feeling a bit like Columbo as he explains how he figured it out, and is ready to continue his speech.

'You sound a bit like Velma in *Scooby-Doo* when she explains how they figured it out,' says Jo.

As Hoppy wrote in his text to Fabien that he has evidence of Jo being followed, Fabien and Mila thought it prudent to bring Jo along. They get a sense that if they want Hoppy's continued support, they need to show him that they trust him, and make him feel part of something. Not feeling part of something is Hoppy's general disposition, and he can never resist an opportunity to change it.

'You looked at every clip?' asks Mila.

'Of course, or at least the ones that hadn't been wiped,' Hoppy replies, 'and these images are the ones where you can most clearly see what is happening.' He clicks play.

'That's him!' Jo shouts. 'I told them, I described him – what he was wearing, how he walked, how tall he was, his build, everything, and your lot–' she points at Hoppy, 'wouldn't even check it out.'

She had described a hooded man, skinny, baggy jeans, peak of a baseball cap obscuring his eyes. She had in fact described half the males that lived around the estate on the edge of Hipton, but this one was most definitely suspiciously only a few feet behind her each time she claimed he had been. The CCTV on the gates of the block Jo lived on showed him loitering, and then following Jo on two occasions. The off-license CCTV shows him waiting outside as Jo buys milk and bread and exits with a bulging blue plastic bag. He's behind her as she feeds the ducks by the fountain in the park. He's on Main Street, his steps matching Jo's.

'Does he plant anything on her?' Mila asks.

'He must have!' says Jo.

'I thought you said he was a stalker?' says Hoppy, glaring at

Fabien, annoyed to be yet again on the back foot. 'Though I did wonder if it was more than that,' he adds, returning to his spy fantasy and wondering if it could actually be the case that something that exciting is happening in his small town.

'Of course you did,' Fabien says kindly. 'I knew I hadn't fooled you for a minute about the disconnect between the requests, or the stalking being the whole story.'

'Quite. But a little more honesty wouldn't go amiss,' says Hoppy, 'saves a bit of time. And although I have my own theory, I'm going to need to hear your version of events first.'

Fabien and Mila have agreed to share everything they know if Hoppy's evidence turned out to be the real deal. Fabien hadn't expected it to look like much at all. But here they are. Mila nods at Fabien, who clears his throat. 'You know Jo was arrested for possession of a fair bit of heroin, amongst other... bits and pieces?' Fabien reminds Hoppy. 'Well, she believes someone planted it on her so that she'd lose her family court hearing.'

'So I'd lose my *baby*,' Jo clarifies. 'They said it was a random stop and search, but then in court the copper said they'd had a tip-off. And my lawyer said to plead guilty, because I was caught red-handed and if I showed remorse and took accountability for my own actions they might go easy on me, might let me have Sarah back anyway. I said no way at first – it isn't right, is it? But then, there was no chance I was going to win by pleading my innocence, so I changed my plea and it still didn't make a blind bit of difference.'

'Pleading guilty at the last minute can, in fact, simply look like an attempt at garnering sympathy,' Hoppy explains, rather unhelpfully, as his three guests look at him dumbfounded.

'I didn't do it at the last minute, Boppy!'

'It's Hoppy–'

'I changed my plea in the interview room, pretty much under duress, because literally *nobody* was on my side.'

'Claiming duress is a very serious matter, Ms Button – are you willing to make a statement?' Jo stares at Hoppy with incredulity, and Mila squeezes her hand, causing her to take a breath. 'Though,' says Hoppy, swiping through something on his screen, 'ah, yes, here. I see your sentence was reduced in line with that plea, which is exactly what I was trying to explain.'

'Are you serious?' asks Jo.

'Always,' replies Hoppy, 'and now I must ask for complete transparency.'

'It's very simple, Hoppy,' says Mila. 'Jo's family court hearing was scheduled, and all reports suggested that the evidence presented would ensure that her baby was returned to her care. The baby had been living with foster parents since birth, due to social services believing that Jo couldn't provide a safe home for Sarah at that time, but since then she had made a good home, had a full-time job, and she had adhered to all the conditions set for her. Then, days before the hearing, the police were tipped off that she was involved in drugs again, and a selection box of substances was found in her handbag, just as she walked back from the shops. You tell me, Hoppy, isn't that odd?'

'UK police receive thousands of tip-offs relating to drugs offences each week, so statistically, it is quite the opposite of odd,' replies Hoppy.

'In places like Hipton? Or Farlington?'

'Not quite so many in rural areas and smaller stations, I grant you.'

'You've looked through the footage of Sarah being followed. How about we look at more footage – see if there's any evidence of her buying, selling or moving drugs?'

'I'm sure she's smarter than that,' says Hoppy. 'You'd be surprised at the savviness of modern criminals.'

'You still think I'm guilty?' says Jo.

'The legal system is very robust. Tip-offs are common. There's evidence of a man following you, but not of any interaction with him – I've studied the footage from the dates you listed in great depth. There's nothing to suggest that he planted anything on you on any of those dates.'

'It would have just been the last date – the day I was arrested! If it was before then, I'd have seen the gear in my bag!' Jo's voice is rising, her frustration bubbling furiously within her.

'You checked the last date, Hoppy?' asks Fabien gently, as Mila rubs Jo's back.

'Of course.'

'But the CCTV isn't everywhere, is it?' interrupts Jo. 'You lot aren't Big Brother just yet. He could have planted it out of sight of the cameras!'

'Yes,' says Hoppy, 'however, there is a more logical explanation for his interest in you, now that I am informed that the stalker story was a ruse, and your connection with this man could be drugs related.'

'What?' asks Jo.

Hoppy opens up another file and presses play. They watch the footage for a few seconds until Hoppy pauses it, and uses his fingers to zoom in closer and closer to the man's neck. With his stylus he rather flamboyantly draws a red circle around something fuzzy.

'He has a tattoo!' says Mila.

'And on his neck, too,' says Fabien, 'I expect he'll regret that one of these days.'

'What is it?' asks Jo.

'I think it's a peace lily,' says Fabien, squinting.

'It's a gang symbol,' clarifies Hoppy, 'and when I combined what it is, where it is, his general stature and demeanour, I was able to identify him.'

FIFTEEN

'And...?' prompts Mila.

'His name is Bradley Pound, and he's a known drug dealer,' says Hoppy, triumphantly.

'Well there you go!' says Jo. 'He must have planted them on me!'

Hoppy shakes his head. 'Or he was keeping an eye on you to ensure you were moving the product and not, say, pilfering any? I believe your file says that the prosecution's theory was that you were newly recruited and taking a few samples to build trust?'

'For the love of Jesus-bloody-Christ!' says Jo. 'What do I have to do to make you see? It's always the same. This other woman, Deb, I met her online. She was about to get her baby boy back, just like me – six months old, he was. They'd taken him at birth because she was drinking early on, but she hadn't touched a drop since, not even in the last trimester, not even when she was crying for him every night, mopping up milk from her useless breasts... and then days before the hearing, they found her drunk – passed out. She said someone spiked her, but no one believed her. Now, course, she's back drinking because... why not? She's nothing left to lose.'

'You were framed and this other lady was spiked? As I always say, the principle of parsimony should be invoked in all matters: *pluralitas non est ponenda necessitate*,' Hoppy says with what he considers to be aplomb.

'Plurality should not be posited without necessity,' Fabien clarifies.

'Wow, for once, I'd actually like it if someone would speak English, please,' says Mila, arms folded, irritated. This was not one of the many phrases she was familiar with.

'It means that the simplest solution is usually right,' Jo explains. 'Don't look so surprised, Fabien, I'm not completely uneducated. I've got a few old philosophy books, or I did, when I had my own place. You can blame Wanda for that, always bringing them over, and going on about some meditation or theory or such while I waited for Sarah to come home, looking for meaning where there is bugger all – just a chaotic world, full of accidents and unfairness and you get what you're given, which in my case is a big steaming pile of–'

'So you're an existentialist?' asks Hoppy, getting rather off point.

'No, as that might suggest I have agency, instead of being tossed around by the universe and its mates. I'm more into Absurdism, I reckon.'

'Interesting,' muses Hoppy.

'Isn't it? So, your theory is that it is easier to assume the drinker drinks, the ex-addict deals, and the law works fairly for all.'

'Quite,' Hoppy says, pleased to have everyone on board, finally. He starts to shut down his screen, satisfied that they can wrap this up.

'There are others like Jo,' says Mila quietly, frowning, trying to catch the thought that's flying around her mind. It's something relating to Jo's story not adding up, but this so-called simple solution is not ringing true either. Not when a private journal so adamantly demonstrates innocence, written in real time. Not that Jo would likely record illegal drug dealing in a written diary, but surely she wasn't such a mastermind that she would have had the foresight to write an entire work of fiction, and just so happen to be tearing it to shreds when she and Fabien walked in. There was nothing intentional about Jo sharing her journal with Mila and Fabien, and lies were nearly always intentional. 'Wanda said so, too.'

'What's that, Mila?' asks Fabien, who is quite keen for Hoppy to be right for once. It would certainly make life easier. For him, anyway.

'Wanda told Elodie and Anna that there had been more cases than usual of sudden reversals in plans to return babies to their mothers. She said usually they could tell from the beginning what the likely outcome would be, but that lately there had been more instances where suddenly, despite months of assessments going one way, everything changed.'

'Did she say all that?' asks Fabien, raising an eyebrow. He seems to remember Elodie saying that she'd made a fleeting remark about there being a few more cases than usual lately, and not elaborately suggesting that anything at all suspicious was going on.

'And then there's Deb. How did you find Deb?' Mila turns to Jo.

'Online. There's a group for parents whose kids have been taken away. Started by someone called Heather, a granny who wanted to adopt her grandkid, but they wouldn't let her because she was too old, so the kid ended up in the care system and they lost touch. Heather campaigns for the rights of families to keep their kids.'

'Were there others? Like you, and Deb? Do you think we could get in touch with them?'

'Well, Deb got kicked out of the group for being abusive to one of the dads when she was pissed, but I might be able to find her.'

Fabien looks to Mila. Jo has just confirmed that the woman is an abusive drunk. Hoppy's conclusion that another drug dealer might have been told to follow Jo on her first few runs seems plausible. Mila is smart, and by God she's been proven right enough times, but she is also biased against everyone and everything even vaguely connected to "The System", and biased in favour of everyone and everything that appears to have lost out to it. According to Mila, the system is incapable of ever getting anything right. In Fabien's view, that is a tad extreme – one would think, even only in terms of probability – that it will, at least occasionally, get something right.

'I think we need to do two things,' Mila says, not noticing Fabien's sigh. 'We need to know why this guy was following Jo, whether someone else was paying him to – see if we can link him to Rob and search for evidence or try for a confession, and we need to hear Deb's story, and see if there are more just like hers.'

'But why?' asks Fabien. At least Jo's claim that Rob framed her to make her vulnerable contains some slim vein of logic, though even that was a push. A broader scheme of an entire system failing to notice that women were falling victim to set-ups and spiking is a step too far.

'I don't know,' Mila admits, 'but the only way we can find out what really happened, whether Jo was framed, or not–'

'I was,' Jo says petulantly.

'–is to find out what this drug dealer was up to. To prove that she was set up, we need motive.'

'Well, yeah, true – we do need proof,' Jo says, nodding, 'and motive. Which I obviously already provided.'

'If Sarah's adoption order was made on the basis of false

evidence, then Jo has a case to get her baby back. And we have a duty to help her. You may say the simplest solution is always the right one, but didn't Sherlock Holmes himself say that, "Once you eliminate the impossible, whatever remains, no matter how improbable, must be the truth?"' Mila had been raiding the old library bookshelves in the hall and had found a real affinity with the often-misunderstood Holmes. 'And I believe Jo.' Mila suddenly realises she does believe Jo, hunch or not; she can feel it through her body that this woman has been failed. And the whole point of Mila and Fabien's Last Chance Cooperative is to remedy where the system has failed the most vulnerable people in society.

Jo sniffs, a tear falls. She wipes it away with her sleeve, embarrassed.

'Sherlock Holmes is a fictional character, Mila,' says Fabien.

'And I'm not sure his methods are as robust as you might like to believe,' says Hoppy. 'You can't believe everything you read in books and watch on television. There's more to policing than these writers know.'

'Isn't it weird, though?' asks Mila.

Fabien thinks, yes, it bloody well is. Here they are harbouring an ex-addict from her violent boyfriend, debating crazy theories about women being framed and spiked, sitting in PC Hoppy's garden shed, surrounded by little painted soldiers and demons, and who knows what else.

'Isn't it weird,' Mila repeats, 'that two fairly local women are claiming they've been set up just ahead of their family court hearings? We should at least look into it, see if there are more women like Jo and Deb. Maybe you could arrest Bradley Pound, Hoppy? See if you can get him to admit to following Jo, and find out why.'

'We don't just go around arresting people willy-nilly,' says Hoppy.

'Though, to be fair, Hoppy old chap, you did say he was a drug dealer,' Fabien reminds him.

'Yeah,' says Jo, 'You can stop and search him *randomly* like one of your lot did to me.'

'Excellent idea, Jo,' says Mila. 'Looks like we have a plan.'

SIXTEEN

Mila is opening and closing the drawers of the huge old desk in the late Lord Gregory Knutsworth's study. The gift sits, unwrapped, on top of the paper, next to the kitchen scissors. Drawers creak and stick and rarely close again on the first attempt. The bottom one on the left is particularly tricky and, having not found what she's looking for, Mila slams it with frustration, upending the stationery holder so that several expensive pens spill onto the desk, rolling and dropping one by one to the floor.

'What on earth is going on?' demands Lady Lydia, the heavy door banging against the wall as she pushes through and marches towards the desk. She bends to pick up a fountain pen. 'This was Gregory's favourite,' she says quietly, looking at it, before shifting her gaze to Mila, who is currently rifling through the third drawer down on the right.

Mila pauses to look up. 'Oh, hello, Lydia. Have you seen the Sellotape?'

'You have no right to be in here!' Lydia bellows in response, and Mila, who has resumed her search, suddenly stops. As quietly as she can, which is not very given the age and state of the desk, she tries to close the drawer. 'You can't just root through my husband's private affairs!'

Mila self-consciously closes her mouth, which she realises is hanging open in surprise at this unexpected and unnecessary outburst. It's just a desk, and Gregory's dead. Who cares? 'I'm sorry?' she ventures.

'Are you?' asks Lydia, still seething. Gregory never trusted Mila, and his investigations into her identity had prompted many to speculate wildly that she might have killed him. Whilst Lydia accepted this was quite untrue, Mila had initially lied to all of them about who she was, and her darling husband had been quite right to question the girl's authenticity. He would have spanked his own child for sticking their nose in his private papers, and would turn in his grave to see Mila doing so, unabashed.

'I am,' Mila says, with more conviction. 'I looked everywhere for the Sellotape and I couldn't find it, and I just thought it might have been tidied away into a desk drawer. I didn't mean to...' Mila searches for one of the phrases Fabien has used when explaining why people always seem so affronted around her, '...disrespect the boundaries.'

Lydia looks a little puzzled. 'Well, yes. I expect you didn't mean anything by it. But, honestly, Mila, why on earth would Gregory have anything so practical as Sellotape? He didn't wrap a present, or *"craft"* anything in his entire life. If something was broken, he would ask Danny to fix it and, furthermore, I'm sure no one has tidied anything away in this house since Anna left. What *is* this?' Lydia peers down over the desk to get a closer look. 'Is it someone's birthday?' The wrapping paper, she notices, is covered in the repeated message of "Happy Birthday!" and Peppa Pig characters, which Lydia recognises from Karlie's birthday last month. 'It isn't Konstantine's? I haven't forgotten? No, that's not for a little boy...'

'No, just a friend. Have you seen the Sellotape? We used it just the other day, but it has vanished. I thought I'd returned it to the kitchen, but–'

'Which friend?' Lydia enquires. Mila doesn't have any friends.

'Someone I met recently, through the charity.'

Lydia raises an eyebrow and smiles. 'How kind.' Perhaps Mila is softening after all.

'I'll walk to the village store,' Mila tells her, retrieving the gift, but leaving the paper and the scissors strewn across the leather topped desk that was so cherished by Lydia's late husband.

Lydia coughs, a gentle signal, and Mila swivels and walks back to the door, collecting the offending items.

The village store sits opposite the green in the centre of the village. Mila heads towards it and spots Susannah sticking a poster on the noticeboard. Tempted to quicken her pace and take the longer route around the green rather than striding across the path as usual and walking straight into Susannah, Mila swallows and decides to be polite, hoping it will be a quick and painless exchange.

'Mila! How lovely to see you! Any news on the playground project? I'm so proud of you and your community spirit, I really am. We all are.' Susannah is also very pleased that as part of Mila's original host family she can claim credit for introducing such a charitable young woman to Farlington... even if she is, at times, a little difficult.

'Um,' Mila begins, thinking they really need to fill out those health and safety forms and get the damned swings installed. She looks around, searching for an excuse. Her eyes first skip over and then land on the face staring back at her from the noticeboard. 'Is that Frederick Fawcett?' Mila points to the poster that Susannah has just pinned.

'Yes, dear,' Susannah says, 'he's doing a talk at the Women's Institute next week.'

Mila starts to speak, but Susannah raises a hand. 'Now, I know you and Elodie and some other young people are not his biggest fans–'

'Susannah, he's a–'

'But,' Susannah continues, hand still raised like a stop sign, 'we do not tolerate this new-fangled cancel culture, and we believe in giving everyone a fair hearing – besides, Jenny Beard met him at a National Trust stately home in Yorkshire and she was quite charmed. Once she had asked him to speak, we couldn't really say no. He's doing the rounds, you know, now he's standing for parliament.'

'He's not standing here, though, is he? Thank God.'

'No, but he's very keen by all accounts to speak to women – especially influential women – leaders of communities, like ourselves. Perhaps you should come, listen to what he has to say. I really wonder if Elodie and the other protesters have got him rather wrong. Taken him out of context.'

'No.'

'No, what?' Susannah asks.

'No, I'm not coming, and no, they haven't got him wrong.'

'Of course, I'm all for inclusivity, just like dear Lydia. We were saying just the other morning over coffee, inclusivity means everyone, not just the people you support. That's why it's so un-inclusive for that awful Gareth Davies to keep writing such dreadful things about the Knutsworths. Anti-aristocracy is classism too, wouldn't you say?'

Mila doesn't know what to say, so she just tries to process what she's heard, her forehead creasing with the effort.

'We had a socialist in September. Well, he was a local historian actually, but he used the word comrade at least three times, and poor Mrs Bentham was very upset by his comments about Mrs Thatcher.'

Mila is still furious when she arrives back at Farlington Hall, though she congratulates herself on how efficiently she managed to end the conversation with Susannah without causing undue offence. She wraps the present at the kitchen table – not in Gregory's prized study – and makes her way to the wing where Jo is set up with an old laptop, wi-fi, and a mission to find and connect with the women who claim to have had similar experiences online.

'How's it going?' Mila asks.

'I scrolled through bloody pages and pages of chat to identify the ones who seem to have similar stories, and I'm DM-ing them one by one, like you said, to keep it discreet. Though I'm not sure how any of their experiences can be related to mine. Rob wouldn't have had anything to do with Deb, or the others. Why would he? I still think we should focus on nailing *him*.'

'It could show a chink in the system, which we might be able to use to demonstrate that the process itself was faulty, and that the evidence given at the family court wasn't robust. It might give us a way to reopen your case.'

Jo sighs. 'I guess, but honestly, their so-called systems are guarded like the crown jewels, and none of them can do any wrong or ever make a mistake. I'm telling you, they just drown you in paperwork, and nobody can work out what the hell is going on.'

'Here, I got you something,' Mila says, handing Jo the gift. 'Sorry about the kids' wrapping paper.'

Jo tears it open. 'A new journal!'

'Thought maybe you'd still find it helpful, you know – to put your thoughts down on paper. I know you must be going mad, stuck in here.'

'Oh, thank you, Mila!' Jo says, hugging her.

Mila's phone vibrates. She breaks the embrace and takes it out of her pocket, grimacing as she reads the message from Fabien.

> Where are you? Mother having a fit. What did you say to Susannah earlier?

'Everything okay?' asks Jo.

'I'm in trouble again.'

SEVENTEEN

Mila kills the radio in frustration. 'Do they always relentlessly play sickly love songs all the way through February in this country?'

'Yep, well, at least until Valentine's Day,' replies Jo, as Mila rolls her eyes at the stupidity of the concept. Jo checks her hair in the mirror above the passenger seat. 'God, I look a mess.'

'Not true, but it really doesn't matter. You know, a low-key appearance can help gain trust,' Mila tells her, glancing left, indicating right. 'Okay, we're nearly in the town centre – can you direct me in from here?'

'Low-key?' Jo laughs. 'I look about fifty-three years old, and like I live in a hole in the ground. At least Anna had something normal to lend me to wear.'

'My clothes are normal,' says Mila, who had failed to find anything in her wardrobe that met with Jo's approval. She is currently dressed in her trademark skinny black jeans adorned with chains, and her favourite chunky boots. Today's T-shirt depicts a murder of crows eating a corpse.

'You look like you worship the devil. You should probably keep your jacket zipped up,' Jo says. 'Anna has good taste, though.' Jo fingers the soft wool of the sage green jumper she borrowed earlier, admires the quality of the long denim skirt. 'Though I could really do with going back to the bedsit and getting my stuff.'

'No, Jo. What if Rob is there? We don't want to make it easy for him to find you, or see you're with us, or in any way get a head start on our investigation.'

Jo looks out of the window, towards the grey sea, which meets the grey sky. 'Next left,' she says, directing Mila to leave the main promenade speckled with amusement arcades and chippies shut down for the winter. She isn't scared of Rob – what more can he do to her that he hasn't already done? There's nothing left to take. 'Straight on here,' she tells Mila, as the streets narrow and the tiny houses get closer and closer together, their pleasant journey to Deb's flat in Morecambe almost at an end. Jo has enjoyed herself these last couple of days – being with Mila, being out of that room – but now she's anxious again, as she has been each time they've arrived at one of the women's homes. 'Left,' she says, and then, 'I hope it goes okay.'

'Don't worry, just be yourself – you've been doing great and I have some questions prepared. You said she was okay when you chatted online, and she's expecting us. Nothing to worry about.' Mila sounds more confident than she feels.

Yesterday was mixed. Daisy had slammed the door in their face despite agreeing to meet, whereas Leann had invited them in and told them a long tale of woe, which didn't take much unravelling, especially when Jo's old dealer appeared downstairs wearing a pink fluffy dressing gown. A few probing questions ascertained that Leann had not been framed, as she had suggested, but that she 'just bloody hated social services and was happy to help bring them down'.

Jo had asked her if she hoped to get her baby back, and the

woman had just shrugged and told her that the ship had sailed, before casually lighting another cigarette.

Then there had been Kaye. Like Jo, she'd had a troubled past, but before things had gone awry, she had a place at university and a promising future playing football at national level. A car accident had whipped it all away, left her in agony for months, and she'd fallen foul of the painkillers. When they ran out and she was signed off, and she looked elsewhere to numb the pain of lost hope. She hadn't managed to stay totally clean throughout the pregnancy, and there had been incidents – arrests for soliciting, and for shoplifting. Kaye had cried with shame recounting it, as they sat in her neat living room, in pride of place a huge blown-up photograph in a lovely frame of Kaye holding her baby, a picture taken shortly before the final adoption order was signed.

Kaye explained that her baby boy Bobby was given to foster parents at birth, with a view to him most likely being returned in a few months, when the assessments were complete. She had proved herself addiction-free, and able to provide a safe and loving home. No promises had been made, but she had harboured no doubt that she would succeed.

'And I did,' she explained earnestly, 'I really did. My aunt got me into rehab, my parents supported me too, they couldn't wait to be grandparents.'

Shortly before the family court hearing, the social worker had paid a final visit to her home alongside the new Director of Children's Social Care. They had asked to see the nursery. 'I was excited to show her, to show anyone – I was so proud of it. I decorated it myself,' Kaye told them. The visiting professionals had admired the cot and the mobile, and the pretty changing table with the safari-themed changing mat resting on top. One of the social workers opened a drawer idly, admiring the workmanship, which revealed a range of pharmaceuticals – and not the kind you get over the counter in Boots. 'And that was pretty much that,' she'd said. 'The thing is, they weren't mine. Someone put them there.'

'Who?' Mila had asked, as Kaye didn't have an abusive or vengeful ex-boyfriend wanting to regain control of her.

'I don't know, Mila, and that's why I didn't stand a chance.'

Kaye had insisted throughout the family court hearing that she wasn't back on drugs, that tests said as much, but with the drugs in the changing table and her long history of abuse, the final decision was made that baby Bobby would be better off with his foster parents, who were desperate to adopt him. The Director of Children's Social Care had been congratulated on her good luck in opening the drawer and saving Bobby from the imminent danger his mother posed.

'I blamed those poor people who had done nothing but love Bobby, but who else would want to sabotage me like that? I haven't made many friends over the last few years, and I guess I even made some enemies, but by the time Bobby was a few months old and I was on track I'd lost touch with most people from my old life. I was only really seeing my family.'

Kaye's parents haven't disowned her, but relations are frosty, and her aunt doesn't want to know her anymore, saddened and hurt to have invested in a liar and a cheat. As with Jo, nobody really believes her version of events, because why would they? Drugs in an addict's possession paint a pretty clear picture to most people. Despite losing her baby and feeling at rock bottom, Kaye has somehow stayed on track, keeping down her job, studying sports science part-time in the hope of becoming a physiotherapist, and she remains determined to prove she is telling the truth.

'I'm all over the internet day in, day out, looking for something that can explain what happened,' she told them. 'I can't afford a solicitor, so I'm constantly trying to make sense of the legal system, but honestly, I'm getting nowhere fast... and then I'm googling, wondering if anyone has had something similar happen, and found that online group. But I keep thinking, maybe the drugs *were* mine, and I just forgot I put them there? After the birth, with no baby to hold or feed, I was going mad at times, and I wonder – did I find them in an old hiding place and just unthinkingly put them in a drawer? Could I have done? Wouldn't I have remembered? I told myself I was mad, paranoid, crazy, but honestly, I think I'd do worse – if I had to – to get my boy back.'

Mila and Jo had left Kaye's house with so many questions whirling around their heads that they had driven back to Farlington Hall in near silence. Mila had suggested they let the information sink in, speak to Deb, their final contact for now, and then try to make sense of the facts and stories they had managed to unearth.

'Just up here, on the right,' Jo says now, as Mila swings into a housing estate with roads too narrow for all the double-parked cars. At the end of the road is a small block of pebble-dashed flats, the bottom windows protected by bars. 'This is it, she's number six, second floor.'

Mila is glad her car is what Fabien describes as an old banger, and therefore unlikely to be of interest to joyriders, and then feels bad for even entertaining such a thought. She worries, not for the first time, that the Knutsworth's family's prejudices are rubbing off on her. A ball flies past Mila's head as she looks up, and bounces off the windscreen.

Jo throws it back to the kids. 'Good job your car's such an old rust bucket, or you'd worry about it getting nicked around here,' she tells Mila, who then feels a little bit better about her own judgements, though not much.

'Right, let's go,' Mila says, as the ball comes flying towards her again, this time with perfect aim, as it whacks her in the side of her head.

'Got the weirdo!' the kids yell, high-fiving each other, until Mila over arms it so hard that it bounces off at least two kids' heads, who look back bewildered.

'This is what this weirdo does to their victims, so begone!' Mila says, cackling and pointing to the gruesome image on her T-shirt. The kids scatter and Mila does her zip up to the top. 'Shall we?'

Deb takes an age to open the door, and when she finally does, Mila and Jo can see why. Mila coughs from the stench of booze, and Jo allows Deb to lean on her as they try to get her inside and close the door behind them.

'I was just having a nap,' Deb slurs, 'just coming round.'

Mila and Jo share a look. While Jo goes to dig around for some coffee and a clean cup, Mila starts to talk to Deb. By the time Jo returns with a black coffee, explaining she can't find any milk, and isn't sure the fridge is working anyway, Mila has ascertained that they're not going to be able to interview Deb today.

'I think we should take her back with us. We can't leave her like this,' says Mila.

'What will Fabien say?' Jo says with a cheeky smile. 'Has he forgiven you yet?'

'I was completely reasonable with Susannah,' Mila replies. She has taken to confiding in Jo when she feels like an outsider in her own home, which is often. After her run-in with Susannah in the village, the apparently furious mayor had been straight on the telephone to Lydia, who had immediately collared Fabien, who had been tasked with "trying to make Mila see sense for once", again.

'You did call her a Nazi, though, right?'

'No! I simply explained to her that those who are willing to give a platform to fascist and reductionist ideologists have – in the past – been called Nazis. I honestly don't know why she was so upset by a simple historical fact. After all, she was the one shouting up for the rights of everyone to say whatever they like.'

Jo laughs.

'Fabien's just pissed because he thinks he has to be the village diplomat, and although he likes to think he's progressive, he can't help his upbringing. He likes life to be ordered, conversations to be civil, and relationships to be simple. He likes things in their proper place.'

'So he's going to love housing another addict in the east wing,' Jo says, shaking her head, as she prods a now snoring Deb, the black coffee next to her untouched. 'Come on, Debs mate, let's get you up,' she says, as she and Mila help Deb up and out the flat, finding the keys in the door, locking up, and heading home to try to disentangle the increasingly strange mystery surrounding three vulnerable yet determined young mothers.

EIGHTEEN

Deb sleeps the whole way home, head lolling in the back seat like a child. Mila calls Fabien when they're a few minutes away and tells him the latest news.

'No,' Fabien says, already doing as he is asked and checking the coast is clear before heading to the driveway, where he will assist Mila and Jo in getting Deb quickly into the house and into the rarely used wing, where Jo and now Deb will now both be staying. 'She's drunk?'

'We've all been there,' replies Mila.

'Not the same, Mila.'

'We need her story, her evidence, Fabien, you know that.'

Fabien thinks Kaye's story sounds suspiciously similar to Jo's, and part of him briefly considers that maybe something strange is going on, though what or why or for whose benefit, he cannot yet fathom. The other part remains resolutely sceptical and he wonders if Jo has just found an old druggy chum to add weight to her story, and ensure Mila's continuing support. Still, Fabien helps get Deb settled on a chaise longue beneath an old cashmere blanket.

'Is that thing loaded?' she slurs, pointing at the antique gun above the old fireplace.

'Shush, don't worry,' Jo says, 'you're safe.'

Fabien, Mila, and Jo drink hot chocolate next to a noisy plug-in heater, afraid to build a fire in case the old chimney is blocked, or smoke coming from where it usually doesn't alerts Danny to their presence.

'From the combination of Kaye's experience and yours, Jo,' Mila summarises, 'the best argument we currently have is that the assessment was unfair, which might mean we could appeal the hearing. Yours was unfair because there is evidence you were being followed by a known drug dealer, which corroborates your given evidence and your real-time diaries, none of which was taken seriously by the authorities at the time. Taken together with Kaye's negative drug tests, which prove she wasn't using despite having drugs in her possession, it could demonstrate a bias in the judgements against the mothers. It is possible we could claim discrimination and prejudice. If what Deb tells us shows the same sort of bias, three women – three victims of systematic class discrimination – it could be enough to make an actual case.'

Jo stays with Deb, offering her water when she stirs, and covering her with the blanket when it slips off her as she tosses and turns. Mila and Fabien have a quiet and awkward dinner with Lydia, during which Mila is forced to apologise to Lydia and promises to apologise in person to Susannah at the soonest opportunity. This is the deal she had to strike with Fabien to reward his ongoing cooperation.

Finally, Deb is awake and sober, and Mila and Fabien have rejoined the women in their wing. 'I'm so sorry, Jo,' she says, looking mournful and pathetic. Mila and Fabien sit quietly. 'I was so nervous about you coming, thinking you wouldn't believe me, that I'd look stupid again, I just thought I'd have a bit of Dutch courage. Shouldn't have, eh? I can't, you see, just one or two sends me into a different place. I think I'll have just one more, I'm feeling okay, I can handle it. You'd think I'd have better tolerance. Thing is, the nurses told me it builds up in you, makes you worse.'

'It's okay,' says Jo, looking at Mila.

'Of course, don't worry, we understand,' says Mila, looking at Fabien.

'You're most welcome here,' says Fabien, looking at the floor.

Deb begins. Her story is the same. She had her problems, she had the same Foster to Adopt order placed upon her baby from birth. Just like Jo and Kaye, Deb had turned things around. For Deb, the moment of clarity came when she'd first held the grainy scan of the tiny person she already loved most in the world, and whom she now stood to lose forever. She attended all her visitations, she hadn't drunk for months. Her social worker was sure baby Jacob would be home in weeks. And then, just before the family hearing, she went out to a small local music festival in a nearby park, and stayed totally sober, until she wasn't. After that, she remembers very little, but she woke up drunk, was late for her visit, her social worker was banging on the door. There was no hiding her hangover; she stank of booze, and there were empties all over the flat. Bottles she hadn't bought, brands she didn't usually choose – couldn't afford, for that matter. But naturally, no one believed her, and with her addiction appearing to be back, she lost the family hearing and her baby.

Mila takes notes furiously, draws diagrams, doodles, asks questions. 'We have a case,' she says, confidently. 'All three women had been rehabilitated, all three are convinced someone set them up or sabotaged them, all three were then dismissed as liars, paranoid or plain mad, by the authorities. It is sexist, classist, prejudiced bullshit, and we have to find out who is behind this.'

'Rob is behind mine, I worked that out already,' says Jo.

'I'm not sure anymore,' Mila tells her. 'There's no link between Rob and Kaye or Deb, or anyone you know, right?'

The women nod; they've been through this.

'I know it was him. When they arrest that Bradley Pound git, they have to get him to admit who told him to follow me. It will be Rob.'

'Fabien, can you chase Hoppy on that?' Mila says, before turning back to Jo. 'The thing is, Jo, I think it might be bigger than Rob. I just don't know how big.'

'Are you sure, Mila?' says Fabien, who wonders if Mila's conviction that there is a connection that puts the authorities and the system in the middle as the wrongdoers is all she needs to find one, substantiated or otherwise.

'Yes, are you sure?' asks Jo, confrontation oozing from her body language. She knows it is Rob. She is starting to think that Fabien might have a point... Maybe Deb is just a drunk, and maybe Kaye's suspicions about herself putting the drugs in the drawer are correct. Obviously, he isn't right about *her*; she *was* set up. 'Mine's a clear case and all we need is proof that Rob framed me – he has a motive, it's in all the books about coercive control. They make you feel like you're going mad – it's called gaslighting. And they'll stop at nothing to undermine you and make you fail, so that you need them. I made notes on it.'

'I'm not saying Rob didn't do terrible things, Jo,' says Mila.

'But you don't think he framed me?'

'I honestly don't know. But I think we need to look for a link, a common thread, or even a common person – an agenda or motive that connects all three cases.'

'There might not be one,' Jo says, thinking that even if there is, they might never find it. What if Mila cares more about proving the system is broken than she does about proving Rob is guilty? What if she cares more about being right than about getting Sarah back? Jo simply isn't prepared to let Mila's lofty plans to prove some "bigger picture" get in the way of her being reunited with her baby, before it is too late.

10 February 2025

Seeing as you bought me this journal, I guess I should address it to you, Mila. It was over a year ago that I started writing my thoughts down, all through the easy bit of chucking my gear down the toilet and all through the pain of staying clean, living with my parents who despised me and wished it was me who had died instead of my sister. I wrote nearly every day, as things got better, and I learned to cope. I wrote all my plans down for me and Sarah and our perfect future life, and then I wrote down everything as the whole thing came crashing down around me. I wrote in prison, and I made my plans to catch Rob out, to get to the truth so that I could be with my baby again. I think of her every second of every day. She's seven months old now, and soon she'll say her first word. "Mama", probably, but she won't say it to me. She'll be learning to roll over, and I won't be there to catch her.

When you came into my life Mila, I thought you were just looking for a charity case so you and your fancy family could feel good about yourselves, but then you showed me you weren't like that... except now, I'm not so sure. Thing is, if we don't go after Rob, I don't think I'll ever see Sarah again, even if you do prove the system is biased or whatever. Nobody apart from you cares about that stuff. Nobody cares about people like us. We have to get our hands dirty, Mila. I hope I can make you see that this isn't about the big fight, this is about me and my baby, and I don't care if that sounds selfish. At the end of the day, I'll do what I have to do to get her back.

NINETEEN

FEBRUARY 2025

'No comment? Ah. The whole interview,' Fabien says, nodding, as he and Mila walk towards the Town Hall steps. Fabien puts his phone back in his pocket and turns to her. 'Hoppy says there isn't much more they can do.'

PC Hoppy Atkins has finally lived up to his word and with his fellow bobby on the beat and long-term crush PC Helen Phillips, brought Bradley Pound in for questioning after persuading Jo to make a formal complaint. They had stopped and searched him previously, but Pound had been totally clean. With Jo's complaint, an increasingly sneaky Hoppy had slipped the whole thing past DI Cora Payne, who had been involved in Jo's case last year and didn't believe a word that came out of her mouth. Hoppy worries constantly about the erosion of his principles.

'He said he put it to Bradley that he had been accused of following a vulnerable woman, and CCTV evidence suggested as much, at which point Bradley asked for the duty solicitor and stoically continued with his No Comment strategy.'

'So obviously he *was* following her?'

'Seems that way, but Hoppy says that the CCTV evidence

only shows he happens to be walking in the same direction; it's circumstantial. He never attempts to make contact. There's no obvious reason why he would be following her, as they have never been known to one another.'

'Apart from the fact he was trying to plant drugs on her at the exact right moment before a tip-off that got her put in jail.'

'Except there's no evidence at all that he did that. Hoppy said even his colleague Helen suggested he might be following her to check that she was delivering the product and not stealing it, given her background and the notes in Jo's file. And Pound's not going to admit to that, either.'

'Helen is even straighter than Hoppy. No imagination.'

'I'm not sure imagination is required, Mila. As you keep reminding us, we need to deal in facts.'

'You still don't believe her, do you?'

'Can you say, hand on heart, you do?'

'I admit, I have had my doubts,' says Mila, as they stop at the bottom of the Town Hall steps, waving at Security Stu, 'but it is too weird a story to be fabricated. And now Kaye and Deb... There's clearly something going on.'

'He couldn't hold Pound. The solicitor was running circles around poor Hoppy, apparently. Said he had nowhere near enough evidence to even suggest the complaint could be upheld, let alone to charge him. He also mentioned harassment, given the recent fruitless stop and search.'

'Hmmm,' is all Mila says, perpetually baffled by a world in which one cannot do whatever they need to, in the pursuit of justice. So much red tape.

'Now,' Fabien says, turning to Mila and taking hold of her shoulders, 'are you going to play nice?'

'Oh piss off, Fabien,' Mila replies, checking her watch, and glancing around. Susannah is expecting them at three for a catch-up on the playground project. But, according to Fabien and Lydia, it is an opportunity for Mila to apologise in person and explain that she does not, contrary to Susannah's impression last time they met, think that the mayor is a Nazi.

'Hey, what the–' says Fabien. 'Isn't that Jo... and Kaye, and drunk Deb?'

'Don't call her that! She's been sober since she arrived with us.'

'That's less than two days. And, also, not the point! What are they doing here? How did they get here?'

Fabien wasn't supposed to have noticed them yet. 'I gave Jo my car keys. Told her to be discreet.'

Fabien raises an eyebrow. 'Mila...' his voice carries warning, 'we are just here to say sorry to Susannah, right? And update her on the dates for the swings project?'

'We are most certainly here to do that. Come on,' she says, as they climb the steps. But Fabien stays static at the bottom. 'Okay,' Mila says with a sigh, 'you got me. We need their files. That's why they're here.'

'Excuse me?'

'Well, they're not allowed to know who the adoptive parents are, but we need to know, as that's the best place to start in terms of looking for a link. Their social workers were all different, but their files will show who else was involved in the decision making and assessments and who the adoptive parents are, so we can cross reference all involved parties and figure out why three women ended up in such a bizarrely similar situation.' Fabien stares at Mila. 'Come on, Fabien, or we'll be late.'

But they are already late. Jo, Kaye, and Deb haven't noticed that Fabien and Mila are not yet ensconced inside, so they walk in calmly.

'Shit, they're in, we have to go. Now!' Mila runs up the steps, calling hello to Security Stu before slipping into the lift with the three women, leaving Fabien in the foyer.

'Ah, Fabien,' Susannah calls, 'I thought I'd just pop out to the foyer to see if you had arrived. Come through, come through. Where's Mila?'

The lift doors open on floor three and, as planned, the women scatter. Jo, known in the department for causing a fuss, runs towards the adoption team's office shouting obscenities and knocking fake pot plants off desks. While Wanda tries to reason with her, and Julia emerges from her office next door, calling for security, Jo appears more and more unstable, throwing a stapler at the window and knocking over two chairs. She pushes Julia, and Mila doesn't think that bit is an act. Jo picks up some scissors and threatens to hurt herself, and then, as planned, runs down the corridor. Wanda and Julia fly out in pursuit behind her. Deb appears then, and does an Oscar worthy performance of collapsing, shouting far more energetically than an unconscious person normally would, but it does the trick, and the last of the team members in the office rush out to her assistance. Mila slips into the office unnoticed, and crouches behind a filing cabinet. Kaye, situated down the hall, next to the fire alarm, smashes it, and runs down the fire escape. The building empties, except for Mila.

Fabien and Susannah are shivering on the Town Hall steps with about four hundred other people shuffling around them, taking up the whole pavement, some spilling out onto the square. Cigarettes are lit, gossip is shared.

'Mila!' says Fabien, as his girlfriend strolls towards them, somehow from the direction of the square, and not from the building she must have been in this whole time. Her capacity for deception is an ongoing concern.

'I'm so sorry I'm late,' she says, kissing him on both cheeks, before turning to Susannah. 'I just couldn't come before I had chased up the health and safety team so I could give you the fullest update you deserve, Susannah.' Mila's smile is wide and genuine, her eyes are begging for forgiveness. Her charm is insurmountable, although Susannah is still pretty annoyed about being compared to Goering. 'I am so very sorry for what I said the other day. I didn't mean it at all. You are nothing like Hitler.'

Susannah isn't quite sure what to say to that, but people are starting to look and definitely listen in, so she says, 'Thank you.'

'And wonderful news,' Mila continues, clearly glad that bit is signed off. 'I have a signature, and the new swings can be installed before Easter.'

Fabien shoots her a look; he got that signature three days ago.

'All clear, all clear,' a fireman shouts, and team leaders start to usher their workers back indoors.

As Fabien and Mila walk away, waving cheerfully, Mila turns to Fabien and says, 'I got the files.'

TWENTY

It isn't difficult to persuade Deb to cover for her. Jo has always been good at making an argument. At school, before she'd started getting in trouble, she used to be head of the debating team.

'Why should Mila decide what we can and can't see or know?' she demands of Deb. They have done everything she asked – bared their souls, made themselves vulnerable to yet more trouble from the authorities at the Town Hall – they could have been arrested. Deb almost ended up in an ambulance. But Mila won't show them their own files. 'It's outrageous,' Jo declares. Mila insists it is the right thing to do – that it would be only natural for them to be tempted to seek the adopters out, and then, how could they stay away? The authorities would then find out about the theft of the files and be able to link it back to them. And that, Mila had explained, would be the end of everything.

'Thing is,' Jo argues, 'she assumes we're stupid, and lacking in will power.'

'To be fair, people have thought that about me my whole life, and I've done a fairly decent job of proving them right.'

'Rubbish,' Jo tells her, 'they put you down so that you stay down. It's called a self-fulfilling prophecy. What we need to do is manifest positive feelings about ourselves, so that they become true instead.'

'Does that work? Sounds like a load of airy-fairy hippy-dippy biscuits to me.'

'Whatever. Mila has no right to treat us like children. You've heard how she talks. She hates the authorities, and I'm starting to think this has less to do with our battle than with her own agenda to prove the system is, as I think she put it – "built on endemic class bias". Even if she does manage to prove that someone at the council didn't assess us totally fairly, they won't reverse the decision; they'll just promise some crap about internal investigations and learning lessons for the future. I know Rob set me up, it's the only logical answer, but she's not interested in looking at that anymore. That dorky policeman happily let Pound go, and nobody plans to finish the job I started. And you need to give some hard thought to who spiked you. Or, you know, it could just be one of those things – happens at festivals all the time.'

'But then I *do* need Mila to prove I was unfairly assessed, don't I? I mean, proving Rob framed you will help you, but I need Mila.'

'I'm not saying Mila isn't helpful, Deb. I'm just saying what she's doing right now isn't enough. Not for me. I'm not going to let that bastard get away with it. And I don't think proving the system is biased is going to do anything to make them believe I was innocent after I've pleaded guilty and done the time. It's different for you. If she proves the system is shit – which obviously it is – then spiked or not, she could argue one slip-up was unfairly used against you. I need so much more than that.'

The rooms Mila has organised for them in the rarely used wing of Farlington Hall consist, in part, of three connecting rooms, which are all variations on the living room concept, which normal people might think require just the one set of four walls. A drawing room, a breakfast room, and Jo can't think what the third was meant to be, and nor could Mila when she'd asked. A lunch room, perhaps, or a nap room. A mini-fridge has been procured and is full of snacks, supplemented by proper dinners squirrelled in by Mila each day. There is a cloakroom with a loo and a sink, but Mila has been sneaking them to the nearest bathroom for a proper bath when she can.

Deb is sitting in their communal living area, under strict instructions to tell Mila and Fabien, should they pop in, that Jo has a migraine, and is to be left alone in her makeshift bedroom. Mila has set them up with wi-fi and an old laptop, and Deb is planning on watching re-runs of *Friends* all day. It helps to keep her mind off really wanting a drink, which she needs to stop the endless grinding pain of being separated from her precious boy, his chubby cheeks imprinted onto her eyelids, his infectious giggle a constant and delicate echo in her ears.

She hasn't told anyone she has checked every dusty old cupboard in these strange old rooms already and discovered there is not a drop to be found. She tells herself she was ensuring there is no nearby temptation. Anyway, she can just go home via the off license whenever she wants, but she has promised Jo she will stay and cover her, and Mila has strongly suggested that if they are able to prove wrongdoing, and Jacob is allowed to come home to her, that Mila and Fabien's ability to vouch for her sobriety would be a very good thing indeed. She desperately wants to go back to the person she was last year: sober, focused, and ready to be the best mum she can be, but it isn't easy. It's never easy.

The camping kettle on the coffee table clicks, and Deb pours hot water on top of the instant coffee in the mug. She settles into the armchair, and hits play on *The One At The Beach*. That jellyfish scene cracks her up.

Jo's heart races as she spots him, just where Hoppy had let slip to Fabien that they'd picked him up. He's arguing with someone on the phone. 'I told you, I didn't say anything.' Pound scowls as he listens to the phone at his ear and Jo follows him down the high street, hopping between passers-by and deftly avoiding the lampposts. 'No idea, but they've got nothing except the ramblings of that junkie Jo, so don't fret, yeah? No charges, couldn't hold me.'

Jo. Her name. She already knew that Rob had paid him to follow her, plant drugs on her, ruin her, but hearing him say her name, confirming her suspicions, sends shivers through her whole body and makes her stomach flip. She feels sick.

'There's no link back to you, mate, none,' says Pound, stopping to fish a vape from his tracksuit pocket and inhaling deeply. 'On my way now,' he replies to whatever the caller says in the pause. He is talking to Rob, Jo is sure of it. Bradley Pound starts to cross the road. 'Okay, I'll be there in ten.'

Jo feels for her phone in her bag. This is her chance to get the evidence they've been searching for. If she can tie him to Rob in ten minutes' time, if she can record this on her phone, she'll have cracked it.

Her stomach rumbles. She has been out for hours, leaving before six under dark skies to avoid detection. She hadn't thought to bring anything to eat, and since she clocked Bradley Pound, she hasn't dared take her eyes off him, certainly not for long enough to pop into a shop and buy a packet of crisps.

Jo follows Pound across the road, and down three more streets to the newly regenerated market quarter, where they have cobbled the roads and painted the shopfronts posh shades of classic green. He heads towards a recently opened wine bar and delicatessen, where you can get sozzled whilst eating smashed avocado and poached eggs. Jo would not have expected Rob to even know this place existed, let alone be inside sipping a fine Shiraz. She hangs back as Pound enters the pretty little place with gold lettering across its large, gleaming window, and watches him move towards the back corner.

He approaches a tall table with a man already seated. This man is not drinking Shiraz; he has a small beer in a very European looking glass. This man has spectacles and a tie, and an envelope stuffed full in front of him. As Pound reaches the table, the man stands to greet him. They nod, Pound takes the envelope, briefly looks inside, and then throws the bespectacled man a thumbs up and leaves as quickly as he enters. The man sits back down on an uncomfortable looking metal stool, and takes a sip of his beer. The man is young, with neat, gelled hair, and an expensive suit. The man is clean-shaven. The man is many things, but he is most definitely not Rob. Jo holds up her phone and clicks on the camera button.

TWENTY-ONE

Mila is sitting in the late Lord Gregory's study on one of the two antique mahogany leather chairs in the corner, a side table next to each, and a low coffee table between them. On the other chair, Wanda sits with her papers balanced on her knee, and a chewed-up biro between her fingers. She uses a sturdy looking folder to lean on as she writes. Mila cannot believe she is the one being interviewed. She's also surprised that Lydia has allowed the room to be utilised as a temporary base for Wanda to conduct the family consultations.

Wanda looks like she should carry a crystal ball or be reading the leaves at the bottom of her teacup. Her dark purple skirt is velvet and skims the floor when she stands. Now it pools around her feet like a decadent pair of curtains, hiding the black boots that must have little bells attached, as she tinkles when she walks, and even when she crosses her legs.

Although the social worker that Jo had once adored and now despises, looks soft and frumpy, Mila can see she is not to be reckoned with. Her questions are thorough, her gaze piercing. She clearly supports Elodie and Anna's application to adopt, but she isn't leaving anything to chance. She has been interviewing Mila for forty minutes now. Although Elodie and Anna live in the gatehouse at the bottom of the long tree-lined driveway, it is officially part of the hall, which means all adults and children at the address have to be assessed, DBS criminal record checks for adults included. They are all to be questioned and their backgrounds examined, their suitability to help provide a safe home for an adopted child evaluated.

Mila is just dying to ask Wanda some questions of her own, but she has not yet thought of a way to subtly drop the names of three adopting couples into the conversation.

Theodore and Cassandra.

Maximilian and Harriet.

Gordan and Lucinda.

Mila is itching to get back to her laptop and continue her search on these couples, who clearly have class in common – judging by the pictures Google has so far thrown up of garden parties and big hats at fancy events, excellent dentistry, and expensive haircuts. But she will need more of a link than that. All the final forms in the files have the same second signatory, the Director of Children's Social Care Julia Bainbridge, but that is hardly surprising. Each case had a different social worker assigned. Nothing of note there either.

The files also demonstrate that the women were all on track and that their social workers had made recommendations throughout their ongoing assessments towards a "return to birth family outcome", and that conversations had been had with the foster parents to relay this. Everything Jo had told them matched up, which bodes well in terms of trusting Jo's recollections. But so far, there is no indication of any obvious bias or unfairness.

The final reports tell the sad story that had been delivered in the family courts. That despite everyone's best efforts, the women had fallen at the last hurdle, demonstrated that they were still in the throes of addiction or criminality or both, that potentially they'd been managing to hide their activities over the last few months, and that it would be unsafe for the child to be returned to them. These women were all tarred with histories that showed clear patterns of behaviour. And when Jo was arrested, Kaye's drugs were found in the changing table drawer, and Deb fell off the wagon so spectacularly, it had been concluded that this pattern was set in stone. It seemed to have come as no surprise to anyone other than the women themselves. All three were considered last chance cases, and their final chance had been and gone.

Mila's research, along with Elodie and Anna's new-found expertise as they navigate the adoption process, reveals that Foster to Adopt, or concurrent care as it is also known, is generally expected to result in adoption rather than with birth parents being reunited with their child, but there is still always a chance, and adopting parents knew this, and were coached to be able to cope with that outcome should it materialise. Mila can't help but wonder if the link is the parents. How far would any parent go to keep their baby?

Jo is fixated on Rob being the villain in her story, but with three cases sharing so many similarities, Mila is convinced that there has to be a common denominator.

There's a knock on the study door.

'Come in,' Mila and Wanda say together.

'Oh, I am sorry, I forgot for a moment this wasn't my office,' says Wanda, shuffling papers.

'How's it going?' asks Elodie, as she and Anna enter the room with Konstantine holding Anna's hand and Karlie holding Elodie's. Offal overtakes them all in his excitement to get under Wanda's enormous skirts. 'Offal, no!' shouts Elodie.

'Oh, that's okay,' says Wanda, trying to locate the little dog who is now entangled and happily rolling around in folds of velvet. Eventually Wanda stands, and he topples out headfirst, and jumps onto Mila's lap. She scratches his ears as he growls in pleasure, half closing his eyes. 'I think we're all done,' she says, sneezing and then instantly rummaging through her huge sequined shoulder bag, searching for a hanky. 'Allergies...'

'Oh crap, sorry, I forgot,' says Elodie, inwardly cursing herself.

'Not a problem, not a problem,' Wanda says, waving her away, and blowing her nose with her other hand. 'And how are you two little angels?' she says to the children.

They smile shyly, Karlie shuffling slightly behind Elodie's legs, giggling a little as Elodie tickles her out into the open. 'We are very fine,' says Konstantine, both children's English brilliant after only a few months.

'I've got a new doll,' says Karlie, thrusting forward a plastic figurine. Then, noticing Mila in the corner chair, she runs forward and dives onto her lap in a heap. 'Aunty Mila!' she screeches.

Mila gives her a big cuddle and turns her around to face the room, as Konstantine strolls over more self-consciously and pops his bottom on the arm of the chair, allowing his hands to rest on Mila's hair, absent-mindedly fiddling with it like a little monkey.

'Anna and Elodie are so wonderful with the children, they often do school runs and look after them while Fabien and I are working, you honestly won't find two more maternal people better suited to adoption.'

'And the children clearly adore you, too,' Wanda says, smiling.

'And I them.'

Offal, concerned he might be missing out, jumps on the pile of limbs that is Mila and the children, wisps of hairs flying into the air, causing Wanda to begin a new fit of sneezing.

'Oh gosh, let's get you outside, Wanda,' says Elodie, leading her from the room.

'And do you have everything you need?' Anna asks.

'Don't sound so nervous,' Wanda says with a smile, now recomposed as they walk towards the door and away from little Offal and the puddle of people beneath him. 'I have all your family interviews, which went well. Of course, I need to go through it all with the team and the director.'

Elodie smiles as she catches the disdain in Wanda's voice. Ever the professional, Wanda never outwardly criticises the Director of Children's Social Care, but it is clear they have very different approaches. From what the couple can work out – and have discussed at length – this Julia woman takes a black and white approach. Wanda has implied that sometimes it isn't just about adding up a form, but knowing people and understanding nuance.

'We still need to run the DBS checks, and go through your paperwork, finances, health checks and so on, but,' she says, looking around the opulent room and then at the two young, fit women in front of her, 'I would be very surprised if there's a problem.'

Wanda calls her goodbyes to Mila and the children, who are now fighting over the doll on the floor by Mila's feet. 'Konstantine, Karlie,' Mila says, hoping to curtail the chaos that is building, 'let's go find Granny Lydia and see if she has any cookies and milk.' At that the fight abruptly stops, the doll drops onto the rug, and Mila hopes she won't get another judgemental telling off for yet more childcare delegation. She lifts Offal down to the floor. 'Sorry, little man, but I have work to do.'

TWENTY-TWO

The mistake Jo made, she thinks, wasn't initially following Bradley Pound, which had led her to photographing the man who may well be involved in the scheme to plant the drugs on her. She's not even sure it was a mistake to continue following him after he left the trendy wine bar. After all, it made sense to see what he would do next and whether it would provide any more clues about what on earth Pound and the smartly dressed man were up to – if they might still be connected to Rob. She was sure Mila would have done the same thing. She could even reason with herself that it wasn't exactly a mistake getting seen by Pound as she snapped him on his own driveway. That could happen to anyone.

No, the mistake Jo made, she thinks, was agreeing to follow him inside, where, he had told her, they could talk properly. Instead, she is locked in the cupboard under the stairs. He's taken her phone, of course, and will have deleted the photos, not that they matter much now. Jo hopes Deb decides to go against her express instructions to keep her plans a secret, and that Mila storms in any moment now. Jo is gagged and tied up, and trying to figure out what the hell Mila would do, and wondering how long Deb will keep up the cover story before anyone looks for her.

Back at the wine bar she had considered staying and watching the man who had handed over the envelope, seeing as he was clearly higher up the food chain than Pound. But he had a lot of his fashionable beer left, and she really thought that Pound's next stop might be Rob, finally proving her theory correct. But he'd gone straight home, and upon seeing the girl who had accused him of following *her,* he had made the swift and efficient decision to kidnap her until he figured out how to resolve the rapidly escalating situation. At least that's how he explained it to her. She told him she'd not been following long, hadn't seen anything, but he had just narrowed his eyes disbelievingly, and said he wasn't in the mood for risks, and his boss would make the call on how to deal with her later.

Jo is terrified.

She hears Pound pacing up and down in the hallway. His huge dog is barking. Jo is pretty sure that she has seen similar dogs on the news because they like to use humans as chew toys, so when Pound said to be quiet and still and not cause a fuss unless she fancied being Jason Statham's next snack, she decided to obey. At least, she did once she realised that was the dog's name.

As Pound had bundled her in, Jo had noticed there were two doors, one on top of the other. Now she starts to make out the room, she can see why. It is overcrowded with boxes and cellophaned packages that Jo recognises as cocaine, heroin, bags of pills, most likely MDMA and other uppers and downers, and all the stuff she used to take to forget who she is.

Jo stifles a tear. Her mouth is dry, the gag is tight, doubled up like the fake door back to the hallway she might never see again. One gag tears at the corners of her mouth, forcing her tongue down, and the other goes right over her mouth, sealing it from air, muffling any sound she might attempt to make.

From the glimpses Jo had caught of Pound when he was following her, she had assumed he was a low-life dealer, and most likely he was, but business is clearly booming. He lives on a nice street in a fairly decent part of Hipton, not far from where she grew up. His semi-detached has new white plastic windows and a neat garden, and she wonders if he mows his lawn and washes his car on a Sunday morning like a normal person, in between creating addicts from vulnerable people and framing innocent women.

In her mind, Pound had been younger, someone who would agree to work for Rob for a few quid, but Pound is in his thirties at least, and when he spoke to her, he seemed nice, reasonable, articulate. His accent is local, like hers; he doesn't sound like a gangster off the telly, affecting a dialect concocted from movies and rap bands. Jo is terrified but she also has never felt more stupid in her life. And she now seriously doubts this guy was working for Rob... but if not him, then who else?

She leans closers to the door. She can smell the dog keeping guard, and hear Pound on his phone. 'Bloody ring me back, you flaming eejit,' he shouts, as Jason Statham barks along enthusiastically. The barks are getting louder and closer, and Jo realises the second door is opening, a flash of light briefly blinding her, before Pound's silhouette comes into view. He holds the dog back on a lead before pulling him forward towards her, the collar straining around his big throbbing neck, his pink gums and sharp white teeth taking up nearly all of his head.

'You all right?' asks Pound.

Jo says something like, 'Uf cous nah, ya furckin dich.' She is tied to a stiff metal rod attached to the wall. She wriggles pointlessly.

Pound crouches down to her level on the concrete floor. He

says, 'I'm going to remove these gags, but if you scream I will let Jason Statham off his lead and then we'll see if he regrets missing his breakfast this morning to chase that squirrel. Though to be fair, the little rodent had it coming – eats all my bird food, and this time of year poor little things will starve without it, you know?' Jo stares at Pound. 'Anyway, don't get all rowdy, is all I'm saying. And not because I'm worried anyone will hear you – they won't – that end wall is soundproofed.' Jo continues to stare, she tries to gulp. What has she got herself into? 'Nod if you understand. I haven't got all day.' Jo nods. 'And even if it wasn't totally soundproofed – which it is, paid a fortune for it, too – Mrs Felcham next door is ninety-three and deaf and she thinks the sun shines out of my arse, seeing as I take her bins out and mow her lawn every Sunday when I do mine. Let her use my 65-incher.'

Jo frowns at him, a look of horror taking shape on her face.

'My massive telly. Get your mind out of the gutter. The thing is, Jo, if you make a fuss, I'll let him off and you'll be punished for screaming, but you and I need to come to an understanding, and I like to keep things civil. Is that clear?'

Although Jo isn't sure that threat of death by dog attack is what everyone would class as civil, she nods and Pound removes the second gag, and then the first. She tries to speak, but starts to cough. Pound takes a bottle of water from his pocket and squirts it into her mouth. She swallows, breathes in gulps of air, and this time, when she starts to speak, she makes herself understood.

'Let me go,' Jo says. 'I won't–'

'You won't say anything? You were just taking photos for a night class? We can all pretend this never happened?'

'Exactly!'

Jason Statham growls. He's on a short lead, and therefore only inches from Jo's face, next to his owner, who is smiling kindly at his pet. 'Shush,' he tells the dog, who seems to scowl in return, but does at least stop growling. His mouth remains open, teeth on display, tongue lolling, saliva dripping.

'Okay, Jo.' Jo goes to speak, but Pound raises his hand. 'Of course I know your name. I know who you are, and I know you've only recently come out of prison. You're an ex-addict who couldn't be trusted to raise her child, and I'm sorry for you, truly I am, but I'm sure it's all for the best. Now, you *could* have moved on, built a new life, learned from your past, but instead you are fixated on getting what you want – regardless of whether it is the right thing for everyone else – and that's typical addict behaviour. The issue I have is that you've been taking pictures of me and I don't know who else, and this could cause problems down the line, at the very least cash flow concerns for me, and potentially, well, greater repercussions. You've put me in a very awkward position, and I'm afraid what happens next is beyond my pay grade. I can't just let you go; you must know that.'

'I just wanted to prove Rob was the one paying you to follow me!'

'Who's Rob?'

'You framed me, didn't you? Who told you to? Why? I have to know! What did I do to you? I just want my baby back.'

'This isn't all about you. Really, young people are so self-absorbed these days.'

'But who? Who *is* it about? Why did you want me to lose Sarah?'

'Who's Sarah?'

'You don't even know her name!' Jo wails, and she starts to cry loud, ugly sobs.

Pound loosens Jason Statham's lead and says, very quietly, 'Attack.' Jason Statham starts to bark and snarl and growl and pull. Jo stops crying and huddles as best she can into the smallest ball she can make. 'Shush,' says Pound, and the dog stops. 'He's very well trained,' Pound tells Jo proudly. 'Here's what's going to happen, Jo,' he says, in a voice a parent might use on a toddler mid-meltdown to regain authority without further escalating the child's unruly behaviour. 'I'm clearly not going to give you any information about the people I work for, as if I do that then I can't really see any way you're getting out of here alive. You following the logic?' Jo nods, unable to do much else than go along with whatever Pound says, as her silent tears fall. 'I'm going to speak to my colleague, and if – and it is a *big* if – we can find a way to get you out of here and home with absolute assurances of silence and a promise to let this all go, maybe you'll live another day to continue making a great big mess of your life however you choose. But for now, you need to be quiet, and the gag is going back on. Do you want to think about it?'

Jo shakes her head now, and she tries so hard to do as she's told, and at least just shut up, but neither of those skills were ever her strong suit, and a voice rises up from her belly, powered by the visceral pain and endless determination to hold Sarah in her arms and kiss her soft, smooth skin. She howls, 'I'll never give up on my baby!' Pound slaps her hard around the face, but Jo barely flinches, staring into his eyes, cold and murderous. 'Fuck you,' she says.

'Stupid girl.' Pound reties the two gags, checking her binds, and allowing Jason Statham to stand millimetres from her panting and slobbering, his rancid breath catching in her throat.

'Furk yaaaah,' she repeats, the sound barely audible through the thick gag.

He kicks her in her side before yanking Jason Statham away, and exiting through the two side doors to the house, locking each one.

TWENTY-THREE

'God, I love the internet,' Mila tells Fabien.

They sit at either end of the sofa in the living quarters they created in the bedroom next door to their own and opposite the children's playroom. Next to that is the children's bedroom, where they now sleep soundly, the door a little ajar in case they cry out, which sometimes they still do, nightmares of their ordeal of losing their mother and moving to a new country waking them in fear.

'You weren't so sure when good old Hoppy was tracking down your real name and almost getting you arrested and deported.'

'This is very true,' Mila replies, 'but isn't it wonderful when we want to do our own background checks, especially on this bunch of narcissists?'

'Now, now, a few photos and selfies in nice spots does not qualify us to diagnose narcissism.'

'You sure?' says Mila. 'Check this woman out.' She turns her laptop around to reveal a grid of photos on Instagram, the woman's wide smile on repeat like a Warhol painting without the irony. 'She even calls herself the *Real* Cassandra Neville.

Like there might be hundreds of impersonators wishing they could pretend to a bunch of strangers that they have her life, which quite frankly looks tedious.'

'No security on hers either then?' asks Fabien, as he browses her husband Theodore's page.

'None. She uses it to promote her interior design business, so that's probably why, though I expect she absolutely couldn't bear not to show the whole world every detail of her moronic existence.'

'Nice wallpaper on that one, though,' Fabien comments. 'Could be William Morris, we have it in one of the cloakrooms.'

Cassandra and Theodore are Sarah's adopted parents. Gordan and Lucinda have adopted Kaye's little boy Bobby, and Maximillian and Harriet are now officially Jacob's parents.

Mila rolls her eyes and goes back to scrolling and searching and clicking. *Right click-save* for anything that she thinks might contain a clue as to how these perfect looking couples could be involved in the downfall of the three birth mothers. They would have all been aware of the increasing likelihood that their foster baby was going to be returned to its mother, and should have been prepared for that. Could three separate couples really have decided to ensure that didn't happen, whatever the cost?

'Theodore plays golf,' Fabien tells Mila.

'Big surprise,' Mila replies. 'Gordan and Lucinda play pairs, too. I saw them grinning stupidly on a course. Abbey-something, I'll check.'

'Abbeyforde Golf Club? That would be a little weird, as that's where Theodore plays; I recognise it from the photos. Used to go there myself occasionally.'

'I didn't know you played golf,' Mila says, with a note of distaste.

'I used to run a hedge fund, Mila.'

'Fair,' she replies, glad he gave all that up, hoping he did so because he'd changed and wanted, like her, to fight for justice, and not just because his business partner had defrauded him and the whole thing had come crashing down and nearly destroyed him and his entire family fortune. 'Oh yeah, Abbeyforde. Same place,' Mila says, having flicked through her other open windows where photos, posts, company blogs, and the odd local news article present the lives of the couple who adopted Kaye's baby boy. 'Shall we check the other couple for golf connections too, Maximillian and Harriet?'

'Definitely,' says Fabien. 'Although, it wouldn't be a *huge* coincidence that three local-ish couples of their class and wealth would have a prestigious golf club in common, even if they don't all live on its doorstep.'

'Still worth checking. Looks like Cassandra and Theodore only recently moved up to Lancashire. They were in Surrey before; there's all this stuff about hashtag adventures and looking for the perfect place to raise a family.'

'Any mention of the adoption itself?' Fabien asks.

'There's one or two, all teasingly vague, like – *we wish we could share our beautiful baby girl with you, but it's not always safe online for adopted children* – but based on their files we know it is definitely the couple who adopted Jo's baby Sarah.'

'Nothing much from Theodore on that front, either – though a few "Welcome to your forever home, Sarah!" shots of the party they must have thrown after the adoption order,' Fabien says.

'Cassandra has a lot of those too. And they're all so happy, and it makes me so angry for Jo.'

'We don't know the adoptive parents had anything to do with what happened to Jo – and we still don't really know what happened to Jo, if anything. Same goes for the others,' Fabien tells Mila, still struggling to understand how or why these three couples would go to such lengths – potentially *illegal* lengths, at that – and take huge risks for something they could eventually get through the formal process anyway.

'Hmm,' is all Mila responds with, because Fabien's right, but there is so much that is wrong about this mystery, and she never did trust middle-upper-class types, despite living with a lord and his mother.

'Oh, here, on Theodore's company news – they're at an event with that fellow you all despise. Fawcett. Some Christian convention.'

'Urgh, let me see,' says Mila, as Fabien swivels his screen around and she screws up her face. 'You know he's speaking at the Farlington WI tomorrow?'

'So I heard. I expect Elodie will be adding another nail to Mother's early grave by showing up with banners and placards and whatnot.'

'Good. I cannot believe they are tolerating his brand of misogyny at the Women's Institute.'

'You're not going, are you?' asks Fabien.

'Oh my God!' Mila says suddenly. 'You have to see this.'

'What?' Fabien asks, noticing she has not answered his question and wondering if this is a distraction ploy.

'Come here, look at this. I've moved on to look at Maximillian Bancroft and his wife Harriet – and check it out, they've all been tagged at some party together.'

'Who?'

'All three couples, Fabien. They all know each other.'

TWENTY-FOUR

Mila has tossed and turned all night. Yesterday evening, she had been desperate to go and talk to Jo and Deb about their potential breakthrough, but it had been late, and Fabien had persuaded her to sleep on it.

They disagree on the significance of the findings. Mila argues that it has to be more than a coincidence that all three belong to the same golf club, and socialise together, and all three have been able to adopt newborns, all in Lancashire, all during the last year. And two of the couples only moved to the area shortly before they adopted. Most importantly, all three are cases in which the babies had been expected to be returned to the birth mothers, until in the final weeks or days before the hearings, suddenly the three birth mothers had failed to stay clean, legal, or sober, and the adoption orders had been signed, despite months of evidence suggesting the women had turned their lives around... and despite this being very uncommon until now.

Fabien suggests that people like the adoptive parents often move in the same circles, especially in places like Lancashire, where they tend to be fewer in number compared to London, Milan, or wherever.

'But two of them only moved to Lancashire last year! Why move here to set up home and adopt? What was wrong with the Surrey mansion? What is going on?' she had asked herself as much as Fabien before turning to him and adding, 'Do you still have your golf clubs?'

They agree on one thing, at least: a conversation with the fathers might reveal something that can shed some light on one of the strangest scenarios they have ever encountered, and for now, that's the best they can hope for.

Mila kisses Fabien's bare shoulder, and he stirs ever so slightly then lets out a contented and sleepy snore. It is still dark outside, Mila can tell from the thin curtains at the window. Her watch shows that it is only quarter past six, and she has no doubt her restlessness will have kept Fabien awake half the night too. She has about an hour before Konstantine and Karlie need to get up for school, so she very quietly gets up, throws on yesterday's jeans, T-shirt, and oversized hoodie, and creeps downstairs without cleaning her teeth.

She has to update Jo and Deb on their progress. Jo hadn't emerged from her migraine slumber all day yesterday, and Deb had been overly protective about letting Mila see her. Mila's now desperate to know if she is feeling better, understanding the toll the whole nightmare is taking on both women. Mila feels responsible and believes she owes them some hope – she will telephone Kaye, too, as soon as the day properly dawns.

Jo and Deb are still angry about Mila keeping the files from them, but Mila knows she can't risk jeopardising the whole investigation. She doesn't blame them for how they feel, though. If Konstantine and Karlie had been taken, she would risk everything to get them back. Why should she expect any different from Jo or Deb, or even the more measured Kaye?

Mila walks down the wide curved staircase to the large entrance hall, a small round table in the middle, always adorned with a huge arrangement of fresh flowers, which Lydia tells anyone who will listen is her only luxury these days. According to Lydia the family has been cash-strapped for years, and Mila can believe it. The wind blows through the rattling windows, wood rotting around half of them, and the plumbing painfully wails each time there's an attempt to run hot water, which usually eventually emerges from the tap, but not in any hurry.

Mila wonders if Lydia's delay in hiring a replacement housekeeper is partly due to the fact that she couldn't really afford Anna, but would have never let her go. Danny, the gardener, is indispensable. Twelve acres of woodland, fields, and formal gardens need to be constantly maintained, and since Lydia's husband died, Danny also manages the land let to local farmers. Mila is learning about rural English life, and despite her early dislike of the smells, and the lack of convenience, she has fallen a little in love with Farlington village life. And despite herself, she has also fallen a lot in love with Fabien and Lydia.

Lydia offered up her home for charity premises and has become a patron to the degree she can afford to, but more importantly than money she offers connections and influence. Mila is suddenly glad, as she looks around and knows the children are safe, and that she has a space to help others thanks to these people, that she had got the playground swings sorted out for them. She just hopes she can get to the bottom of this other case before Lydia discovers her stowaways and finally decides she's had enough. She loathes dishonesty, which Mila isn't a fan of either, usually. But there's nothing usual about this, and, in this instance, she feels the means justify the ends.

She switches on a light in the corridor leading through to Jo and Deb's rooms and makes her way to their door. She can hear tinny music, and wonders what the hell the women are thinking, playing music. It may be a rarely used wing, but she's asked them not to take unnecessary risks. Isn't she taking enough risks for all of them? Fabien doesn't need another excuse to chuck them out of the hall; he thinks that housing them is going above and beyond, and that working on the case should be more than enough. 'We can't house every client, Mila, what if we take on a class action?' Plus, he has told her, now the swings are sorted they probably need a new official project to ensure Lydia and other interested parties, such as the ever-present Mayor Susannah Wilson, will continue to see value in their work and continue to help them to raise their profile and their funds.

Mila understands that providing a home for the women is potentially taking on too much, and possibly even unprofessional, yet she feels morally bound to do so. Mila is scared Jo would be in danger from her awful ex Rob, and that Deb would otherwise sabotage herself and any chance they had of reuniting her with her son.

At least here, Mila could keep an eye on them, make sure they are safe, and that Deb isn't drinking.

Mila opens the door to find Deb swigging from a bottle of whisky, humming along to an old love song that's playing on her phone.

'What's going on, Deb?' Mila asks. 'Where the hell did you get that, and where's Jo?'

TWENTY-FIVE

Deb is making no sense whatsoever. The whisky is old, and the bottle still dusty despite Deb's handprints, so Mila suspects Deb has been for a wander around the hall – it's a miracle she hasn't woken someone up and been caught red-handed. Deb is very drunk.

She throws half formed sentences around the room, from which Mila gathers that Deb couldn't sleep, didn't know what to do about Jo, was scared, and missed her little baby Jacob, that she needed something to stop the torment of seeing his face, and worrying about Jo.

'She's gone', she tells Mila. 'Jo has gone to find *him*. The one who framed her.'

Rob, thinks Mila. Jo has gone to confront him because Mila no longer believes that Rob is involved, and instead is doggedly pursuing different lines of inquiry. Mila has made Jo feel powerless by dismissing her theory, and now Jo is taking matters into her own hands. Although Deb is talking rubbish and repeating herself, Mila works out that the migraine story was concocted to account for Jo's absence, which means she has been gone since yesterday morning.

Mila calls Jo, but her phone is switched off, and Mila really doesn't think Jo would willingly stay with Rob without sending a message back, even if she thought that was the way to trap him into a confession. Mila has tried to encourage Jo to keep her phone off as much as possible even though she has disabled the tracking app, just in case he was tracking her some other way, or, if she's honest, in case Jo did something silly through the phone – posted something, or texted someone – that could lead to her whereabouts being identified. She should have shown Jo more trust, let her in on her thought processes, because what she has now done is erode any faith Jo has in Mila's own plan. And now, Mila knows for certain, Jo is in trouble.

Mila forgets about waiting for the light to finally illuminate the wintry Lancashire skies, and scrolls to Kaye's name in her phone, hits call, and hopes she keeps her phone on all night. She's always studying or attending classes for her sports science course, or waiting tables and pulling pints in the local pub until late, so it's clear she is always exhausted, but Kaye never complains. She's doing it for her baby, for when he comes home. She has never stopped believing she might find a way to prove her innocence, to be reunited with Bobby.

Kaye answers on the first ring. 'Couldn't sleep, never can. Any news?' Kaye sounds alert and keen, and Mila hates herself for not having only good news to share. If anyone deserves some hope it is these three women.

'There's something, actually.' Mila really wants to skip to the problem of Jo, but she owes Kaye more than that. 'The three sets of adoptive parents all know one another. We think we can get closer to them, uncover whatever it is they know about what happened in the run-up to the adoption orders.'

'That's great, though maybe they don't know anything.' Kaye has consistently had the most realistic outlook, or pessimistic, and Mila can't blame her. Also, Kaye hadn't argued about not finding out the identities of baby Bobby's adoptive parents. She had as much as admitted she doubted she could have stayed away.

'Maybe not, but we are going to try. I really don't believe it's all one big coincidence.' And she doesn't, though Fabien still thinks it very possible, as does Elodie. After all, Elodie explained last night when they updated their gatehouse contingency on their findings, Wanda said that adoption agencies have local get-togethers for adopters to form support networks. It's true, but Mila is still hanging on to a strong hunch that there is more to it; the connections, combined with the very real and very strange files that prove shockingly unlikely similarities in three very unusual cases, have to mean something. But right now, Mila has to hold that thought and find Jo. 'Look, I can explain more later, but can you come over? There's a bit of a problem...'

Fabien wakes up to a punch in his lower abdomen.

'Wakey, wakey, Uncle Fabien! We're going to be late for school!' Konstantine says bouncing on top of Fabien's stomach with gusto as Karlie clambers onto the bed.

Fabien's eyes force themselves to become unglued and he sees it is light outside, and in the middle of February that means Konstantine is quite right: they are late. He grabs his watch from the bedside table while the children crawl over him, their bony little knees and elbows prodding him in the ribs and head. 'Crap!'

'Naughty Uncle Fabien!' the children shout in unison, before launching into a sing-song chant. 'We are going to tell on you!' they repeat, giggling with glee.

It is already half past seven, Mila is nowhere to be seen, and clearly she hasn't got the children ready – they must be the only under-tens in the world who need to be woken up by their parents. They take turns, and Thursday is definitely Mila's turn. Isn't it? Fabien feels like he hasn't slept at all, and he is struggling to get his brain fired up.

Konstantine is in his favourite Spiderman pyjamas and Karlie is still wearing her favourite of Mila's T-shirts, which she has decided to reinvent as a nightie. Fabien isn't convinced the terrifying Slipknot masks are conducive to sound sleep, but Karlie will not be dissuaded; she imitates Mila in every way, and Fabien fears there is probably going to be trouble ahead.

'Right! Up!' Fabien instructs as he spills the children off himself and rolls them onto the duvet. 'Up, now! Teeth to be cleaned, uniforms to be donned, let's go, go, go!' Fabien calls to them as he runs over to his wardrobe, pulls out his neatly folded jeans, and a freshly ironed shirt. He tries not to notice Mila's pile of crumpled belongings strewn over their beautiful antique chairs, some of which have been in the family for centuries.

He quickly inspects the children, neatens their ties, and checks the noticeboard they have pinned up outside the playroom for any extra kit. 'P.E. oh, for goodness' sake!' Fabien mutters, pulling out a gym kit and stuffing it into the drawstring bag the children are all issued with.

The tardy three gallop down the large staircase, Fabien still calling for Mila, who is nowhere to be seen. Honestly, he thinks, he ought to be used to it by now. Just gone eight and they may just make it in time for school register at half past, if he grabs them some fruit for breakfast. He almost crashes into Lydia at the bottom of the stairs, who is checking her reflection in the ginormous mirror.

'Goodness!' she admonishes, and Fabien notices she is rather dressed up for a Thursday morning. 'Are you taking the children today? I thought Mila was. You haven't forgotten

Chris-Whatsit from the BBC and his producer will be here all day? You promised you'd help show them around.'

'What time?' Fabien says, feeling the sweat on his brow, the panic of the morning, his concern for where Mila has got to, combined with the need to hide said panic and concern from his mother in order to not intensify her growing impatience with Mila and his apparent lack of control over the situation.

'Nine, sharp,' she replies, smoothing down her hair, and turning to him. 'I say, you look a little peaky. Are you quite well?'

'Fine, fine, um, I'll drop them at the gatehouse. Elodie will take them, and I'll be back in time to smarten up for Chris-Whatsit.'

'Good boy,' Lydia replies, 'and Mila will be here later? She's very important for our diversity message. Anna's coming, too.'

Fabien isn't always brilliant at thinking on his feet, so the best he can come up with is, 'Come along children, we're late!' as he slams the huge front door behind them.

'Again?' Elodie says, as Fabien shrugs in return on her doorstep. 'Let me get my coat...'

'Good practice? Yes?' Fabien attempts, with a sheepish grin.

'Have they eaten?' Anna calls from down the hallway.

'Um...' Fabien says.

Elodie shakes her head, and Anna runs back to the kitchen, shouting, 'Don't worry, we have croissants!'

'She's going to make a great mum,' Fabien says, bracing himself for the punch on the arm he fully deserves, before waving the children goodbye.

He takes a sneaky detour around the back of the hall to pop in unseen by Lydia, and makes his way to the rarely used wings his unwanted guests are currently occupying, which is where he fully expects to find Mila. No doubt she'll be mid-plot with her so-called clients, her responsibilities clean forgotten in her rash determination to follow up on even the most tenuous of leads – and without even waking him, or, better still, waiting for him to wake up at a reasonable time.

Fabien decides he must talk to her about her lack of team spirit, at least where he is concerned, but for now he will rally her back to the main hall and, for once, they will show up for his mother and her cronies on time.

He makes it to Jo and Deb's rooms, and knocks gently, at first thinking it is early, they might still be sleeping, before realising that Mila is obviously in there creating some sort of complex diagram about whatever new theory she has come up with overnight. He opens the door without waiting for a response, but Mila is not standing gesticulating enthusiastically at a flipchart with a marker pen. Mila is not there at all. Deb is lying on the chaise longue with her head on another woman's lap, sleeping, sweaty hair matted across her forehead.

'I'm Kaye,' says the woman. 'I came to look after Deb, she...'

'Drank my father's seventy-eight-year-old Macallan?' Fabien says, picking up the empty, previously treasured, bottle in horror.

'Yes,' says Kaye, 'something like that.'

'And Mila?' Fabien asks, shaking his head at the bottle in mourning.

'She went to find Jo.'

'You'd better start from the beginning, Kaye,' Fabien says, wondering why she now seems to think she lives here too, and what the hell is going on.

TWENTY-SIX

Mila is standing outside Rob's flat when she receives the first call from Fabien, a little after eight. It was one of Jo's last listed addresses in her file. Mila doesn't answer, because she has a plan.

She will wait, quietly, and sneak in to avoid unnecessary confrontation with Rob. She makes a mental note to tell Fabien about her sensible, low-risk strategy afterwards. He will be proud, she thinks.

Mila is watching Rob emerge with a fresh cut on his eye by the time the third text message arrives, but her phone is on silent and her hood is pulled over her face. She slips through the heavy door to the flats he leaves swinging behind him, just in time.

No one is answering the door to the bedsit. Either Jo isn't here, or she is, and she's hurt. Mila throws her weight against the door until the rotten wood around the latch lock shatters and she's in. A window is broken, and there is glass on the floor. She takes a close look at the damaged furniture, the debris of a night ill-spent, blood on the white plastic folding table in the corner, where an empty bottle of Jim Beam sits next to a couple of glasses and an overflowing ashtray. All the time she is shouting Jo's name, but the bedsit isn't large, and Jo isn't here.

Mila's phone starts to ring. Fabien, again. She has already been too long, she needs to answer, and yet...

It rings out, but within seconds another text arrives. He knows Jo's run off, and she has gone after her presuming Jo is at Rob's. And, as she isn't answering her phone he is about to skip out on his mother and Chris-Whatsit from the BBC to come straight to Rob's bedsit and make sure she's not in danger.

Shit, Mila thinks. It isn't that Mila doesn't appreciate the sentiment, but nothing about Fabien's offer is appealing at this moment in time. First, she's leaving. Second, the last thing she wants is to further rile Lydia, especially in front of Chris-Whatsit from the BBC – that could easily be the final straw. And third, she has somewhere else to be, because if that bastard Rob knows where Jo is, if he has hurt her, he's going to pay, and Mila knows where he works.

Mila replies quickly and efficiently.

> I am sorry, it was gut reaction, but no one is in. I'm just going to have a quick look for Jo around town and I'll be back in a couple of hours. Please cover for me, and don't make it worse by being absent too. Love you xx

Fabien's reply is brief and unfriendly, but it gives Mila an hour to find Jo.

Jo has told Mila that part of Rob's latest ammunition when he belittled her for going to prison and losing their baby to the system was to gloat about how well he was doing at work. Assistant Manager now, at a design and printing firm on an industrial estate on the outskirts of town. Mila had been gobsmacked printing firms still existed, as the only people she knew who still actually printed posters and pamphlets were

Lydia and Susannah and they did all theirs, badly, in Microsoft Paint before printing them out on a loud and creaking old printer in the Old School House that doubled up as their community centre. But whatever, that's where Rob is, and that is where Mila is heading.

'And this is my late husband's great-grandfather,' Lydia explains to Chris-Whatsit and Producer Amy as they walk around the edge of the dining hall, its walls adorned with family portraits going back 600 years. 'And this,' Lydia says, proudly, stopping in front of a hideous painting of a stern looking man with small eyes, a pointy beard, and a very silly hat and collar, 'is the fourth Earl of Farlington. He was a key contributor in the suppression of the Rising of the North in 1563.'

'So, the family has always been political?' asks Producer Amy.

'Heaven's no, nothing so crass!' exclaims Lydia. 'Just loyal, and patriotic. One must keep the Catholics in check.'

'Sorry?' asks Producer Amy, as Chris-Whatsit laughs – before swallowing his laugh abruptly as he receives a sharp look from Lydia.

'It was a Catholic uprising, dear,' explains Lydia carefully, wondering what kind of education one needs to work at the BBC these days. 'The Catholic nobility planned to dethrone Elizabeth I, and restore Roman Catholicism. They wanted Mary, Queen of Scots, on the throne, which would have been quite the disaster, so thank goodness for the contributions of our ancestors. Just think, we might not have had Elizabeth II, then no King Charles III, so no William, and then quite unthinkably, no lovely Catherine. Of course, the Scots tried again in the Civil War, and we actually lost the hall to them briefly, but it was recovered, though my husband never did like the–'

Before she can continue her history lesson, Fabien interrupts. 'Of course, that's ancient history now, and it doesn't reflect the current Knutsworth family values.'

'Darling, ancient history ends in AD 500,' Lydia says, quite disappointed in her son's lack of precision.

'Yes, Mother, just a turn of phrase. Shall we look at some more recent paintings, and perhaps then venture outside? It's a little cold, of course, but the snowdrops are wonderful at this time of year. We were thinking of opening the gardens to allow the whole community to enjoy them.' Lydia looks aghast at Fabien. 'Let's head out, and then we can sit by the fire and take tea to warm up, and discuss the plan for the television programme,' Fabien says, gently leading his mother forward.

'Ah!' she says, stopping so suddenly that Chris-Whatsit and Producer Amy accidentally walk into the back of them. 'There he is! My late husband, Lord Gregory Archibald Knutsworth. He always looked his best with his great big beast between his legs.'

'We should be filming this,' says Producer Amy, elbowing Chris-Whatsit who nods, unable to speak for fear of laughing out loud. He is almost purple with the effort of suppression.

'Solomon, pure thoroughbred. Dead now,' Lydia continues wistfully. 'Sorry, what was that about filming? I'm sure we will need to write the scripts first, dear,' she tells Producer Amy, looking to Chris-Whatsit to explain to this young inexperienced woman how proper television programmes at the BBC are made, 'after all, this isn't a *Real Lives of Desperate Housemaids* production.' Lydia chuckles, pleased she makes the effort to stay abreast of the latest cultural movements. She had quite enjoyed the one set in Essex, although she required subtitles and a thesaurus to hand to follow it properly.

'Actually, we don't plan to script it,' Chris-Whatsit tells Lydia. 'We want to capture the authentic you, the real family.'

'Reality television?' Lydia says, slowly. It's one thing to watch it, quite another to be in it.

'Yes, but–' Amy begins.

Chris-Whatsit speaks over her, 'No, a *documentary*.'

'Called, *The Other Half*,' Producer Amy adds unhelpfully.

'The other half to what?' asks Lydia. 'Because if you are referring to that tiresome phrase, "how the other half live", I really think you need to understand a few things. Firstly, we are *not* the other half, we are far fewer than that. A rarity, in fact, courageously trying to retain the values and traditions that will otherwise be lost. And secondly, it isn't all fur coats and balls. This isn't *Bridgerton*. It's hard work, and community obligation. Why, aren't we going to focus on our wonderful charity work and my modern lesbian daughter and my refugee almost-daughter-in-law?' Lydia's voice has risen in pitch and her breathing has quickened.

'Of course, of course,' Chris-Whatsit placates, shooting Producer Amy a look, 'the title is just a working title, and the *documentary*,' he eyeballs Amy once again, 'will showcase the rich tapestry of modern aristocratic life.'

'Well,' sniffs Lydia, 'that does sound rather more like it.' She turns to Fabien, who she realises is playing with his phone again rather than paying attention. 'What do you think, Fabien?'

He has several missed calls from Hoppy and now one text. Mila has been arrested.

TWENTY-SEVEN

Fabien is not driving as carefully as Mila would like as they make their way back from Hipton Police Station, but she decides now isn't the time to criticise. His hands grip the wheel tightly, knuckles white. He is definitely pretty pissed off. He wouldn't even detour to pick up Mila's car.

'Assault!' he says. 'The police arrested *you* for assaulting *Rob*! At his place of work?'

'It was mainly verbal assault.'

'*Mainly?*' Fabien says, incredulous, having received the full circumstances of Mila's arrest from the arresting officer, PC Hoppy Atkins.

'He got in my face, so I pushed him a bit.'

'Hoppy said you pushed him over and kicked him in the ribs.'

'Not hard, though. And he isn't pressing charges. He didn't even call the police; his manager did. So that proves he's definitely hiding something.'

'It really doesn't prove anything of the sort, Mila. We know he probably has nothing to do with our case, if we even *have* a case, so what the hell were you thinking?'

'Jo thinks he does and Deb told me that is where she had gone – I thought he might have hurt her.'

'But Rob insisted he hadn't seen her for a couple of weeks, right – since you brought her here? And she wasn't at his bedsit. And who the hell does he think you are?'

'Don't worry, he doesn't know who I am, I just said I was a friend. It won't come back to you, if that's all you're worried about. I don't think he reads the papers, or has any interest in the great and good of Farlington.' Fabien silently shakes his head and wonders how one so clever can be so blinkered at times. 'But where is she, Fabien? Isn't that the most important thing?'

'Did you even try her parents?' Fabien asks. 'If, as you say, she's angry with you for keeping the files from her, and for not following up on Rob, maybe she just left. She's entitled to.' And, Fabien thinks, it wouldn't be such a bad thing. Apparently, Kaye is now staying until they get to the bottom of things, to help keep Deb on the wagon. One in, one out.

'She won't have gone there. I was so sure she would have gone to Rob's. I thought he was lying. He said after what she'd put him through even if she did turn up, he'd send her packing, which I don't believe for a second. Then his boss told me to leave, and I told his boss that Rob was a woman-beating bastard who probably had her in the boot of his car. And that's when Rob got in my face.'

'Deb was passed out when I found her a couple of hours later. Are you sure she even knew what she was talking about?'

Mila closes her eyes as Fabien jerks the car off the main road leading into Farlington from Hipton, and finally starts to slow down, the roads narrowing to single track. The niggle gains intensity as she tries to remember Deb's exact words when Mila had asked where Jo was. 'She said... She went to find him.'

'Rob?'

'She didn't say Rob. Oh God, what if she meant Bradley Pound?'

'And you didn't think to check?' Fabien roars. 'This is impetuous, even for you!'

Mila quickly finds Kaye's number and hits dial.

'Seriously?' Fabien says, as Mila holds the phone to her ear.

'Kaye, is Deb awake? Ask her, was it Rob Jo went to find, or Pound?'

As Mila ends the call, she turns to Fabien. 'We have to go to Pound's place.'

Fabien continues to stare ahead at the mountains in the distance, visible beneath the crisp blue sky as they drive down the narrowest of lanes to Farlington Hall. Occasionally, the old Defender scratches against a bare hedgerow branch where there isn't room for the full width of a car.

Mila tries again. 'Fabien, she went to find Bradley Pound. We have to go. She could be in real danger. That guy is an actual gangster. He hurts people.'

'We don't know where he lives,' Fabien replies quietly, steadily navigating the winding lane.

'We know where he operates.'

'We are not spending the rest of the day roaming around the streets in the wrong end of Hipton in the hope of bumping into Pound. And we can presume if that's what Jo's masterplan was that she is still roaming the streets on a wild-goose chase and will soon get bored and come back.'

'She's been gone all night,' Mila says, now seriously concerned and hating herself for getting it so wrong. She also knows she has to appeal to Fabien's innate goodness, and do her very best not to be argumentative or dogmatic or aggressive, the things he often tells her she is.

'She's probably at a friend's or her parents'.' Fabien's face is fixed, his mouth tight. He needs to make Mila see sense. They are supposed to be helping people who have slipped through the net to find justice through legal means. Getting involved with volatile ex-criminals and addicts, embroiled in altercations with thugs and gangsters, had at no point been in the strategic plan.

'We have to look for Pound,' Mila says, 'please. Even if she's really mad at us – at me – and went off to do her own thing, if she has confronted Pound about following her, trying to get him to confess to working with Rob, and he's actually working for someone else, we don't know what he, or whoever he is working for, is capable of.'

'We don't even know if Pound has anything to do with Jo, not really.'

'But we *do* know she went to confront him, and he won't just send her away with a stern word or two. She could be–' Mila, unlike her usual self, looks frantic, sounds hysterical. It's her fault. If anything has happened to Jo, it's her fault.

'Okay, Mila,' Fabien says, to Mila's surprise, 'but we are not going ourselves. If she hasn't found him, then it's pointless, and if he has found her, then it's dangerous.'

'What, then? How will we find her?'

'Hoppy. Hoppy has seen that Pound appeared to be following Jo, and we have good reason to believe she went looking for him to confront him, most likely to prove that Rob was the one paying him. That should be enough for Hoppy to pay him a visit, and scope the place out. It's a start, and it is the best we can do. Do you agree?'

Mila really doesn't agree, but if she and Fabien reveal themselves to Pound now accusing him of all sorts, but he hasn't even seen Jo, then he will flag the whole investigation to whoever is paying him, and that will be the end of the case. 'Can you call Hoppy right now, and get him to go straight away?'

TWENTY-EIGHT

Jo is eating the whole packet of chocolate Hobnobs while Bradley Pound and Jason Statham watch her with judgement in their eyes. Jason Statham is drooling a bit, and Pound is tapping his feet impatiently. He hasn't struck her again since last time, and even Jason Statham seems to be warming to her.

'Don't look at me like that,' she says, 'this is the first food you've given me, and I'm starving.'

Pound twiddles the gags in his hand and looks to the ceiling. 'Fecks' sake, nothing's ever good enough,' he says, shaking his head. That's his last packet and they're his favourite biscuits.

Jo ignores him. She has picked up on Pound leaving irate but cryptic voicemails to whoever he works for, and so long as they don't answer, Jo reckons she's safe. As soon as they do, however, it's a different story. They will never trust her to keep quiet. The longer she thinks about it, the more she understands that what she has seen somehow relates to her case, and maybe even to the others. And that it matters to Pound and his associates a lot.

Clearly, the man in the suit drinking craft beer in the hip wine shop is the boss, and Pound is nervous about telling him he has been followed and photographed, never mind the ensuing abduction... but, Jo figures, he has the phone with the photos and the girl that took them, so she can only presume he will be ordered to "deal" with her, as he keeps implying. Jo doesn't know for sure what "dealing with her" means, but she is fairly certain it will not be anything good, and it is likely to be something permanent. She is counting on Mila working out where she is before that happens. Jo hopes that the suited man's diary is chock-full and he doesn't get a chance to check his messages until she has been rescued. And she will be rescued, won't she?

Jo now realises that Mila is right. Rob is an abomination of a man, but he's not clever enough to do anything so convoluted just to get Jo back in his clutches. She isn't usually so full of herself; how stupid Mila must think her to imagine someone would go to such lengths for her. Hasn't Mila told her the cases have to be connected, that there is someone orchestrating all three – perhaps many more – cases in which women have been tricked, framed or manipulated into losing their family court hearings at the last moment, so that their babies stayed with the foster parents? She should have listened, even if she still can't understand who on earth would have anything to gain from taking their babies. It has to be the adopters, right? Paying the man in the suit to sabotage them.

The doorbell goes, followed by a hard knock. Mila! Thank God.

'Right, party's over,' Pound says, ripping the packet from her hands, and quickly retying her.

The knocking is louder now, three knocks, and then... 'Police!'

Jo starts to shout, and the slap that follows cracks against her cheek, sending her head sharply to one side. She feels the blood run from her nose as the gags are crudely and roughly tied, making her unable to make more than a muffled cry. Jason Statham is growling and barking, his early patience evaporating in the commotion. Pound tugs at his collar and goes to the side doors that lead back into the house.

'Not a sound,' he tells her. 'They won't be here for you. I've got more important things going on, and if I think you're trying to make a fuss, once I've seen them out, I'll be back to take matters into my own hands. I think we both know how this ends, don't we? Waiting for the green light from my man is just a courtesy. And courtesy is not friggin' mandatory.' Pound locks the two doors behind him, and leaves Jo staring at the brick wall which separates her from the front half of the garage. She just hopes that the police *are* here for her, and that it's someone with more tenacity than that halfwit, PC Hoppy Atkins.

Hoppy doesn't have a search warrant for Bradley Pound's house. He has already called in on the parents, who won't report Jo missing and have explained that she is an adult who chooses not to keep in touch, and if she has been staying with a friend and now has moved on, they don't plan to get themselves all upset and "waste police time over nothing."

The boss, surprisingly, has given the okay to check in on Pound, but made it clear that this does not count as a missing person investigation, simply raising her eyebrows when Hoppy mentioned Mila's concerns. DI Cora Payne had enough to do with Mila Kiss and the Knutsworths the previous year, and spent some time repairing the damage caused by the relentless yet unapproved investigations of young Hoppy. She remains constantly irritated at having to oversee the Hipton outpost Hoppy is stationed at from her senior post in CID, but cutbacks have left her with little choice. House guests are allowed to leave, she told him in no uncertain terms, and given that Mila has only known this woman for two minutes, Jo has no obligation to inform her as to her whereabouts.

'Good afternoon, Mr Pound,' says Hoppy, as the front door is finally opened. He can hear the television blaring and recognises "Climb Ev'ry Mountain" from *The Sound of Music,* one of his mother's favourite films, and a regular accompaniment to their Sunday afternoons. He wouldn't have had Pound down as a fan, but then they do say you can't judge a book by its cover.

'All right, PC Atkins, to what do I owe the pleasure this time?' A large angry looking dog shoves his head around Pound's bulky frame to get a better smell of the latest intruder, and snarls, just a little.

'Have you seen this woman?' Hoppy presents the photograph of Jo.

'This again? Do I need a solicitor? I told you before, never seen her in my life.'

'She's gone missing, and we are following up all around the local area,' Hoppy says in his best police officer voice.

'And, what, because I walked on the same streets as her once or twice, you think I'm now privy to her every move? Didn't the solicitor say I had nothing to do with her? She's a druggy, right? Paranoid.'

'Who told you that?' asks Hoppy, thinking there might be an opportunity to catch Pound out in a lie.

'Solicitor, mate, he said she'd only just recently got out of the clink. It was him who said she's a nutter, though he didn't use that term, as it happens. I got the gist, though. Basically, she's on the streets, accusing innocent men of following her, and now she's gone missing, and you're all running about after her, when you should be out there catching real criminals. I feel as sorry for the fruitcakes as the next bloke, and it hasn't passed me by that there's a mental health crisis in this country and the healthcare system can't cope, but you lot – you hardworking police – it's not your job to look after them, is it? Tragic really, hope she turns up.' Pound starts to close the door.

'May I come in?' Hoppy asks, gently pushing the door back towards Pound and smiling his toothy smile that makes him look about twelve. As Pound's face darkens and his glare pierces into Hoppy, he *feels* about twelve, too.

'You got a warrant?'

'Have you got something to hide?' Hoppy asks, trying to keep his breath soft and even, like the meditation app says you should. Hoppy is feeling very brave, but also slightly foolhardy. He double checks his bodycam is on, and feels nervously for his radio.

Pound grins widely, and swings open the door. The finale song to *The Sound of the Music* continues to blare. 'Come in. Cuppa?' he says, as Hoppy steps into the hallway, the dog staring at him, mouth open. 'Jason Statham, come,' says Pound, and the dog trots after him, tail wagging. 'Sorry about the noise, got it on for Mrs Felcham. She likes to see the von Trapps on the big screen at least once a week, but she weren't feeling so well, so I took her home halfway through, and not turned it off yet. Gotta admit, truth be told, it's not a bad film for its time though, hey? Nothing on *The Fast and the Furious,* which is a personal favourite of mine, but that Julie Andrews is a bit of all right, and she can't half belt them tunes out.'

Hoppy is beginning to wonder if he's got Pound wrong, though doubting Mila's instincts in the past has usually resulted in him having a great deal of egg on his face. 'Perhaps I could look around?' Hoppy asks.

'Well, PC Atkins, you know I don't have to say yes, as you've got no warrant or any real reason to be here, have you? But seeing as you asked so nicely, I'll show you about myself, and then you can be on your way, knowing I've nothing to do with your missing girl. Then, maybe you can focus on something more urgent. Like those kids on the estate across town. Always on drugs, did you know that? Terrible shame.'

The television continues to blare out, and Hoppy walks straight past the hidden door to the garage, through to the kitchen. He looks in the bedrooms upstairs, which he notes are tastefully decorated, with maybe just a tad too much velvet and satin, and one too many mirrors on the ceilings, which Hoppy finds very odd, but not illegal. He doesn't find any hint of drugs, and wonders if Pound really has turned over a new leaf, as he'd insisted during his interview, before he'd gone full *"No comment"*, and as his empty pockets during the unsuccessful stop and search had implied before that.

Back in the kitchen, Hoppy takes a polite sip of the strong dark-coloured tea he doesn't really want, preferring fruit and mint teas to the builder's variety. 'Who's that?' Hoppy asks, pointing to a photograph of a young woman on top of a brown envelope, a couple of sheets of handwritten notes underneath.

'Niece, sister sent it the other day,' Pound says, rapidly moving it away, shoving the notes and photo back into the envelope, 'a face only a mother could love, eh? You seen everything now, PC Atkins? I'll show you out, and perhaps you and whoever is pulling your strings about this girl can give me a break. Just trying to get on, you know?'

'Thank you, Mr Pound,' says Hoppy as he steps out of the house into the dark February chill, the sun long gone by five these days. 'Ah,' he says, swivelling around halfway down the garden path as he notices the red garage door attached to the house, 'mind if I peek into the garage?'

TWENTY-NINE

'She definitely wasn't there?' Mila asks, unconvinced.

'Hoppy looked everywhere, even in the garage. But it's good news, Mila. It means she is somewhere of her own accord. Safe.'

'Or he's already dealt with her.'

'It is far more likely she didn't even find him in the first place, and she's staying locally in Hipton while she looks,' Fabien says, still scrolling and tapping away on his tablet.

'I don't understand why her phone is still off, something's not right, and yet, nobody seems to care.'

'It isn't that we don't care, Mila, but you have to accept that she isn't there, and we really don't know her at all, or her friends. She could have gone anywhere.'

'She never mentioned any friends,' Mila says, 'not proper ones, anyway.'

'You've known her for two weeks; you hardly know anything about her life beyond the baby and the adoption. Hoppy said the neighbour confirmed she had visited earlier to watch *The Sound of Music,* and Bradley Pound was alone. Well, with his dog.'

'I mean, does that sound likely to you? *The Sound of Music*?'

'It is a classic, to be fair.'

'But how many gangster drug dealers watch old musicals with their elderly neighbours?'

'Maybe he really is a changed man.'

'Bollocks. He's just trying to make himself look good. What did he say the old lady next door was called?'

'Mrs Doris Felcham.'

'Unfortunate.'

'A little.'

Mila sits cross-legged on the bed, propped up by pillows and wrapped in Fabien's great big towelling dressing gown. Her laptop balances on a decorative cushion between her knees as she scours online for an address for Pound's elderly neighbour. Old people always have landlines and, for some reason, like them to be listed alongside their home address in digital versions of the old-fashioned telephone directories.

Four bowls licked clean of raspberry ripple ice cream clutter the bedside tables, a treat for the children following their chaotic morning. They'd wholeheartedly bought into the story that Mila had been ill. Lydia had simply raised an eyebrow and insisted on Mila taking her miracle cure cough medicine, which Mila had noted was at least thirty years out of date. With Fabien's encouragement – *insistence*, more like – she swallowed it down, retching. 'You enjoyed that, didn't you?' she had asked him.

He just smiled and said, 'It's good for you, given you were too ill to speak to the BBC earlier.'

Now, the children are sleeping across the hall, and Mila and Fabien need to figure out how to move forward.

'I am sorry about forgetting the children needed me this morning,' says Mila, and she really is. Her failures as their surrogate mother are not lost on her, and as soon as she realised what she had done, which was when Fabien reminded her and not a moment sooner, she felt a familiar ghost kicking her in the stomach. She will not forgive herself for this or for any of her mistakes when it comes to Konstantine and Karlie, yet she thinks there will probably be more to come. 'Really, I am.'

Fabien looks at Mila and smiles. 'And for being arrested?'

Mila nods. 'But I'm more sorry about the kids.'

'They're fine, Mila, don't beat yourself up about *that*.' There are definitely other things Fabien thinks Mila would be better off focusing any self-reflection on.

Mila still feels awful about forgetting her sister's children needed her. Still, there's nothing like a fight for justice to keep her mind off her losing battle to be a better parent, girlfriend, in-law, person. She goes back to squinting at her screen.

'I believe that the evidence has started to stack up against the adoptive parents,' says Fabien, 'and we have worked too hard and risked too much – especially you – not to follow up on these leads. We can't waste time, or any more favours, looking for someone who doesn't want to be found. It still might be a coincidence that the three couples know one another, and all had permanent adoption orders instated at the last moment, with three birth mothers claiming to be framed in very similar ways, but it seems increasingly unlikely.'

'You've changed your tune,' Mila says, looking sideways at Fabien.

'Maybe,' he says. 'You're very persuasive. Also, Kaye just seems so normal and committed, the more I speak with her, the less likely it seems that she would make such a monumental error. She had only recently assembled the changing table in which they found the drugs, so she couldn't have simply forgotten they were there. They must have been planted.'

'Why wasn't Jo's story enough, or Deb's?' Mila asks.

'They don't make a great first impression, do they?'

'Snob.'

'Yes, probably, but ranting on the Town Hall steps and getting thrown out of online support groups for being abusive doesn't build a great deal of confidence in their reliability. And now Jo's done a runner – these sorts of impulsive behaviours are exactly why the courts fail to find their stories credible. They can be their own worst enemies.'

Mila can't argue with that. She also can't shake the feeling that even if Jo is angry and making a point, she would have checked her phone and at least texted to let them know she is safe. Jo *is* impulsive, she is furious, emotionally damaged, and perhaps even reckless, but she isn't cruel. Mila is sure of it. Jo would have been in touch if she were able.

'At least Deb seems to have recovered her determination to stay sober. It beggars belief how someone could trick an alcoholic into relapsing. Kaye said she'd been sober for months, but something like this – the spiking followed by the loss of her child – would inevitably have set her back.'

Mila raises an eyebrow. 'I said that from the beginning!'

'But you say things so fervently, darling, so fanatically, that sometimes it sounds rather, well, fantastical.'

'That is so–' Mila begins, outrage in her eyes.

'Right!' he announces, placing down his iPad. 'I'm in. Golf tomorrow, at one.'

'They're definitely going to be there? All three adoptive dads?' Mila asks, a little sulkily.

'Yup, I called earlier, spoke to the manager, double checked my "pals" will be there. I'd already figured out they usually played on Fridays, from their social media accounts, and the rest was easy.'

'He gave you private client information, just like that?'

'People will tell me anything. I have a natural charm,' Fabien replies.

'You have a title, you mean?'

'And that. The hardest part was filling out the ten-page membership form, not to mention parting with the best part of £2,000 for the pleasure.'

'Shit, I'm sorry.'

'Don't be, I actually quite like golf and now you'll have to let me indulge without rolling your eyes or calling me bourgeois, seeing as it is all for the greater good.'

They hear footsteps and giggling from outside the door. There's lots of loud whispering, and then a knock on their bedroom door.

'Bro!' Elodie whispers exaggeratedly and with a slight slur. 'Are you two still awake?'

After Elodie and Anna fall into the room, Offal padding in behind them, delighted at the midnight excursion, they jump onto the bed almost dislocating Fabien's left knee and get themselves comfortable.

'We couldn't wait to tell you!' Elodie says. They had been to the Women's Institute talk to protest against Frederick Fawcett, they explain with glee. Susannah had been beside herself, and thank goodness Lydia had opted not to attend, having been worn down by Elodie's explanations of why Fawcett should not be given a platform or endorsement by the family, as she might have had a funny turn had she been there. Fawcett had been sucking up to what Elodie and Anna describe as "the old-fashioned values of the collective WI's hive mind", waxing lyrical about how their traditional marriages and well-brought up children were the reason the economy was thriving.

'The economy isn't thriving, though, is it?' Mila asks.

'You seem to be mistaking Fawcett for someone concerned with actual facts,' Anna says.

'He told them that mothers were pillars of the community, even got them to give themselves a round of applause, saying they were responsible for the success of future generations,' Elodie says, then standing on the bed, wobbling precariously, she throws her arms into the air, and impersonates Fawcett's speech. "A return to traditional values, led by women – the women in this *very* room – is the only hope for our great nation!"

'My God,' says Mila.

'Sit down before you do yourself a mischief,' says Fabien.

'Oh, you should have heard them,' Elodie continues, now sitting on Fabien's foot, 'they lapped it up! It was actually frightening. So we pressed play.'

'Play on what?' asks Fabien.

'We compiled a series of clips from Hitler, Mussolini, and Stalin who had all said pretty similar stuff, drowning him out. Anna had connected to the speaker in the Old School House, you know – that Councillor Beard had installed for the Summer BBQ? And not one of the pillars of Great Britain knew how to switch it off!' Elodie rolls around on the bed, laughing like a schoolgirl. Fabien and Mila smile, and Anna shakes her head fondly at her girlfriend.

'Then what?' asks Mila.

'Well, we assumed he would carry on regardless, but his PA had to take some urgent call, and suddenly they made their excuses and left, saying something had come up – on a Thursday night, hardly,' Elodie says. 'They just couldn't take the heat, hahaha!' she slaps her thigh in glee, and rolls straight off the bed with a thump. 'Owww,' she says from the floor, as Offal licks her face, causing more giggling.

'Then,' Anna says, 'as you *may* have gathered, we went to the pub.'

'But that's not all...' Elodie says in a sing-song voice as she pulls herself back up with the help of the wooden bed post. She jumps back onto the bed, almost breaking Fabien's ankle, and wraps her arms around Anna. 'We came home to a letter.'

'And?' asks Fabien.

'We've passed stage one of the adoption process!'

'Oh, congratulations!' Mila and Fabien cry, removing laptops and iPads from their path to lean forward and hug the two women. 'That's wonderful news,' Fabien adds, 'Mother will be over the moon for you; it might take her mind off the rather disastrous meeting with Chris-Whatsit from the BBC.'

'Oh, well, we may not have done much to help the PR strategy actually,' says Anna. 'Gareth Davies from the *Farlington Gazette* was there too, so guess who will be front page news again?'

16 February 2025

Where are you, Mila? Wanda was right about one thing at least – writing a journal is good for anxiety – but my journal is back at the house, and my hands are tied so all I can do is close my eyes and talk to you in my mind. I never believed in God, but I'm praying now. I never believed in telepathy either, but it looks like my best bet now. I'm sorry Mila, for everything. I heard Pound leave messages for someone, saying there was an urgent problem that needed to be dealt with. Not the first time I've been called that, but I'm beginning to think it might be the last. Hurry Mila, because I think when he finally talks to this guy, I'm a goner...

THIRTY

Mila is not interested in beauty, her own or that of others, but she is not blind to it either. So today, Mila has blow-dried her hair into soft, smooth curls, and found an old lipstick of Lydia's to paint her lips red, her Cupid's bow popping more than ever. She has cobbled together an outfit by raiding Elodie and Anna's wardrobes, claiming she needs something less grungy for some meeting with the playground committee.

Elodie had raised an eyebrow at that; since when has Mila ever tried to fit in? But on balance, she decided she'd prefer to know as little as possible about whatever it was Mila was really getting up to.

Mila checks out her reflection. She's hitched up the skirt with a belt, and left several more buttons than necessary undone on the shirt, revealing a hint of lace bra, the very gentle curve of her pale skin above it, two beauty spots drawing the eye. Today, she has someone very important to introduce herself to, someone she suspects will like this ludicrously insufficient clothing in the middle of British winter.

'What do you think?' she says to Offal, who perks up from his doze upon hearing his name. Mila had offered to walk Offal earlier, and texted Elodie to say he was happy staying at the main house for the afternoon. 'But actually, little man,' Mila tells the fluffy white teddy-bear of a dog, 'we are going on an adventure.'

'This is it, Offal,' Mila says, closing the car door, where she has parked up around the corner from Mrs Felcham's house, right next door to Pound's, and according to the online satellite map, its perfect mirror image. She clips on Offal's lead, and they walk around the back of the house, where a narrow footpath leads to the back garden gates. She gently opens Mrs Felcham's gate a few inches and unclips Offal's lead, throwing a small stick inside, and closing the gate behind him as he runs to fetch it. 'I'll be five minutes, Offal, don't worry.'

Mila hurries around to the front of the house, and rings the doorbell, which loudly plays a song Mila vaguely recognises. A television soap theme, Australian, she thinks, that Lydia pretends not to be glued to every teatime. Through the bubble glass she sees Mrs Felcham's form shuffle towards her slowly and unlock the door, chain too, and Mila thinks she ought to be more careful. There are all sorts of scammers and tricksters about, people who will say anything to gain access to your home.

'I've lost my dog!' says Mila, holding up the lead. 'Have you seen him?'

'Oh dear,' Mrs Felcham replies, twiddling something in her ear. 'Just turning my hearing aids up so I can hear you, but I gather you've lost your dog?' she says, pointing at the dangling lead.

'Have you seen him? He's white and he's called Offal.'

'What a good name. We lived on offal in my day, nobody likes it now, young people only want the finest cuts, don't they?'

'Have you seen him?'

'I haven't seen a dog, but then, I've been watching *Bargain Hunt*. The Blue Team had an absolute stinker! Lost twenty quid on the most hideous figurine I've ever seen. Chipped as well, it was, don't know what they were thinking. I could have told them it was worth bugger all.'

The conversation, taking slightly longer than anticipated, was suddenly interrupted by the unforgettable sound of Offal's high-pitched impression of a lost wolf cub.

'That's him!' Mila says. 'Did you hear him?'

Mrs Felcham twiddles with the hearing aid again, just as Offal gives his call another go. 'Oh, I did that time. I wonder where he could be...'

'It sounds like it came from back there,' Mila says, pointing down Mrs Felcham's hallway.

'I'm sure I would have noticed if he was in my house, young lady. I might be old, but I'm far from daft.'

'Do you have a garden? Maybe he got into the garden?' Mila asks, wiping a fake tear from her eye.

'Of course! Silly me. Come through, come through.'

Ten minutes later, Mila perches on a floral sofa facing an electric fire in Mrs Felcham's front room. Offal sits happily by her feet eating a custard cream bestowed on him by Mrs Felcham, who cannot fathom how the little dog had got in when the gate was closed.

'Perhaps it blew open and then shut?' says Mila.

'That isn't good. It's not what it used to be, this area. When I first moved in fifty years ago it was considered very upmarket, these houses were brand new. Everyone wanted one. I'll ask young Bradley to take a look at the catch.'

'Bradley?' Mila asks, blowing on her tea. 'Grandson?' she adds, smiling sweetly.

'No, not family, actually. My husband and I weren't blessed

with children. But the young man next door is a life saver, just like a grandson to me. Helps me with the garden, the bins, and any odd jobs. We watch *The Sound of Music* every week together. Isn't he an absolute angel?'

Well, that bit *was* true, Mila thinks, perturbed but undeterred. 'He sounds great. Anyway, I think it's a lovely area, you know. I'd really like to live somewhere like this. I'm saving up for a deposit. I don't suppose I could have a look around?'

When Mrs Felcham closes the door behind Mila and Offal, Mila has one more stop: the most important one, and now she knows exactly what she's dealing with. After the disaster with Rob, Mila can't afford to make any more mistakes.

She takes a few steps down the street until she is at the bottom of Pound's front garden, and swings open the gate. She takes the tennis ball she has stuffed with treats by making a small hole on one side out of her handbag. These treats are Offal's everything. She subtly clicks open the garden gate and chucks the tennis ball hard against the window, really hard, but not hard enough to break it. Offal dives up the path to retrieve it, and on discovering the treats inside he immediately lies down to devour them.

'Offal! Offal! Come back, you naughty boy!' Mila shouts, far more loudly than necessary. And when nothing happens – thank goodness for Elodie's relaxed attitude to training and Offal's dedication to his favourite treats – she lobs a second ball, this time against the door.

Finally, the door opens and there stands the man from the grainy CCTV images who has been following Jo. The man who gave a No Comment interview. The man who Jo has gone to find, and who, Mila is convinced, has caught Jo on his tail, and either now has her against her will while he figures out how much she knows and what to do with her, or much, much worse. 'What the bloody hell is going on out here?' he says, a large dog barking behind his legs, the door only ajar.

Mila flicks her hair back, and juts her chest out. One leg poses proud and bent in front of the other, making her legs look even longer than they are. 'I'm so, so sorry,' she gushes in a girly, apologetic voice, 'my little dog got through your gate and I didn't want to trespass so I was calling him, but he's such a naughty boy.' Mila giggles, twizzling her hair in one hand. 'May I?' she asks, Offal totally oblivious to the danger lurking behind Bradley Pound's knees as he hoovers up the treats having ripped the ball open.

'Yeah, yeah, course, darlin',' Pound says, watching Mila wiggle up the crazy paving , and slowly bend over provocatively to clip Offal's lead on once more.

'Good, good boy,' she whispers, in her normal voice. She stands, slowly rising from her core, giving Bradley a good look down her top. Mila is a little appalled she has decided to use these tactics, but as far as she's concerned, you've got to know your audience, and play to their weaknesses.

'I'm Sophia,' she says, holding out her hand as if she expects it to be kissed. Pound takes it awkwardly in his and shakes the loose limb, her slim wrist floppy and delicate.

'Brad,' he replies.

'Oh, you have a dog too, how cute!' says Mila, as Jason Statham growls at her.

'Not how he's normally described,' says Pound.

'Bet he's a softie really? Can I stroke him?' Mila starts to bend forward a little, her head getting dangerously close to Pound's crotch. 'Go on, let me stroke him,' she more or less purrs, wondering when the hell she learned how to do this and how it is coming so naturally.

'Aye,' he says, 'go on, you're right, he looks the part and sounds the part, but he'd do anything for a stick of carrot and a game of fetch. Loves a tummy tickle. Roll over,' he tells the dog, who does as he is told.

Mila crouches down, strokes his belly, and sneaks him a couple of treats. 'What's his name? He's gorgeous, just like his daddy,' Mila says, almost making herself vomit.

'Jason Statham. Tough guys, innit?' Pound winks, and Mila giggles. She's not sure who she hates more at this moment; him or herself. 'He likes you,' Pound adds.

She looks down at Jason Statham who is now in his best begging position, panting and drooling. 'Ever been on a doggie date, Jason Statham?' she asks, before looking back up at Pound, drawing his gaze into her deep, seductive eyes. Offal, now full and bloated, flops to the floor with the crushed up, torn tennis ball between his teeth and she quickly scoops him into her arms, just in case Jason Statham takes an immediate liking to Elodie's most treasured creature, lying down as if dinner on a plate.

'A what?' says Pound.

'You, me, and the dogs go on a walk. It's like a date.'

'But without any of the good bits of a date,' he says, laughing, liking this sexy, forward woman in front of him, thinking it's been too long since he had female company.

'Well, maybe if the first date for the pups goes well, we can talk about a second date with all the good bits...' Mila really doesn't know how she is keeping her breakfast down.

'You wanna go on a walk now?' he asks, raising his eyebrows.

'I'm already on a walk, just asking if you want to join me.'

Pound shakes his head, smiling, but then says, 'Ah, why not. Let me just get my coat.'

'Yay!' Mila squeals, imitating her young niece, and then with Oscar-worthy enthusiasm, she launches into a severe coughing fit. 'Water,' she splutters, 'need... water.' She grabs her throat and continues to cough, staggering into his hallway.

'Come into the kitchen. Christ,' he says.

Mila drinks the glass of water, making a speedy recovery as she confirms the back door leads from the kitchen directly to the garden, just like the one in Mrs Felcham's house. Pound grabs his coat and a lead from the hook on the wall, and the now placid Jason Statham watches on, wagging his tail in anticipation. As Pound bends to slip the lead over his dog's thick neck, Mila quickly and quietly turns the key in the back door and unlocks it.

Mila and Pound stroll out onto the street, and head towards the park. She takes her phone from her pocket, and texts Kaye her instructions.

THIRTY-ONE

Kaye and Deb are keeping a low profile in the back of Mila's car when the text comes through.

'We're on,' says Kaye to Deb. 'You ready?'

'Fuck yeah,' Deb replies, grinning widely.

When they arrive at Bradley Pound's house they push the back gate open and tread lightly as they walk through the garden, which is littered with fluffy, cute dog toys, alongside the odd turd. The door, as promised, is unlocked. Safe in the knowledge that the house is otherwise empty, they begin to make some noise.

'Jo! Jo!' they shout over and over, running from room to room. They don't hear a reply. 'Jo! Jo! JO!'

'Shush a minute,' says Deb. 'I think I hear something.' They go into the kitchen and listen for a moment, then head back into the hallway where the sounds seem to be louder. They press their ears to the wooden panelling under the stairs, and they think they can hear some scuffling, muffled and unclear.

'I hope it isn't rats,' says Deb.

'I reckon it's her,' Kaye says. 'Jo! Don't worry, we're here. Pound's gone, I'm going to work out how to reach you.' She turns to Deb. 'There must be some kind of understairs cupboard behind here...' But no obvious door, she thinks, not liking where the thought takes her.

'Or a basement?' Deb says with a shudder.

Kaye traces her fingers all over the panel, squinting to find a keyhole. Her hands run up and down the wood, finding nothing. 'You go search the kitchen and tops for a key basket or something,' she tells Deb, who runs off and starts to look for any random key she can find. 'Aha. This could be it!' Having pulled at the carpet, she spots a very small bolt right at the bottom, fastening the door into the floor. It is obscured by the hallway carpet, but it doesn't even need a key. She unlocks it and the door swings open.

'What the...?' says Deb, joining Kaye in the hall.

'Another door,' replies Kaye, disheartened.

'It's like a creepy version of *Alice in Wonderland*.'

'Actually, I thought the original *Alice* was pretty creepy,' Kaye remarks as she examines the second door. This one *does* require a key. 'It's one of those old-fashioned types, Deb,' Kaye tells her, examining the lock, 'probably long and thin with a big fat tooth on the end, you know?'

Deb runs back into the kitchen to search. 'I can't find any keys at all! He could have them with him, couldn't he?' she calls back to Kaye, still rummaging in drawers and cupboards, not caring about the mess. It won't matter if they succeed. It won't matter if they don't.

'Jo!' Kaye shouts again. 'Can you hear us?' Please let her be here, safe, unhurt.

'Mmmmmheeeere,' says a very quiet, strained voice as Kaye presses her ear to the door, her face squished against the wood.

'Thank God!' Kaye screams in delight. 'Deb, forget the key, there's no time – come help me knock this bastard door down. We're coming for you, Jo!'

At first, they plough into the door with their shoulders, like they've seen on telly, the heroes making it look easy. It isn't, and it hurts like hell. Then they get imaginative. Two broken kitchen chairs later, the women are beginning to get desperate.

'The coffee machine!' Deb says, as they look around for more instruments to use in place of their bruised shoulders and the chairs that really weren't made to last. 'He's got one of those huge ones you put beans in.'

'They cost a fortune. I swear to God, I can't believe I lined people like Pounds' pockets, while slowly losing everything. And they just get richer and have nice kitchens.'

'And good coffee.' Deb adds, 'It's the right shape, too.'

'Right shape for what?'

'Like a knocking post, it's a big bulky cylinder and I bet it weighs a bit,' Deb says, running over to it, and unplugging it. 'Yep, this is it, let's go. Let's smash the bastard's stuff up and save our Jo.'

With one drive, the wood on the door splinters, and with the second push, they have made a hole. By the third it is a big enough hole to climb through. Deb and Kaye clamber through, find a light switch and illuminate the brick-walled room, full of shelves stacked high with packages and pills. A money counter sits on a small desk in the corner. And in the other corner sits Jo, gagged and tied, and dirty. She's crying, and her lips are chapped from the gag, blood lining it from where the rags have cut into her.

They run over and touch her gently. 'You're safe,' says Kaye.

Deb goes to untie the gag, but Kaye stops her. 'What the hell?'

'Just one second,' Kaye replies, quickly getting her phone out of her pocket and taking a photo of Jo as they found her, and snapping all around the room. 'Okay, now,' she says, quickly sending the photos to Hoppy, with only a few words – "Jo *was* at Pound's" – before dropping to her knees to help release Jo from her binds and sending Mila the subtle confirmation of their find she'd requested.

They run from the house, and back to the car – in case Pound comes back before the police arrive, in case the police don't take them seriously, in case Mila is in trouble – following her directions to the letter. Send the photos, get in the car, and get home to safety, or if Jo is hurt, go straight to the hospital. Jo seems okay, and is playing down the bruises on her face, so they head back to Farlington Hall. Kaye rings Hoppy back, who had immediately responded to the text with several calls. She tells him they've escaped and where to find Mila and Pound. He promises they are on their way. The three women are silent as they drive, hearts pumping, praying to any god that will have them that the police can finally get Pound and the answers they need to prove that they were all followed, all framed, all wrongly accused. Only then can they hope to get their babies back.

It turns out Jason Statham is a very well-behaved dog, well-trained and sweet-natured. Unlike his owner. Pound is showing off his command of the dog, how he never wanted a dangerous dog, just one that looked and acted tough. 'You know, for protection?' he says.

'Protection from what?' Mila replies, shrugging his arm from her shoulder for the third time.

'Can't be too careful,' Pound says. 'We have a bond, me and Jason Statham, so he has my back and I have his.'

'So, what is it that you do?' Mila asks, buying time. Pound has already suggested they find a pub and get in from the sharp frosty cold and the bitter wind, but this is where she needs to be, for when the police get here and finally catch him. That will wipe the smug look off his face.

'Gotta say, Sophia, I think I preferred the flirty version of you back at mine.'

'Oh, you!' Mila says, slapping his chest playfully, and batting her eyelashes. 'I just wanted to get to know you a bit,' she tells him, smiling, reminding herself to keep up the act for as long as it takes for them to get here and get the cuffs on those wandering hands. She has received a thumbs up emoji from Kaye, which is all she requested to confirm they had Jo and she was safe and alive, without risking Pound catching sight of anything incriminating. 'That okay, Bradley?'

'Only my mother and the old dear next door call me that, and only when I've been very naughty.' He winks, and Mila uses all of her strength not to roll her eyes and say something she would definitely regret.

Instead, she says, 'Well, best not be naughty then, and tell me what you do so I can work out if you're worth my time.' Mila thinks she heard that line on one of Lydia's dating shows.

'Sales, imports, exports, plenty of cash for treating a princess like you, don't you worry,' he says, as Mila hides her shock at his lack of offence at being asked about his earning power on a first date. 'Hold on,' he says. Pound's phone vibrates in his pocket. 'Mrs Felcham?' Mila freezes. This probably isn't good. Pound listens quietly, frown deepening, for a few seconds. 'Thank you, Mrs Felcham,' he says, hanging up, and looking at Mila. 'You?' he says.

So, Mrs Felcham wasn't calling about her garden gate.

'You...' he repeats, eyes wide, fight or flight rippling through his shocked expression as he almost dances, staggering back, lurching forward in anger, then back again as realisation dawns. The audacity of some girl to trick *him*, a mastermind criminal.

The absolute cheek of it, the humiliation, the fucking disaster of the whole bleeding thing.

'Police!' shout the police. 'Stay where you are!'

But they are metres away, and Bradley Pound does not stay where he is. Flight wins. He forces Jason Statham's lead into Mila's empty hand, and runs, shouting back, 'You better make sure he's looked after, you lying bitch!'

THIRTY-TWO

Statements are taken, Jo is checked over and patched up, and Fabien has three stiff brandies to take the edge off his fury about being left in the dark yet again while Mila put herself – and Kaye, and Deb – in grave danger.

'But I was right, Jo *was* there,' is Mila's response, and the worst thing is, she *was* right. Nobody had listened to her, again. Hoppy had failed to get past Pound's practised deception, and Jo had been exactly where Mila had worked out she would be. If Mila had not gone rogue, it isn't certain what would have happened to Jo. It isn't certain, and it isn't something they can begin to understand yet, because Pound has got away and is still on the run.

Fabien doesn't know what to think. Do they all have to go along with Mila's every whim now, seeing as she keeps on being proved correct, no matter how crazy it seems, how dangerous? However much it puts others at risk?

'What if he hadn't fallen for your seduction?' Fabien asks Mila, still a little sore about that part of the plan in particular.

Mila just shrugs nonchalantly, oblivious to Fabien's hurt look, as though the very idea of Pound not falling for her isn't worth entertaining. 'I would have pretended to be ill or something.'

Fabien says nothing. Her confidence is both breathtaking and dangerous. He's exhausted from covering up the hidden guests, making excuses as to why they're driving in and out of the grounds and spending little time in the same room as Lady Lydia, who is beginning to take it personally. Though, thank heavens, she hasn't picked up on any of the chaos around her, busy as she is with now writing her own script for the BBC show, despite not having been asked to. In fact, despite specifically being asked *not* to.

After individual statements have been taken, Jo, Deb, Kaye, and Mila sit together with DI Cora Payne and PC Hoppy Atkins in the family room at the station. They ask if the police now believe their version of events: that the women were framed so that their babies could be adopted permanently. DI Payne's face says it all: *not really.*

DI Payne is clearly trying to be gentle as she explains that it isn't for the police to speculate over motive, nor to believe or disbelieve theories and stories. It is their job to collect the facts, and so their number one priority remains to find Pound and, she attempts to reassure them, they have all their resources on that. He is wanted on charges of abduction and false imprisonment, not to mention possession with an intent to supply a staggering amount of Class A drugs. The CCTV evidence of him being in the vicinity of Jo in the run-up to her arrest now can be seen in a more compelling light. But they can't jump from an attack on one woman to a conspiracy against three, when there is no evidence to show he had anything to do with Kaye or Deb, and thus far has no clear connections to anyone involved in the adoption of the three children. 'But we will find him, and we will question him, and we will explore what relationship, if any, he may or may not have had to the other women, and why. If this goes beyond him, we will try to find out who else was involved.'

'I saw him get an envelope!' Jo cries. 'I saw the bloke give it to him.'

'Officers are looking for the envelope, but we haven't found your phone with the image on – most likely, he destroyed it – and the chances are it was an envelope of cash, nothing more. He's a drug dealer. There's no reason to assume the man you saw in the bar was related to your abduction.' DI Payne shows them out, offering referrals to counselling, giving the women a card with the number for Samaritans on the front.

'I'm not suicidal,' Kaye mutters, 'I'm bleeding furious.'

Back in the safety of the rarely used wing that now doubles up as a temporary home for Kaye, Deb, and Jo, as well as being Mila's investigation headquarters, Fabien joins the women. His day of subterfuge at the golf club now feels far less heroic than it had done earlier. Elodie and Anna sneak in too, demanding the whole story about where Offal has been all day.

With Offal's gallant part in Jo's rescue fully recounted, Elodie and Anna insist on staying for the remaining part of the evening, in a moral support capacity, and, Elodie admits, in part because it is "pretty bloody exciting". And surely now the actual police are involved, and Mila is no longer sleuthing perilously, the risk of jeopardising the adoption application by accidentally breaking the law or getting in with the wrong types is limited. Anna isn't so sure; she knows Mila a little better than that, and wants to know what Mila Kiss is planning next.

'What happened to his dog?' asks Elodie, scratching her brave baby Offal behind his ears. She'd given Mila a telling off for putting Offal at risk, but as soon as she understood Mila's plan and the real risk of Jo being murdered imminently, she decided to forgive her and instead focus on Offal's rewards and recovery. So far, he seems okay and is lapping up the extra attention and treats.

'Mrs Felcham took him in. She doesn't believe a word of the accusations, apparently. Said I was shifty, and probably had some vendetta against him. I believe she said, "Those foreign types can't be trusted,"' Mila explains.

'Jesus,' says Anna.

Fabien squeezes Mila's hand. Can he really blame her for never taking the easy path when hers has always been so hard? She's conditioned to fight, and so far, she's always won.

'So, what's next?' asks Jo. 'Now the police are only looking at Pound, who is probably in Marbella by now with all the other dealers on the run. How do we find the guy with the envelope?'

'That's a good question,' Mila replies, 'though they put Pound's name out to border control straight away, so the police are pretty sure he's still in the country.'

'Or in a container on a ship, going the long but unchecked route,' says Deb.

'But...' Mila begins, 'Fabien did get some strong insights from the three adoptive fathers today: Theodore, Maximilian, and Gordan.'

'Right,' Fabien says, clearing his throat and opening his notepad.

'You took notes at the golf club?' Mila asks.

'Of course not, I was all laid-back and natural there, but I was afraid I'd forget something so I took notes in the car park. Don't worry, they didn't see me, looked as though they were settled into the bar for the night. So...'

Fabien starts to go through his findings. He bought a few rounds, and feigned interest in their home lives. The proud fathers showed a few snaps on their phones of their new babies, and Fabien had decided to take a leaf out of Mila's book and attempt an act. He'd sadly looked into his pint, and told them he and his wife couldn't have children.

The conversation quickly moved on to adoption, and the pros and cons of the system. They eagerly shared their wisdom with the desolate lord, their new friend in high places, not that they were short of those already, judging by the competitive name-dropping. They ranted about the difficulty of adopting newborns in a system that values the rights of addicts and criminals and hopeless young women unable to care for a child over the rights of the child to enjoy a loving family.

'They want you to take an older kid usually,' Gordan had said, 'not that I have a problem with that, but they've usually been through the ringer by then, as the mother will have been trouble since they were born, but she'll have had chance after chance, and the poor kid – well–'

'Damaged,' interrupted Theodore, 'and Cassandra – well, both of us – we wanted to start from day one with our baby.'

'We all did,' said Maximilian. 'That's how we came to be friends, actually, through the online forums – shared beliefs, shared frustrations in the system.'

Fabien had bitten his lip, the soft, caring words of Wanda explaining the importance of the birth mother bond in his mind, swirling with the memories of the heartbreaking pain in the eyes of Jo, Kaye, and Deb, and the facts that he can now see clearly: these women *hadn't* been hopeless, they had triumphed over adversity. Fabien knows many don't, and he is delighted that the children who genuinely need a loving home will find one through the system, with caring people just like his daft sister and the lovely Anna, but something has gone very terribly wrong in these cases, and it seems that they are getting closer to understanding how, and why.

Fabien had asked the adoptive fathers how they all came to

be so lucky, against the odds, three newborns in a year. For a moment, Fabien thought they looked guarded, but they quickly guffawed and patted one another's backs, telling him and the world they were just born lucky, and batting around words such as perseverance, patience, and faith.

'You see, Fabien,' Theodore had leaned in conspiratorially, the stench of whisky on his breath, 'May I call you that, m'Lord?' he'd added, laughing and smacking Fabien hard on the back. With Fabien's nod he continued, 'You have to be strong. And you have to believe. And lastly, do whatever it takes to realise your dreams. God, two of us – he pointed at himself and Gordan, moved counties so we could adopt here, in Lancashire.'

'Why here?' Fabien had asked.

'More babies in need. Poorer area,' Gordan said loudly. Fabien started to think, in that moment, that these people may not have adopted their babies in a way that would be deemed fair by anyone's standards, and the accusations that Jo, Kaye, and Deb had relentlessly made might actually be true. He couldn't quite believe it, and yet...

Fabien flicks through his notes, and holds up a page with a website address written across the middle, which he passes around to Mila and the others. 'They invited me to join some private forum for people hoping to adopt but struggling with the system. It's run by a church group.'

'I'm impressed,' says Jo.

Fabien chooses to ignore the obvious surprise in Jo's tone. 'I'm going to start there, see if anyone is offering some other way into the system, or suggesting they can somehow manipulate it, either by pairing certain people with certain children, or by sabotaging women with newborns in the system.'

'I can't see them admitting that online in writing,' says Mila, thinking aloud.

'No,' Fabien says, 'but I think it is a good place to begin.

Without a doubt, these families have somehow played the system. I don't know what their role is exactly, or who else was helping them. It's possible they just paid some money to get the result and have no idea what getting that result involved.'

'Or they masterminded the whole thing,' says Elodie. 'I just can't believe it. The system seems so watertight. So thorough. It's blinking maddening at times, though honestly, this makes me glad it is.'

'I really can't see these guys masterminding anything,' replies Fabien, 'but all I can do for now is dig deeper.'

'Thank you, Fabien,' says Mila, 'this is such a huge step forward. If this forum is where they met, then it's likely to be the place where anyone else involved met. And if not, and these three buffoons have somehow orchestrated the whole thing with no outside help, then we'll find out. Let's keep at it.'

'Will do. They mentioned some fundraiser ball they are going to, said they'd check with the organiser and see if they can organise a table for us. It's not far off though, so they weren't too sure. If that falls through, I'll just have to play more golf.'

'Poor you,' Mila says, sticking her tongue out at Fabien.

Suddenly Mila, Fabien, Elodie, and Anna's phones all ping at once. They take a quick look. It's Lydia on the WhatsApp family chat she had recently insisted on someone setting up for her.

'It's time for Celebrity Gogglebox,' says Mila, looking up from the message.

'Come on, I can get on these forums while I watch, we can't leave her alone all night; she'll start hatching all sorts of plans, and then you'll think the BBC fly on the wall is a good idea,' Fabien says, standing up, and brushing down the creases in his trousers.

'We're not going,' says Elodie. 'She's still cross about the article after the WI thing, and she'll only make scathing remarks all the way through.'

'Oh, I didn't see it, sis! Did they get your best side?' Fabien teases.

Mila taps away on her laptop, and brings up the online version. 'Oh, there you are!' She laughs, turning the screen. 'Fawcett looks livid. Brilliant!'

Jo suddenly jumps up and dives towards the screen, her head almost touching it. 'That's him! The man in the suit, with the envelope!' she says, pointing and jabbing furiously, as the others gather round to see who she means. Her finger rests on the face of the young man in a shiny suit standing next to Fawcett.

Elodie gasps. 'Fawcett's PA, the one who took the call when we were protesting and suddenly legged it.'

THIRTY-THREE

Susannah takes the croissants out of the oven and clatters the tray onto the counter before lifting them one by one with tongs to arrange them prettily on the large serving plate. She walks over to the kitchen table and places it down in front of Mila and Fabien.

'I can't tell you how lovely it is to have you both at the table again, it has been far too long,' she says, topping up their coffee cups from the cafetiere, 'and with such exciting news as well.'

Mila and Fabien worked into the night to cobble together a launch event plan for the new swings in the village park so that they had a valid reason to visit. Online searches for Frederick Fawcett's PA revealed only that the man was a bit of a digital ghost, which was odd given his boss's profile. You would think he would at least be listed on Fawcett's website as staff, but that was just pages and pages about Fawcett himself, with only an online form to get in touch.

'Please, help yourself,' Susannah tells them.

Mila and Fabien take a croissant each and Mila stuffs half of hers into her mouth at once. She has agreed she might be better off as the silent partner this morning. They need a name for this

PA, and naturally Elodie and Anna had not been formally introduced at the Women's Institute. A bit more digging could probably get them what they need, but they are starting to feel the pressure of being onto something, and they are pretty sure Susannah will be a direct line to the information they need.

'So,' Fabien begins, 'about the other night, at your WI meeting.'

'I wasn't going to say anything to you, Fabien, as I realise it isn't your fault. But Mr Fawcett was our guest, and regardless of his political or social views, he deserved some common courtesy at least.'

'Quite,' Fabien says, 'and I would like to apologise on behalf of the Knutsworth family for my sister and Anna's behaviour. Elodie is headstrong and takes his views rather personally, given that she is gay, unmarried, and planning to become a mother.'

'I'm not homophobic, of course, you see. I don't think Mr Fawcett is either, I–'

'I wouldn't dream of suggesting you were, Susannah,' Fabien says gently, as Mila fills her mouth with the other half of her croissant and takes another from the serving plate as assurance, should she be tempted to say something that would not help their cause.

'I do believe he is simply championing the traditional family, and that's not to say one can't do it another way, but you see, the LGBT... erm... something-something community have fantastic advocates, quite loud ones really, and so Mr Fawcett just wants to bring balance to the debate, and recognise the hard work more traditional mothers do in raising the next generation.'

Mila takes a huge swallow that almost gets stuck in her throat. She swallows again and again until her airway is clear.

Fabien firmly puts his hand on hers, and says, 'You have a crumb just there, darling.' He gently dabs her mouth and looks into her eyes: *Please, just hold that thought a couple more minutes*. Mila tears more croissant off, spilling specks of pastry onto the table and floor, and throws a big chunk into her mouth, which is starting to dry out. She takes a large swig of coffee to wash it down, burning her throat in the process and sputtering a little. Susannah pulls a face at her manners, but says nothing except for an almost imperceptible tut.

'We had a pride event, remember, on the village green. I wore a rainbow headband,' Susannah reminds him.

'A splendid event!' Fabien says, smiling widely. 'You and my mother did an excellent job.'

'Elodie wasn't even a lesbian then,' Susannah adds.

'You mean she wasn't out?' Mila says, with her mouth still half full, receiving a sharp kick from Fabien under the table.

'Um, yes, yes, I think that's what I meant. More coffee?' Susannah says, pouring before an answer is given.

'Well, I do hope Mr Fawcett and his team were not too offended,' Fabien says.

'They'll come to pride this summer, right?' Mila adds.

'What Mila means, Susannah, is I do hope we haven't burned your bridges. Perhaps we could reach out. He has a PA, doesn't he? If you let me have his details, I'll write to him personally and ensure that he feels very welcome, as all your speakers and guests ought to, in our wonderfully diverse village.'

With the PA's name, number and email address saved in Fabien's phone, Susannah shows them to the door.

'Do give our best to Martin,' says Fabien. 'Sorry to have missed him.'

'Of course, goodbye, and thank you both so much for making the swings a priority for the Last Chance Cooperative. I know you often have bigger fish to fry, as they say – all your amnesty type projects – but I do think it is so easy to forget the little things that can make an enormous difference to the lives of ordinary, *local* people.'

'Like two straight, middle-class parents with the ability to set up a trust fund?' Mila asks, smiling. She can feel Fabien seething, but they have what they need. The croissant has digested and the words are finding their way out. 'Because there is plenty of neglect and alcoholism and issues in those families too. And there are many children growing up with single mums, or with wider family members – like our children, for instance – or in families with little money spare, and they are loved and nurtured as much as any child in a boating hat and blazer. If not more so!'

'Well, I–' Susannah stammers, a little taken aback. The morning has been so pleasant up until now, but Mila has always been a loose cannon, and although Susannah isn't particularly fond of the move to blame every ill of the world and all bad behaviour on poor mental health, she sometimes wonders if Mila isn't a little, well, mad. She supposes it could be a cultural thing.

Fabien knows he should step in but it takes him a few seconds too long to think up a wet blanket to throw on Mila's latest pyrotechnics.

She goes on, 'The Guardian actually ran an article based on a report that suggested middle class parents drink and consume more drugs than their poorer counterparts.'

'I wouldn't believe everything you read in The Guardian, dear,' Susannah says, on surer footing now. 'It's run by communists, and I think even you would agree they can't be trusted.'

Mila scrolls through her meagre search results as Fabien drives them back from Susannah's house.

'You shouldn't wind her up like that. You know we all

despise everything Fawcett stands for, but people like Susannah Wilson just don't see the world the same way. She gets carried away and easily flattered. She's not a bad woman, you know that from personal experience,' says Fabien.

'She's not bad, but she is vain. And stupid.'

'She's from a different world.'

'She's from a different planet.'

'Do you ever think it might be easier to just let some things go?' asks Fabien.

'No.'

Fabien sighs, thinking of their hurried getaway before Mila had a chance to draw them all into a political debate. 'If nothing else, constant conflict is very time-consuming, not to mention tiring. And I do hope you realise that sometimes adoption with another family is actually the only way – and the best thing for the child. Think of everything Elodie and Anna have told us!'

'Yes. But whoever is behind all this is using the system against the people it is supposed to protect. They're saying: you have seen mothers with addiction problems before, so this woman here must be the same. And they use those similarities, the shared troubled past, and then they say she can't change. They manipulate the decision-makers into being blind to her studies, her stable job, her loving home. It is the easiest lie to tell, because in the past it has been true for so many others.'

'I never thought I would say this, but I'm glad we met Jo that day, and then found Kaye and Deb. Without seeing the three cases together, it would have been impossible to believe something so sinister was going on,' says Fabien.

'Because it's such an everyday story! Parent relapses after one chance too many, and they take the child, and I know you're right – in those cases, it has to be done for the sake of the child. I mean, didn't Wanda repeat the message enough? Removing a child from a birth parent is a *last resort*. And I know in the majority of cases the right decision is made, and most adopters, who I can see go through terrible, long, exhausting journeys, are amazing. But in our three cases... it's far from ordinary.'

'Exactly. But to prove any of it, we need to start linking the people involved otherwise, as Payne would annoyingly say, it is just *conjecture*.' Mila smiles as Fabien imitates DI Payne's official sounding voice. 'Right, cop-face on, facts out, what do we know?' asks Fabien.

'We know the adoptive parents benefit from the lie, and that they are entitled types who would possibly take a favour, pay some money, to – as you lot would say – jump the queue, but we don't know whether they would understand the extent of what is going on,' Mila begins. 'I think there's definitely money involved, but I also think it's more than that, like we said last night; it's all leading to one person with a very dangerous agenda.'

'Any more luck on this PA?' Fabien says, glancing over to Mila, who is reading from her phone.

'Mr Stephen Grey, PA to Frederick Fawcett, previously employed by Fawcett's Think Tank, and before that was at the London School of Economics, where he studied Politics. Clearly the two of them are pretty close. But other than a slim profile on LinkedIn – no blogs or anything – I still can't find him anywhere on social. No sign of him on your adoption forum, either. At least not under his own name. He's either shy or hiding something.'

'I think we pass Mr Stephen Grey to Hoppy and Payne,' says Fabien, readying himself for a fight, as he turns into the long driveway leading up to Farlington Hall.

'You're right.'

'Sorry?'

'You're right. If they trust Jo's memory of seeing Fawcett's PA handing the envelope to Pound, maybe the police will at least consider the theory that his abduction of Jo could have been ordered, rather than random or drug-related male violence – which, you know, I get would be their go-to assumption, it happens.'

'This could be enough to get Payne and Hoppy to look harder for the envelope, and if they find it, it could contain evidence that Jo, Kaye, and Deb were set up.'

'And I think we know who could be behind it,' says Mila, turning her phone screen to Fabien, zoomed in on the picture from the local news. Fawcett is in the foreground at the WI meeting, flanked by Susannah and four other committee members, with Stephen Grey lurking in the background looking distractedly at his phone.

Fabien pulls the handbrake on, unclips his seatbelt, and turns to Mila, leaning forward to kiss her. 'Let's go get the bastards.'

THIRTY-FOUR

The wood burner in the lakeside holiday pod is roaring. The entire front panel of the otherwise wooden structure is made of glass, so whatever the weather, the guests can look out onto a pretty lake surrounded by wildflowers in summer, but today it is just a field of boggy grass. The rest of the holiday park is still closed for off-season, and it seems unlikely the swinging seats on the front porch will get much use in the sideways rain splattering against the window, but, Mike, the landlord of Fabien and Mila's local pub, owns the pods, and he has made an exception for the day.

'This is heaven,' says Deb, pulling the tartan blanket over her knees as she snuggles deeper into the sofa she shares with Kaye.

'Isn't it just?' says Kaye.

'I'm going to bring Sarah, one day,' says Jo, reminding everyone of why they are here. 'Reckon he'll do mates' rates?'

Fabien and Mila have been harbouring their guests for several weeks now, and quite understandably, the three women are going stir-crazy. Jo stays because she had nowhere else to go and she wants to be on the case, and privy to every bit of information as soon as it comes in. Deb stays because these women – and Fabien – have reminded her why she needs to stay sober, and with them by her side, she won't fail again. And Kaye stays for Deb, and for Jo, and because she believes that together, they – the underdogs, the down-and-outs, the misfits – can actually get justice, and most importantly, get their babies back.

'Thank you, Mila,' Kaye says.

'It was Fabien's idea, all this,' Mila replies, gesturing around. There's a little self-catering kitchen, a huge sitting area crammed with deliciously comfortable soft furnishings, and then three bedrooms off to the sides. 'I didn't know they made caravans this grand.'

'It's a pod,' Fabien corrects her.

'Whatever it is, it's perfect.' Mila squeezes his knee.

They all have a device, be it a laptop, an iPad, the children's tablet, a smartphone, and they are connected to the internet. There is hot chocolate, five different types of tea, all the snacks you could dream of, and Fabien has promised to roast marshmallows later, under the porch, no matter how horizontal and angry the rain becomes. Everyone needs something nice every now and again, even in the midst of a serious criminal investigation.

Fawcett is the main target, given he has a much more accessible digital footprint than his shady PA. Their plan is to find out everything they can about him and, ideally, link him to the parents and the PA with digital evidence plus, if at all possible, a money trail. Mila and Fabien have reasoned that a lot of information can be harvested in the public domain.

'Aha!' Fabien shouts with glee, only five minutes into the group's quiet research. 'I knew it!'

'That was quick, Brains,' says Jo.

'Well, it's not much, but, well...'

'Go on!' says Mila.

'Spit it out!' commands Deb.

'An email from one of the adoptive fathers.'

The women shift a little uncomfortably, knowing that they are the only ones still in the dark about the identity of the people who currently have custody of their children. They have also agreed to keep it that way for now, for plausible deniability regarding Mila's theft of the documents from children's social services, but also in case the lionesses within them were to rage free and try to retrieve their cubs. They could be close to justice now; they have to stay strong.

'And...' prompts Kaye.

'It's about that fundraiser they were being a little prissy about; said they thought all the tables might be sold out, and no point revealing the cause and host and so on if that were the case,' Fabien explains.

'Didn't they realise that sounds a bit weird?' asks Deb.

'Yeah, but also mysterious – like, who is the big celebrity...'

'Let me guess,' says Mila, as they had, of course, suspected who it might be all along, given the numerous photos on social media and the obvious overlapping of networks.

'The one and only Frederick Fawcett. And we have a table for his big fundraising event.'

'Why do we want to go to that, for Pete's sake?' asks Deb.

'We need to get closer to him to get evidence. This is good,' says Mila. 'The more connections between Fawcett and the parents, the better. We just need the PA's link to Pound to be solidified, and then Fawcett's role should become clear. But we still need the paper trail,' says Mila.

They start at the end, with Fawcett's most recent escapades, which are naturally easier to find online, particularly as he is standing as an MP at the next election. His PR machine is running at full speed, and his website is slick.

There's a button to donate as large as the one to join his list of subscribers.

'Would it be too obvious for the adoptive parents to have donated to his party campaign? Presumably it must have been in the making long before he made the announcement, which could fit with the timing of adoption arrangements being made,' says Fabien.

'Yes,' Mila says, 'and you would normally find lists of large donations, anything over £10,000, I think, on the Electoral Commission's website, but it is only updated every six months, and they could have given a number of smaller donations to stay below the radar.'

'You've already checked and you know they're not listed?'

'Yes, sorry, I should have said,' Mila replies. She's been moving so fast through the list of possibilities in her mind that she sometimes forgets to update the team.

'I wonder how much our babies are worth,' Kaye says quietly, to herself really, and Deb squeezes her hand.

'Everything, more than anyone could pay,' she says.

'I'll make a list, and we can take one lead on Fawcett each,' says Mila, feeling the need to regain order – the whole case has felt so urgent and slippery, and moved so fast, it has felt more like drowning than swimming. She needs to take control of her thinking as well as the process if they hope to create a solid and irrefutable case. 'His recent political campaign belongs to one thread, his think tank organisation is another, although he seems to have slightly distanced himself from that since announcing his political interest – I suppose to look more independent and ensure any of its more extreme policies don't put off the voters who are fast falling for his return-to-great-British-traditions rhetoric.'

'Rather than the "let's-throw-single-mothers-in-the-workhouse" actual policy,' Kaye quips.

'Absolutely. The third avenue is his previous life as a vicar – we know at least one of the families was photographed at a Christian convention with him, so they could go way back. Everything is worth looking at.'

'I'll take politics,' says Fabien. After his success charming the golf club into giving out their clients' private information, Fabien is feeling quite the undercover expert, at least on the end of a phone. 'I have an idea.'

'I'll look at the think tank,' says Mila. 'I'm pretty familiar with Companies House and looking into hidden funds bouncing between businesses and individuals.'

'Then I guess it's the sinners on the vicar,' says Jo.

'Lucky old Reverend Fawcett,' Kaye replies.

Deb laughs, looking around, and although she wishes she had never made the mistakes she did, never been vulnerable enough to be one of the targets of this evil scam to take their children, she'll never be sorry she met this group of people. She beams at them, ready to roll her sleeves up and make a difference. 'Let's do it.'

They get to work. An eclectic playlist plays in the background on the music system integrated into the luxury lakeside pod. Mila's trademark thrash metal gives way to Fabien's Chopin, which in turn flows into Kaye's choice of nineties Britpop, inspired by her mum's infatuation with Liam Gallagher, Deb's country mash-up, and Jo's *High School Musical* soundtrack, which reminds her of better times singing into the hairbrush with her big sister, before everything went horribly wrong.

Up and down they get, wandering to the fridge to retrieve more tasty snacks – sausage rolls, which they warm in the oven and serve with mustard, rounds of cheese on toast with HP Sauce, and a vat of Mila's home-made spiced cauliflower soup simmering away on the hob. The kettle is boiled over and over, tea is poured again and again. More logs are added to the burner, and blankets are shared, discarded and reclaimed, as they work away, stretch, open the front doors to feel the fresh air and smell the rain, before battening down the hatches once more. And with every hour that passes they uncover something new, everyone finding something, and everyone feeling part of something. Something big.

THIRTY-FIVE

Hoppy opens with, 'It isn't good news, I'm afraid,' when Fabien puts him on speakerphone in the pod.

He explains that he was sanctioned to bring Stephen Grey, PA to Frederick Fawcett, in for questioning.

Jo is amazed that based off her witness statement the police believe that the PA had met with Pound on the day she had been abducted, or at least considered it believable enough to bring a smart, suited, trendy craft-beer-drinking professional man into the station for an interview.

'You were the victim of an abduction,' Kaye says when she notices Jo's look of surprise, 'of course they're taking your statement seriously.'

'We take *all* statements and witness accounts seriously,' Hoppy adds, insulted on behalf of the entire police service. He goes on to explain what they already know from Susannah: that Stephen Grey no longer works for Fawcett's think tank, but is employed as his personal PA, paid out of Fawcett's own pocket. It is no great secret or revelation.

It gets worse. Stephen Grey is quite certain that he has nothing to hide, and he said as much to Hoppy in the interview.

He doesn't know Pound, doesn't recognise him. The wine bar's CCTV may well show the PA and Pound both entering the building, but they do so separately and leave separately too. The PA had sat at the back, unseen by the cameras. During his interview, Stephen Grey calmly and politely acknowledges he had been in the bar, but that the man they were looking for – this ghastly criminal who Stephen very much hopes they will catch soon – being there too is nothing but a coincidence.

'There's no evidence, you see,' Hoppy explains.

Jo rolls her eyes; so much for her credible witness account.

Stephen Grey told Hoppy that he is Fawcett's personal PA, organises his diary and runs his errands, supporting him across all of his work as a lobbyist, Christian activist, as well as in his charity work, and now in his campaign to stand for parliament. He clearly looks up to the man, adores him, even, but there is no crime in that.

'We had to let him go,' Hoppy tells them.

'The envelope!' Jo shouts. 'Didn't you ask about the envelope?'

'Oh yes,' says Hoppy, 'and he said he often deals with Fawcett's correspondence, but he wouldn't have handed it over to some stranger in a bar and the young lady must have been mistaken. He actually wishes you well, Jo,' Hoppy adds, 'says you've obviously been through a lot and that must have been very traumatic, and perhaps that's why you are confused.'

'Are you serious, Hoppy?' Mila says through gritted teeth, as Jo lets out an exasperated growl.

'I'm just relaying the facts,' Hoppy says, wondering why he's always getting it wrong, 'and I haven't finished.'

'Maybe get on with it then, Hoppy old chap,' Fabien says, softly.

'We still view Stephen Grey as a person of interest with regards to locating Bradley Pound, although we are also looking into other ways of finding Pound – his family, his rivals, his clients. So far, nothing. But we had to let Grey go because we don't have anything solid that connects him to Pound, other than a single witness who saw them from a distance, through a glass front of a busy shop. And DI Payne still thinks Pound should be our focus. There isn't anything to suggest Grey was involved in Jo's abduction, or in Pound's business. Yet, anyway.'

Jo sighs. Mila sighs. Fabien sighs. Kaye rolls her eyes. Deb kicks the pouffe her feet were resting on earlier, and stubs her toe, not realising how hard it is. 'Ow.'

'Did you look for the envelope?' asks Mila, an impatient note in her voice.

'Oh yes,' Hoppy says, 'I suppose that's the good news bit.'

'What?' Mila and Fabien shout out in astonishment.

'I'm a little embarrassed to say I think it is the envelope I saw on his kitchen table when I visited him.'

'You saw an envelope on the table when you were looking for me, and I was literally behind the door in the hallway, and you didn't look at it?' Jo says.

'It was a double door, to be fair,' Hoppy reminds her, 'and very well disguised. Besides, I didn't have a warrant.'

'Get on with it, Hoppy,' Fabien tells him.

'Anyway, I did look in the envelope at the time. Or, at least, he showed me the photo from it. Said it was his niece. That's why I didn't connect it with the envelope we were looking for, which we thought was full of drug money.'

'*You* thought it was full of drug money. *We* thought it might be something linking him to their crimes against young vulnerable mothers in the Foster to Adopt system.'

'Yes, well, you'll be pleased to know you were absolutely right there.' There's a shocked silence. 'So,' Hoppy continues, 'we found the envelope and its contents in the bin, shredded. It took ages to put it back together. I've done 10,000-piece jigsaw puzzles full of sky easier than that, but we did it.' Hoppy pauses for praise, but none comes, so he carries on. 'It appears to be part of a file on a young woman whose baby is in the Foster to Adopt programme, with notes on her background, and a suggested timeline linked to her court hearing. It is pretty solid evidence that Pound was being tasked with framing women to ensure they lost their hearings, and that their children would be placed in permanent adoption homes with the foster parents. The young woman in question and her social worker have been briefed and are being looked after.'

'So, you do believe us?' Jo says, in barely a whisper.

'Oh yes, indeed, it looks like it might well add up. Strange world,' Hoppy replies cheerfully.

'You couldn't have led with this?' asks Fabien. 'The good news breakthrough bit that might actually prove the case?'

Hoppy is quiet for a moment, and makes a note to start with good news in future. 'It's not all good news though,' he says, 'as Pound is still at large, and as we can't link Mr Grey to the envelope we found, we still can't be sure who was instructing Pound. We're trying to get a fingerprint from it, which is very difficult as it has been shredded and put back together – very skilfully, I might add – but if we do get a print, we can try and match it to Stephen Grey.'

Mila and Fabien have not yet mentioned their suspicions about Frederick Fawcett being the ringleader, given the police's insistence on hard evidence, and their ham-fisted methods that could result in compromising the amateur sleuths' own increasingly valuable hand. After all, employing someone as your PA isn't a crime – nor is being an utter bellend, as Deb had pointed out – so, until now, the investigation into Fawcett had lay with them and them alone. But with the envelope in play, things could be about to change.

'What's your theory on Grey's motive?' Mila asks.

'Money, plus we gather from his politics he wouldn't be ideologically opposed to helping to create more nuclear families,' Hoppy replies. 'If we can prove his connection to the envelope, we can get a warrant to check his bank account. We suspect the adoptive parents may have paid him, and whilst we would like to bring them in, the people in question are well-connected and very wealthy. Payne thinks they will lawyer-up, so to speak.'

'If they're in an American legal drama on telly,' says Kaye.

'In short, we need more evidence before we can bring them in for questioning. On the surface, there is no link whatsoever between the parents and Stephen Grey.'

'Though we know at least one of the couples knows Fawcett...' Fabien begins, and Mila shoots him a warning look. She doesn't trust the police not to spook Fawcett.

'Of course, it has crossed our mind, but we can't even link his *employee* at this stage, and without any evidence he had anything to do with Pound's activities, we may have to reconsider the entire theory.'

'And go back to the old "Pound's a drug dealer who just happened to abduct a woman randomly who believed he had been following her and had helped to frame her for a crime that resulted in her losing her baby, and there's no more to it than that,"' says Mila.

'Quite,' Hoppy says, glad it is starting to make sense to everyone. He knows that the general public would like to be able to arrest and jail people on a hunch, but Hoppy has been well-trained. They only deal with tangible evidence. And so far, the facts only provide evidence for Pound's actions, and don't point conclusively to anyone else.

'You reckon it is Fawcett, though, right?' prompts Kaye.

'We only deal in tangible evidence,' says Hoppy, primly.

'Hoppy...' warns Mila.

'DI Payne and I doubt Stephen Grey was acting alone, having met him and seen his clear dedication to his boss. So, yes, Fawcett is another person of interest, but I can't make any solid assertions or promises. There's just not enough evidence.'

After Hoppy hangs up and everyone breathes a sigh of relief, they work late into the evening. Mila muses that in the unlikely event that Hoppy and Payne actually get some sort of useful breakthrough from their investigation, it would be through the PA's confession, which at this stage seems impossible.

Exhausted, they take a break outside, wrapped up in jumpers and hats and blankets, and sit on the porch. The sky is clear, making the night even more bitterly cold, but the stars are bright and there are so many above them they hypnotise the group as they sip hot chocolate and eat toasted marshmallows, and think about how long ago those stars existed, and how small they all are, sitting here, hoping they have enough. And daring to believe they just might, because their own research has been very fruitful indeed.

THIRTY-SIX

Fabien is particularly pleased with himself, and his stern, official tone with Fawcett's campaign agent as he demanded to know all recent donors for the campaign. 'Do you think we should have told Hoppy what we found?' he asks, as they rake over the day's work.

'That you tricked Fawcett's campaign agent into providing financial details he was not obligated to share?' says Mila.

'Is that illegal?' asks Jo.

'Yep,' Mila replies.

'But the stuff *you* found was just on Companies House. *That's* not illegal,' Kaye says to Mila.

'And our stuff is in a church newsletter publicly available online,' Deb adds, 'and that smug git Theodore couldn't help but gloat about the donation his firm gave to Fawcett's Christian group.'

'All very true, but these people are smart. They're hiding in plain sight. There's nothing at all illegal about the way they have given money to Fawcett, and although I'm loath to say it, Hoppy is right when he says there's no hard proof of a connection between Fawcett and Pound, not even via his PA, unless they get that fingerprint.'

Sighs are emitted, and heads thrown back in frustration.

'What are we even doing this for?' mutters Jo.

'Don't say that,' Mila says, sitting up straight. 'What we have is a lot. It's everything we need to make the next step, and it's the next step that will prove our case.'

Although they have been unable to find listed donations to Fawcett's new political campaign on the electoral register because they haven't yet been posted, Fabien has been able to pretend to be the tax man looking into discrepancies in political campaign reporting, to get a list of recent donors. It was an easy win, as the agent had no reason not to provide the list of donors, who are all legitimate and above board, and who include Gordan and Lucinda, the adoptive parents of Deb's baby boy.

Companies House lists Maximillian as a shareholder in Fawcett's think tank, and subsequent web-trawling has shown him grinning widely on a venture capitalist website, reporting him to be a major investor in the business. Now Maximillian and his wife Harriet are the proud adoptive parents of Kaye's baby. In theory, there is nothing strange about that, as Fawcett, and even Grey, have no links to Kaye or her little boy Bobby. Nor do they have anything to do with the adoption services, or with Pound. The two elements of their life: business (and their generosity to Fawcett), and parenthood, are entirely unrelated.

Then there are Theodore and Cassandra, adoptive parents to Jo's baby Sarah, who Mila and Fabien have seen online posing at a charity convention with Fawcett and handing over a large cheque to Fawcett's church group. Although he is no longer a vicar, Fawcett is clearly still central in leading the church group's charitable work, if the newsletters are anything to go by.

That's where it starts to get really interesting. Jo, Deb, and

Kaye have scrolled through the church group's online archive of newsletters, going back years, getting slicker in more recent times, from the early days of badly formatted Word documents and clip art. Someone in the group is clearly keen on admin, as their diligent records proudly boast about all the good work they are doing in the community on a monthly basis, never missing an edition.

It takes hours of clicking and reading about boring bake sales, carol singing, group prayer sessions, and family fun days before they land on an interview with Fawcett, from back when he was still a vicar, and the church group was celebrating its first anniversary.

14 July 2009: One-Year Anniversary Celebrations Continue for the LCFF!

We're delighted to celebrate one whole year of the Lancashire Christian-First Family, which has grown in strength and love under the guidance of Rev. Frederick Fawcett, our founder and leader. Read on to find out more about what inspires Rev. Fawcett, and why he is so committed to making positive change in the world.

Rev. Fawcett, thank you for agreeing to be interviewed. First of all, congratulations on the one-year anniversary of our group. What first inspired you to create it?

I'm proud to be a vicar at St John the Baptist Church, and the work we do there is incredibly rewarding. However, the group is for those of us who feel the need for an even deeper connection, and who share the values and drive to work tirelessly to create a better world, even when our views may go against the grain, or might not quite fit with the common trend towards acceptance of social ills that are slowly eroding the fabric of our society. I'm forever grateful for the energy, love and support everyone in our growing group brings to our mission, and I know that together we can achieve great things and truly help people live happier and more worthwhile lives.

You have always focused our work on the need to help children thrive. Could you tell us more about that?
Of course, Marjorie. I didn't have a happy childhood myself, and it would have been so easy for me to lose my way. Luckily, I found God, and the church, but without that support I am not sure where I would have ended up. We owe it to the next generation to ensure they are nurtured so that they can grow up to add value to our society, and go on to raise the next generation of children. Our country, our world, our moral compasses, are all only as strong as the children in our society.

Such a simple theory, yet so powerful. Thank you. You say you didn't have an easy childhood; would you be able to share the experiences that shaped your outlook?
Although it is painful for me to recollect that time in my life, I am happy to share my experiences, so that others know that they are not alone and that there are people out there, like us, fighting for their right to a happier life. My mother was an alcoholic and my father was not around; I never even knew him. I should have been removed from her care as a baby, but I was left, neglected, hungry, with no toys or books, and even less affection. I struggled in school, and acted out. I could have been a clever boy, but instead I floundered. Until a kindly vicar saw me stealing sweets from the local shop and took me to the vicarage for a hot meal. He taught me the importance of family – both God's family and the love of one's own parents – and I soon understood what I had been missing. I vowed to fight for other children like me, and their rights to a loving and safe environment.

A worthy ambition, indeed. We've been lucky to support you in this goal, working alongside local children's charities. What are you most proud of in that space?

We have managed to donate over £10,000 this year to a local charity that provides days out for children who are in the care system, but are too old to be considered for adoption. These children have had their right to a normal, loving homelife whipped away from them, through the inaction of a system that allowed their parents too many chances until it was too late for them to start again. We have hosted a number of fun days for the young people, welcomed them into our group, and organised lessons in everything from fishing to cookery to woodwork – all the things their parents might have taught them had they had a proper family life. Here's me in a photo with a lovely boy, young Stephen, who will remain in care until he reaches adulthood. This is, of course, a tragedy, but our group, and myself personally, are committed to being his surrogate family... not only until he reaches eighteen, but always. Because that's what a loving family should do. And we will do this for as many children as we can. That, Marjorie, and young Stephen here – who has overcome the most terrible start in life – is what I am most proud of in our group.

There's a photo next to the article, showing a young Stephen Grey holding a brown trout towards the camera, smiling from ear to ear, as Frederick beams next to him, his arm over the boy's shoulder, looking every inch like a proud father. A little more digging around St John the Baptist Church reveals that Fawcett had left very suddenly the following year, presumably no longer falling into line with official church views, or perhaps just too busy with his own highly personal, yet tragically blinkered, mission.

'So, we have motive for both Fawcett and Grey, and it is clear why Grey would do Fawcett's dirty work,' says Mila. 'We can also financially link the adoptive parents to Fawcett, though not in any illegal capacity. But it is the next move that will make or break this investigation.'

'Go on,' says Fabien.

'A confession,' Mila tells him, 'a complete admission of guilt, with every word recorded.'

'Shit,' says Jo.

'Really?' says Kaye.

'How the hell are we going to manage that?' asks Fabien.

Mila smiles, and says, 'Just you wait and see.'

THIRTY-SEVEN

Jo, Kaye, and Deb are once again holed up in their quarters in the rarely used wing of Farlington Hall, thankful to the Lancashire February darkness for the ease of coming and going unseen from the lakeside holiday pod, and for the rest of the household's desire to remain indoors with the curtains drawn as much as possible.

There is little more they can do to aid the next steps of the plan, but Mila has given them another task for when, she says, inevitably, the police can use their evidence to arrest Fawcett, Grey, Pound, and the three sets of adoptive parents, and they need to build the case to make it robust enough to withstand the scrutiny of a trial. The three women wish they had Mila's confidence, but life has somewhat knocked that out of them, made cynics of them, prepared them for the worst. Yet, they're determined to try, and so each woman is trying to recount her journey as a timeline; her commitment to overcoming her demons, the work she has done, and her successes as well as any hiccups along the way.

The hardest part of getting any jury to convict on this case will be complete bafflement as to why anyone would be motivated to do such a thing. There's a system in place for childless couples to adopt, and even to adopt babies as newborns, despite Gordan's explanation to Fabien that there were far fewer small babies for adoption than older children and sibling sets. So why not just apply, like Elodie and Anna were doing? And why make a woman who is about to be a good birth mother fail, when there are plenty of children who genuinely need a new loving family, because, sadly, their birth parents have *not* been able to care for them, and never will? A sense of entitlement is the easy answer, but it'll be near impossible to prove.

In his strange, twisted way, Mila thinks Fawcett is convinced that he is doing the right thing for the babies. Furthermore, she speculates, Fawcett and his cronies perhaps conclude that the mothers who have overcome their addictions from the start of their pregnancy will give birth to healthy children, which the adoptive parents might well stipulate as important to them; their demands being taken into consideration, given what they are paying. It makes the women feel sick to think of their babies as commodities, with specifications and ratings.

But if Mila is right in her theory, pulled together from many sources and woven like a messy patchwork quilt, then the women's stories will matter. They will matter just as much as Fawcett's sad childhood and Grey's adoration of the father figure who saved him, taught him everything he believes today about how his life could have been different if he had been adopted by a Cassandra and Theodore, a Harriet and Maximillian, or a Lucinda and Gordan. Because Jo's story, and Deb's, and Kaye's, will show another side to the story, one in which people – *mothers* – may not be perfect, but they are able to love and provide, despite having had problems in the past. It will show the world that the strength that it takes to overcome these sorts of obstacles is the same strength that will make them wonderful parents.

While Jo, Deb, and Kaye wrack their brains for forgotten details and wrangle with painful memories, Fabien and Mila are busy stalking Fawcett. The golf-playing fathers easily let slip which member's club Fawcett attends, and Fabien has managed to obtain a week-long guest pass for himself and Mila, who he claims is a wealthy socialite in her home country. With the right clothes, all pertained from Lydia's wardrobe without her realising, and taken in with funky belts, adorned with modern jewellery, and chunky boots, she looks easily bizarre enough to be an heiress-slash-influencer.

Day in, day out, they turn up, charm the staff, sip the odd flute of vintage champagne or a small aged whisky, and eat the olives offered, occasionally ordering a plate of Iberico ham or a whole Époisses cheese served with white truffle honey. This part of the plan is not too arduous, though it is starting to stretch their budget. They had been hoping he would have been in by now. The way the fathers had spoken, you would think Fawcett practically lived here, lunchtimes and post-work being his favourite drop-in times.

It's lunchtime now, on the fifth consecutive day of Mila and Fabien's visits, and he isn't here. The plate of ham is empty, the cheese sits heavily in their stomach, and in place of the bowl of plump, juicy green olives is a bowl of stones. Fabien's glass contains no whisky, and Mila is trying to eke out the last inch of her drink to avoid being offered another. But it's only a matter of time; the staff here are very attentive.

One starts to walk towards their table, but Fabien gestures

they are fine for now, his hand hovering over his glass. They are sitting in a booth for four, in the hope of Fawcett arriving and being persuaded to join them, despite the room seating around fifty patrons and only currently being home to a handful. Their table has an excellent vantage point, with a clear view of the entrance to the bar and casual dining area. It is wood panelled, with mahogany leather chairs and dark furniture. Side tables are adorned with Tiffany lamps, and newspaper racks are full. An open fire roars in an enormous and beautiful fireplace, surrounded by ancient, patterned tiles in perfect condition. The club is old-fashioned by design, its members old men mainly, with boxes of free cigars that you can no longer smoke even in private clubs, much to the irritation of the clientele. However, you *can* stand outside beneath the large covered porch, looking to the manicured formal gardens as a doorman holds an umbrella for you, should you be willing to sacrifice your right to the comfort of warmth and a chair for a puff of Cuban magic.

'Another two days, and our trial membership runs out,' says Fabien, picking at an almost non-existent morsel of ham fat, and swilling his empty glass.

It is almost two, getting past traditional lunchtime in a place like this. Mila throws back the last sip, and starts to stand. 'We can come back later, I guess.'

As they start to leave, Fabien suddenly reaches for Mila's arm, and gently pushes her back into her seat, as he retakes his own. 'He's here. With a woman.'

Mila looks over to the entrance, and there he is: Frederick Fawcett, church group leader, think tank owner, parliamentary candidate, and wrecker of women's lives. They gape for a moment, watching him hand his coat over to the concierge and touch the small of the woman's back as they are led to their own booth, only a few feet away from Fabien and Mila's.

Fabien manages to get a photo on his phone.

'Who is she?' asks Mila.

'No idea. He's unmarried, or "married to the job", so he says online. Girlfriend?' says Fabien, to himself as much as to Mila. 'Funny that,' he adds, 'being so fanatical about the traditional family and not even having a wife, let alone children.'

'God complex. He is a father to all children in need of a father,' says Mila. 'I think we'd better order another drink.'

'And ham. I could definitely eat more ham.'

Two hours later, Fabien has welcomed Fawcett into their booth. The woman has left, seemingly irked by the interruption and repulsed by the entitled and very drunk young lord and his spiky girlfriend. Mila is furious that during their one chance to manipulate Fawcett into a confession, Fabien has loaded himself up on expensive whisky and blown a good chunk of their budget on throwing it down Fawcett's neck too. Fawcett is clearly delighted about hobnobbing with an actual hereditary lord with such a fascinating, traditional family history.

Fabien has regaled Fawcett with tales of his family's legacy including killing Scots, especially the Catholic ones, beating the bloody French countless times, and being consistently well-connected to the great and the good of the clergy, with the last Archbishop of Canterbury performing his baptism. When he gets onto his late father's connections with former Prime Ministers and members of the House of Lords, and his own personal admiration for them, not to mention his plan to host a dinner party – and of course, Mr Fawcett must come – Fawcett is practically drooling.

Fabien clicks his fingers obnoxiously at a waiter, and asks for more whisky.

'More?' says Mila, who managed to make her first glass last

another good hour after Fawcett's arrival, before switching to sparkling water. 'I suppose I'll be driving home,' she mutters, wishing she could storm out as she would normally in such a situation, and leave him to make his own way back, but still holding out a slither of hope that they can get something useful out of Fawcett. That was the plan, after all. Act like a Cassandra and Theodore, all pompous and proper, and see if he offers up his services. Right now, Mila cannot imagine that Fawcett would believe that Fabien was serious about becoming a father, nor would he risk making such a highly illegal proposition to someone as loud and drunk as her errant idiot of a boyfriend. Mila tries to switch back into the conversation the two men are almost having, the train of thought veering around erratically, hoping she can find a way to rescue the afternoon, and get what they came for.

'Course,' Fabien slurs, 'these days we're so controlled by the bureaucracy, the petty civil servants and council workers, the common man with his *ways*,' he says, as though having "ways" is a bad thing, regardless of what said ways are. 'There used to be respect for the establishment, the aristocracy. We upheld tradition, proper moral values, a good Christian way of life... but now, it's gone. Soon we'll be run by a bunch of lesbian single mothers making a living from growing cannabis and protesting. Still, I don't suppose there's much we can do, just ride out the wave, and hope one day we come full circle...' Fabien makes an exaggerated shrugging gesture, and knocks his phone, which clatters to the floor.

He practically falls beneath the table to retrieve it, while Mila tries to recover from almost spitting her drink out. She is starting to wonder what Fabien is up to...

Mila's phone vibrates, indicating a message. 'I'm sorry,' she says, smiling at Fawcett, as she takes it from her bag. Fabien bangs his head violently on the table as he tries to sit himself back up on the chair, and knocks Mila's drink into her lap. 'Fabien!' she shouts, standing and brushing the liquid from her dress.

'Sorry, sorry, sorry, at least it's only water,' Fabien says, winking at Fawcett for no discernible reason, but he winks back all the same, men together, laughing at the hysterical woman with her water. 'Is your phone okay? So,' Fabien turns back to Fawcett without waiting for an answer, 'you're standing for parliament, you're a man of the clergy, what would you do about this dastardly situation, old chap? I tell you what, I'm disillusioned with the Tories, to be quite honest. You know, I was just reading an article in *The Spectator* that said it's been more than ten years since a Prime Minister gave a speech promoting marriage, whereas eighty per cent of British people believe children are better off within a traditional family. If things continue this way, there'll be no marriage left by 2060. Imagine that!' Fabien roars, slamming his glass on the table, spilling some of it. 'And to think my father was such a generous Conservative Party donor, and now I must find my own path, for the sake of our future children.'

Fabien is loud, and slurry, but his memory with regards to some old article seems remarkably thorough. She reads the text as Fabien babbles on, not letting Fawcett get a word in edgeways.

Start recording now. Tap when ready.

Mila smiles inwardly: clever boy. She shouldn't doubt him so readily. Mila hits record and taps him gently on the thigh.

Fabien continues on, seamlessly. 'So, Mr Fawcett, are you a brave man? An original man? Can you do what it takes, *whatever* it takes, to get this country back on track? Tell me, how far would you go to have my cheque in your campaign's pocket?

Because I'm looking for an innovator, a disruptor, someone who isn't afraid to shake things up and take risks for the greater good. Is that you, Mr Fawcett?'

Finally, Fabien takes a breath, and Frederick Fawcett begins to speak.

THIRTY-EIGHT

'That was pretty impressive,' Mila says, as Fabien, the stone-cold sober and terrifyingly good actor and liar, drives them back from the private members' club, 'though will it be enough?'

Frederick Fawcett had not, as Fabien had, surreptitiously poured most of his whisky onto the expensive carpet beneath their feet under the table, but he had been able to hold his liqueur. Whilst clearly tipsy, very flattered, and unable to resist an opportunity to climb onto his soapbox, he had not admitted to any specific illegal activity.

'He confirmed our theory, in a way, and that he did so with little prompting has got to mean something,' says Fabien.

Mila bites her lip. It's a good start, but they need more. Fabien's improvised plan, he tells her, came about when he realised in the club as Fawcett finally entered that the original idea of posing as a childless couple in need of a fast-track solution to their greatest desire might not work as quickly as they needed it to. Fawcett would almost certainly have them vetted, and even then, they weren't sure how much the adoptive parents would be told. They may well think they are simply queue-jumping in return for a donation, and that Fawcett has links in the adoption service.

'Why didn't you just tell me the new plan?' Mila asks, irritated. 'Am I not receptive to other ideas than my own?'

Fabien swallows before answering. 'It occurred to me, literally as he stepped into the club for the first time all week, that it might trigger suspicion to immediately start talking to someone about personal fertility issues... If we'd seen him on a few occasions, built up a rapport, well.' By the time the woman Fawcett had arrived with was making her excuses, Fabien was already well into plan B and rather enjoying himself. 'After all,' he tells Mila, 'he may think he's driven by ideology, but I'll bet you power and money come first. It's always the way, and I knew I could convince him I had both to offer him.'

With a little more coaxing and a couple more drinks, Frederick Fawcett had spoken openly, but theoretically, about the ideal family structure, and early intervention into non-viable family units, namely abusive or neglectful parents. 'You see, young man, there is untold emotional and mental damage in a child left with addicted or abusive parents, and the longer they are left with them, the worse and more irreversible that damage will be, rendering their lives forever hindered, and their contributions to society forever curtailed.'

'Shame we can't just whip those kids to safety at the first sign of trouble, eh?' Fabien had said with a laugh, as though something like that were impossible.

Not for a man like Fawcett, though, who had replied, 'I believe we can, we should, and we will. Whatever it takes, whatever it costs. The children's futures must always come first.'

'I think we need more,' says Mila, 'before we can go to Hoppy and Payne. They won't question him on this; he hasn't said anything incriminating yet, and they can't link the PA to Pound as it is.'

Fabien's phone beeps and he nods towards it, not taking his eyes off the road. 'Could you check that for me?'

Mila takes the phone from the middle cup holder between the two front seats, opens it with Fabien's pin and reads the message. 'It's your mother again. Wants to know what time we will be back. They started filming at three, and it's nearly five now.'

'We said it would be about four or five, didn't we?' Fabien asks. 'Honestly, sometimes I wish we'd never met Chris-Whatsit from the BBC.'

'And it's only the first day, or afternoon, really. Apparently they spent the morning getting the lighting set up, and running through plans. Susannah is there, and they were going to do Elodie and Anna's segment in the gatehouse before we arrive. Even the social worker Wanda is getting her five minutes of fame, according to Elodie. She wasn't keen at first, but they convinced her. Of course the real reason Lydia agreed to allow Wanda to be in it was to show how normal the family is, you know – having a social worker visit rather than, say, the King.'

'Ha ha,' Fabien replies. 'Do the texts sound increasingly frantic?'

'Of course.'

'Nearly there,' he says. 'You really think we need more from Fawcett?'

'I do, but honestly, Fabien, you were brilliant. You've established a friendship, and exchanged numbers; you will get everything we need next time. He will trust you, and we will finish this, once and for all.'

Susannah and Lydia are having a gin and tonic in the drawing room, which is perfectly respectable because it is now five o'clock and they have done an absolutely marvellous job of co-ordinating the filming, the scripts, the camera men and women, as well as delivering a word-perfect interview each. Lady Lydia Knutsworth and Mayor Susannah Wilson are in their element, and Chris-Whatsit is losing his mind.

Their large drinks, ice gently clinking crystal, the soothing fizz of the bubbles, the slight, sharp aroma of fresh lemon, are very well deserved. Shortly, Lydia expects Chris-Whatsit from the BBC and Producer Amy will have finished in the gatehouse, Fabien and Mila will arrive home, and they'll all reconvene to congratulate themselves. Wonderful.

'Do you know, Susannah,' Lydia says, 'I have been wondering if we should show some of the shabbier rooms to the BBC?'

'Oh?' says Susannah, taking another refreshing sip of her perfectly mixed drink. Lydia knows how to fix a cocktail.

'Well, part of the narrative,' she says, emphasising the word *narrative* having done her research on documentary making and storytelling, 'is how the upper classes are caretakers of these ancient homes and gardens, and that we toil to enable them to survive. There's a ridiculous assumption that we are simply rolling around in cash, like the *nouveau riche* lot, which couldn't be further from the truth.'

'Naturally,' Susannah says, being neither upper-class and cash-poor, nor lower-class and rich, when either, she sometimes thinks, might be nicer than being middle-class and boringly comfortable.

'So, I thought we could show them how we carefully maintain parts of the house we can't afford to live in all the time – I mean, heating more than a quarter of the place would require the selling of one's vital organs. Wouldn't that be a clever idea? Don't you think, Susannah?' Lydia asks.

'Selling one's vital organs?'

'No, darling. What I mean is, wouldn't it be a clever idea to be warts and all?'

Susannah isn't sure it is a good idea. Warts are usually better off well hidden, in her experience. 'Very clever indeed,' she says.

'Let's show them before they go. We can go and choose some ideal filming locations, ones with good anecdotes, and then when they join us, we can have a little rest and then take them through so they can amend the scripts ready for the morning. There are a couple of rooms in the rarely used east wing, right on the other side of the house, that have some quite fascinating artefacts. There's an old Purdey rifle hanging above the fireplace that my great-great grandfather had specially commissioned and used in the Boer War, not to mention my Great Aunt Celia's chaise longue, which she had made in Paris. A beautiful thing, indeed.' Lydia stands with nothing less than gusto, and Susannah takes a big gulp of her drink and quickly decides to bring the rest with her. It's too good not to.

Lydia chatters incessantly as they stride down corridor after corridor, as the carpets become shabbier, the dust thicker, and Susannah thinks she has finally made it, past the formal invites, even past the drawing room teas and drinks and pleasant entertaining. If they were schoolgirls, this would be the equivalent of a sleepover. She is personally invited to see Lady Lydia Knutsworth's warts. The fact that the BBC, and subsequently the rest of the nation is also being invited is not the point. Susannah is there first, alone, and trusted to advise on which particular eyesores and family secrets to reveal. If that doesn't make them best friends forever, Susannah doesn't know what does.

'What on earth?' Lydia says in a panicked whisper, stopping suddenly in a narrow corridor, causing a slosh of Susannah's drink to hop onto the front of her pretty cream blouse, leaving an unattractive damp patch.

'What?' asks Susannah.

'Shush,' Lydia says, putting her index finger to her lips and narrowing her eyes. She takes her other hand to her ear, and leans towards the left, in the direction of the suspected interlopers.

Susannah freezes. Voices.

'Intruders!' Lydia mouths dramatically, eyes widening.

Susannah feels for her phone but realises she left it in her bag back in the drawing room. She points in the general direction from where they came, but Lydia doesn't notice, because she is already doing a strange tiptoe dance towards the door, crouching as if lasers are about her. Lydia turns towards Susannah, who quickly tries to work out how to change the direction of events; confronting dangerous intruders was certainly not in her diary for today. Besides, lovely Chris-Whatsit from the BBC is only half a mile away down the driveway, and would surely be heroic given half a chance. No need for two delicate ladies to put themselves in peril.

Too late.

Lydia swings open the door with a bang and starts shouting like Honey Bunny in the opening scenes of *Pulp Fiction* – if Honey Bunny spoke like the late Queen. Susannah realises that despite her better instincts, she must follow. Imagine if the film crew show up and she is cowering in the hallway while her friend takes on the burglars? She just hopes that Lydia won't escalate the situation. It's important to stay calm and in control...

Lydia has unhooked the old gun from above the fireplace and is pointing it at three improperly dressed women. Two are sitting on the Parisian chaise longue, and one is smoking. Her cigarette starts to burn a hole in the fabric as she stares at Lydia in shock.

'We can explain,' says Jo, wishing she had double-checked the status of the gun. The ones the posh people put on walls aren't loaded, are they? Can you be sure? The woman in front of her, Fabien's mother, she presumes, is clearly unhinged.

'Hands up!' Lydia demands. 'And move, move.' She prods Deb first, who jumps up. Kaye and Jo follow.

'Please,' says Kaye, 'we can explain.'

'Out, out, out, out, out!' shouts Lydia, using the gun to poke and prod. 'You don't think I'll use it?'

Jo, Deb, and Kaye think she probably won't, and they suspect it isn't loaded, but when a huge rifle is pointed at your head it feels natural to do as you are asked.

And when Lydia pulls the bolt back and clicks it back into place, the action recalling the old Westerns that Deb's dad used to watch on repeat just before the bang and blood splatter, she shouts, 'Run!' and they do.

Susannah grabs the fire poker. She isn't quite sure why, but being armed seems to be the way forward, and she does not like to be an outlier. The three young women run down the dark corridors, chased fervently by Lydia and less enthusiastically by Susannah, as both women's weapons stretch out before them, the three young women in front with seemingly endless energy, in pyjama short sets with messy hair. It starts to cross Susannah's mind that it's rather odd for intruders to be sitting around in loungewear eating ice cream from a sharing tub and smoking, but there really isn't time to question the unfolding events, and it would be impossible to compete with Lydia's tirade.

'My great aunt had that chaise longue *commissioned*!' she yells, 'in *Paris*! And I work tirelessly to preserve my late husband's estate! You think you are just *entitled – entitled!* – to squat here, to *take!* We *earned* this life! Over hundreds of years! Our ancestors *toiled!*'

The entrance hall doors swing open and the women, who Susannah now notices are barefoot, run down the driveway, towards Elodie, Anna, social worker Wanda, Chris-Whatsit from the BBC, Producer Amy, and a quiet cameraman whose name they do not know. The rain clouds and advancing afternoon hours have made the skies black. The barefooted women in pyjamas have wet tangled hair and are panting with exertion as they barge towards the people they hope will save them from the crazy posh women with guns and pokers who will not listen to reason.

'What the actual...?' begins Elodie, as Jo falls into her open arms, and Anna gathers Kaye and Deb into hers.

The cameraman moves slowly and deliberately.

'Stop that!' says Lydia, starting to realise she may have made a mistake. He does not stop, and Lydia suspects he's actually zooming in on her enraged face. She tries to subtly relax her features, but realises she is still pointing a locked, albeit decommissioned and unloaded, gun at a young woman in the arms of her daughter, in front of a BBC camera.

She lowers the gun as a car pulls up beside them. Mila lowers the window.

'Jo?'

The camera swivels towards the open car window.

'Fabien,' says Lydia, 'what is this?' Her son leans across Mila, his brow furrowed, trying to get a sense of the situation, but realising all sense has gone.

The cameraman, now in danger of becoming dizzy, moves around to capture the scene. Susannah drops the poker onto the ground. It clatters.

Wanda's training kicks into action a little late. 'Shall we all just take a deep breath?' she says. Wanda is looking at Jo, this woman who she has cared for since she was a girl until she couldn't, until she let her down somehow – something she has never forgiven herself for. Why is she here, bedraggled and in nightwear, with Deborah and Kaye, another two similarly clad women?

Just then, a police car pulls up, and Hoppy jumps out, also looking frazzled. 'There's been a development,' he says, taking in the scene. 'Um, what's going on?'

'We can explain,' says Mila.

THIRTY-NINE

Stephen Grey, personal PA to Frederick Fawcett, believes he has turned his life around.

When Frederick Fawcett's church group first came to his care home all those years ago, and suggested that some of the teenage boys could go over to some religious group's fun day, he had initially refused. But he was on thin ice, they had explained, and showing willing might help ensure he isn't moved to a more specialist home. He'd recently been done for shoplifting again, and he'd given Aaron in fifth form a black eye, which was the last time he had bothered to show up for school. And so he had been in danger of being expelled for his apparently unrivalled truancy record. He went along to the stupid fun day, and was surprised to find it was actually fun, although he hadn't let his mask slip for even a moment, and had almost broken the coconut shy, such was the force he used as he threw.

It had been then that Frederick Fawcett had introduced himself. He'd fetched him a cola and a chocolate bar, and said, 'So what's your story?'

Until then, Stephen Grey hadn't thought of his life as a

story. He hated books anyway, and nobody had read to him as a child.

'You can write your own ending,' Frederick Fawcett had explained. 'This is only the beginning.'

And with Fawcett's help, he did. He started attending Fawcett's church, and joined the group that met separately. He didn't get expelled and instead got some decent GCSEs, and went on to do A Levels. Fawcett helped him to apply to university and get a loan, and he actually got in, and managed to get a 2:1 in Politics. Then he went straight to work for Fawcett, who was no longer a vicar, but still leading the Lancashire Christian-First Family group, and running a think tank lobby group.

Now he's helping Fawcett progress his political career. Stephen Grey owes everything to Fawcett. He is the closest thing to a father that Stephen has. He taught him everything he knows about family and faith, and the importance of morality in society. Fawcett is bold, and brave. He's a maverick, unafraid to do whatever it takes to make the world a better place, and to help make sure children don't go through the pain and trauma that Stephen himself went through. How can that be a bad thing?

And that's why Stephen Grey is saying "No comment" over and over. He hasn't done anything wrong by helping Fawcett ensure those babies were able to stay with their loving new parents, rather than allowing a broken system to send them back to a life of neglect and instability.

They have prepared for this unlikely moment carefully. Fawcett has ensured Stephen will be protected – he doesn't have any online profiles linking him to Fred, which is to help keep him safe. All Fred had asked is that if he's ever questioned, to just say nothing. So, he's doing "No comment" like he's seen on television, and he knows it'll all be okay; it isn't like he's actually been arrested, or anything. This is just an informal chat, and when it's over he will ring Fred, and Fred will help him. Only, he hasn't been able to get hold of Fred in days... he hopes he isn't in any trouble.

Stephen doesn't think he is in any trouble, or not immediately, anyway. He trusts Fred implicitly to make sure he is safe and loved, and sheltered from the terrifying world around him. Except... Stephen Grey's fingerprints are on file from his shoplifting days, so actually, as the little chat progresses, it would seem to Stephen that maybe he *is* in trouble, after all.

It started with a knock on his door. Stephen has been keeping a low profile since Pound had been almost caught, in case there was any connection found to him. When the woman claimed she had seen him with Pound and the police had brought him in, initially he had panicked, but he went over everything Fred had told him last time they spoke. They had picked the meeting spots carefully; there would be no evidence, no CCTV. Just a confused woman with a history of addiction seeing him in the same bar as Pound. They had nothing. He had been let go without charge. Fawcett was sure it would all blow over, but told him to stay hidden, both offline and online. Obviously, their work wasn't totally above board, and you couldn't be too careful. They were forging a new way forward, and that involved risks, subterfuge, and other exciting things.

Besides, no one had listened to Jo before, so why would they start now? Just stay tight-lipped and quiet for a while, Grey had been instructed. Their future projects were on hold indefinitely until it was safe to work again. Fawcett had seemed incredibly relaxed and confident; it was contagious. But regardless, he hadn't picked up a call or replied to a text from Stephen since.

Now, Stephen Grey is beginning to understand why that might be.

Hoppy explains to him that there was a fingerprint found on

an envelope in Pound's house. It matches his fingerprints, which are on record from his shoplifting days. This links him to Pound, when previously he denied knowing him, but more importantly it links him to their next target. A woman whose baby is happily living with a wonderful couple desperate to raise her and give her everything she needs. The birth mother has been riddled with addictions for half her life, and as Fawcett always says – there is a great deal of scientific evidence to back it up, too – she will almost certainly relapse, and then her baby will be bounced around foster families, missing her chance of a normal, stable, happy life.

But as Hoppy and Payne explain this woman's journey to sobriety: her apprenticeship as a sous chef in a local bistro, her attendance at AA meetings, and her newfound religion and role in the church choir, Stephen Grey starts to get an uncomfortable feeling. She sounds like the sort of person Fawcett would usually help. Since they started their project to unite children with their – as Fawcett put it – ideal families, saving them from a life of abuse and trauma and neglect, occasionally he has worried about whether they might get it wrong, but he hates to question Fawcett and whenever he has gingerly asked, Fawcett has been quite angry. Stephen believes in the project, he truly does, but he also believes in redemption and forgiveness.

'It's only yours and Pound's fingerprints on the envelope, and only Pound's on the documents inside. So either you are working alone, or whoever gave you this envelope has been very careful to protect themselves, but not quite so protective of you,' DI Payne says, gently. Almost kindly.

Fawcett never met or spoke to Pound, that was Stephen's job. Fawcett procured the files and handed them over to Stephen to deliver to Pound, having arranged his extraordinarily well-paid employment via a coke-fuelled business associate.

Stephen handled the payments to Pound, and any other communication. 'Do I need a solicitor? Is this still just a little chat?' he asks.

'Perhaps you do, actually, Stephen,' says DI Payne, 'because it would appear that we may be able to make a strong case that suggests you handed over an envelope instructing someone to harm a young woman, and that you were acting alone in this.'

Stephen Grey owes everything to Fawcett, and even if Fawcett has got it wrong this time, at least they didn't go ahead with it. The other women, though... the babies are better off now, thanks to them, aren't they? Fawcett is only doing what is necessary to save the children. Life isn't always simple; he has taught Stephen that. Sometimes you have to break a few eggs, as they say. He can't let Fawcett down now, it would ruin him, and it would break his heart. But Stephen Grey is frightened. Will he go to prison, lose everything he has worked for? Will Fawcett abandon him then? He might have to. A tear escapes from the corner of his eye.

'Before you call your solicitor, may I show you just a couple more things? You don't need to say a word,' says DI Payne.

Stephen nods, and Hoppy spreads out some printouts and photographs.

'This is Jo, Deb, and Kaye,' says Hoppy, 'but we think you already know that.' Stephen Grey stays still and silent in his uncomfortable plastic chair. 'I'm going to share their stories, if that's okay with you, Stephen?' Hoppy says.

Stephen nods, another tear escaping, embarrassing him. His heart is beating too fast, his stomach is churning. He may need to use the bathroom.

'The thing is,' DI Payne says, once Hoppy has finished telling Stephen Grey the truth about Jo, Deb, and Kaye, and has passed him a tissue, 'we don't think you did act alone. It could be, Stephen, that you didn't even know what was in the envelopes, not in any detail. You're a PA, and PAs assist with correspondence, run errands... and so we might be inclined to believe you, if you were to tell us someone else was pulling the strings, manipulating you.'

Stephen Grey is shaking; he doesn't know what to do or what to think. Everything he has just heard is absolutely at odds with the stories that Fawcett has told him. Where is the truth? He can't see it; he can't grasp it. He loves Fawcett, he doesn't want this new story to be true. The police are lying. They must be. But why?

'Here's what we think, Stephen. We think that someone with a very warped view of right and wrong has coerced you into behaviours that do not come naturally to you. You seem like a nice person. A good person. We think this person has his own agenda, one in which he seeks to sabotage single mothers with troubled backgrounds to further his own misogynistic, hateful worldview. With yours and Pound's help, he has hurt these women, torn families apart, and we suspect, become richer. I believe you have been tricked into believing you are helping people, but you have been set up to take the fall should you get caught. We don't believe a good person, with a true desire to change the world for the better, would do something like that to someone they really love.'

Stephen Grey drops his head to the table, his hands on his hair, tugging a little.

'If you give us this person, if you help us to locate Pound, then you might find your role in all this mess is greatly reduced,' says Payne.

'Would you like us to call the duty solicitor now, Stephen?' asks Hoppy. 'And perhaps you'd like to make a phone call?' They still hope he won't call Fawcett before they have a chance to get to him. If he chooses to make a call, they may have to swoop in and arrest Fawcett before they're ready, before they have any real evidence, otherwise he'll disappear before the pips indicate that Stephen's phone call is coming to an end.

'No,' says Stephen, quietly. Those three women have made mistakes, but they have turned their lives around, just like he has. Why aren't they applauding them, supporting them, inviting them to join the group, instead of ensuring they fail, and sabotaging them? Why is he the only one linked to Pound and the files? Why isn't Fawcett helping him more? He abandoned him as soon as the police first questioned him. Would he even answer if he called him now, from the station, like any young man in trouble might phone his dad?

Which story does he believe now? The three women, the two police officers, the sickness in his belly? Or the father figure who has transformed his life so remarkably? The father figure who let him become vulnerable to arrest and told him, in no uncertain terms, should the worst ever happen, to never mention Fawcett's name, so that he could continue their good work, unimpeded. They must all always do what they can for the greater good.

Stephen Grey loves Frederick Fawcett, and he definitely owes him a lot. But maybe not everything. And Stephen Grey can see these recent photos of the three women in front of them; he has heard their stories. A mature student who's dedicated to sports, a future nurse with dreams of making her little girl proud, two of them had bravely helped the other escape from grave danger. And that had been something that had done more than make Stephen feel sick. He'd actually vomited when he realised what the message he had passed on to Pound about Jo had really meant. Now, hearing all the evidence together, the women's lives laid out in front of him, remembering the sordid details of everything they had done – that he had excused as necessary, for the children's futures, he is feeling very strange indeed.

'Stephen?' DI Payne prompts. 'Shall we call the duty solicitor, or do you have your own legal representative to call?'

'We told Pound to make it look like an overdose,' Stephen says, looking down at his hands, resting on the table between him and the officers.

'What?' says Hoppy.

'Jo, the girl in his garage. Once interest had died down, he said it would be best if Jo met her fate sooner rather than later. That she'd be found in an alleyway one day, like everyone always predicted, and this way her family would be at peace, and so would she.'

'Who said that?' Payne asks, knowing the answer, hoping it comes.

'Fred. Frederick... Fawcett,' replies Stephen, a sob escaping his mouth.

'It is your right to a solicitor,' begins Hoppy once again, but Stephen suddenly sits up straight.

'No. I don't need a solicitor or a phone call. I'll tell you everything,' he says.

FORTY

Wanda has insisted on rearranging the furniture in the drawing room so that they are all sitting in a circle, much to Lydia's annoyance. Lydia draws the line at holding hands. She's upset enough as it is about the lies and hidden women in her house, without taking part in some sort of inappropriate hippy nonsense. Wanda has made tea, her years as a social worker giving her an unmatched ability to find a kettle, cups and teabags in under five minutes, even in a grand hall. Fabien, Mila, Lydia, Susannah, along with Jo, Deb, and Kaye make up the trusted circle. Elodie and Anna have decided to leave them to it. Chris-Whatsit and Producer Amy have reluctantly agreed to stop filming for the day, packed up and left, with footage Lydia is sure will ruin her. She and Susannah are sticking to very large gin and tonics. Susannah suspects the footage will put a swift end to her political career, too.

'I would have agreed to let these poor young women stay here,' Lydia lies, quite convincingly, as she sniffs, and looks hurt in Mila and Fabien's direction. 'There was no need for all this sneaking around.'

'I must concur; transparency would have been more conducive to teamwork,' says Hoppy, also looking meaningfully at Mila and Fabien, irritated that yet again they have consistently behaved as if he and his superiors cannot be trusted to tread carefully.

'I think the fact that they were almost shot on sight by Lydia, and had all been previously dismissed by the police, who seemed more interested in Pound's stash of Class A drugs than their experiences, justifies our decision to keep some things under the radar,' says Mila.

'Don't be so dramatic,' Lydia says, her drink clinking as she gesticulates, 'the gun wasn't loaded.'

'We thought they were squatters,' adds Susannah.

'We were in fear for our lives,' Lydia clarifies, taking a sip.

'And *we* were just following the evidence,' Hoppy explains. 'We always knew there was likely to be more to it, but as I said, we can only go where the facts take us.'

Jo, Deb, and Kaye raise their eyebrows, though they are not surprised at the judgements and cynicism being thrown their way.

Fabien, ever the peacekeeper, and in fear of another clash between Mila and Lydia, intervenes. 'Quite right, we are terribly sorry for not being completely honest, but we were dealing with very sensitive information and didn't want to put anyone in an awkward position. How about we go over everything that we have again? Hmmm?'

Lydia folds her arms, and Susannah, next to her, pats her hand in solidarity. Why these young people have to get themselves mixed up in such dreadful situations, she doesn't understand. What is wrong with sticking to new swing sets for the playground, if they want to help children and young mothers? She is also shocked that Fawcett has turned out to be quite the villain that Elodie, Anna, and Mila had insisted all along... but of course, Susannah couldn't have possibly known, as she wasn't party to all the facts, as usual.

A rapid yet thorough verbal debrief from Hoppy had given Mila and Fabien the missing piece of the puzzle. Stephen Grey has confessed everything he knows – which is a lot – placing Fawcett front and centre of the entire operation. Frederick Fawcett groomed Stephen from a young age, to believe anything he said, and to do anything he asked. As the police had gone over the women's true stories and the devasting impact of what Fawcett had really done, the image had slowly shattered for Stephen Grey and, combined with his fear of going to prison for a long time, this had compelled him to tell the whole truth.

Fawcett had a long-term goal, and for a long time, Stephen Grey had believed it was a beautiful ambition. His aim was to rid the country of single parents, or parents with a history of what he called "unsavoury behaviours", thereby ensuring no child suffers as Fawcett did as a child, or as Stephen Grey did, too. He told Stephen they were a catalyst for change, and were simply speeding up the inevitable; the women relapsing to their old ways. The benefit to their method was the child being removed as early as possible into their forever homes with their ideal parents, giving them the best possible chance of avoiding upheaval and emotional trauma.

When Fawcett suggested that Jo's demise needed to go a step further, that she might need to overdose in Pound's garage, in case she were to cause alarm and hinder the whole programme, Stephen had started to find it increasingly difficult to sleep. Jo was selfish, Fawcett had said, and was putting her own needs above the welfare of her baby girl and the opportunity they had to save so many children. Could they allow one woman on a mission to destroy their far greater goal?

It always came down to working for the greater good, doing God's work. Saving the children.

Jo's baby didn't need saving though, nor did Kaye's, or Deb's. Stephen had only realised that in the police interview room earlier that day. But Fawcett believed that social services was too slack on birth parents, that the ones who successfully won their family court hearings were going to ultimately fail their children anyway, and that more permanent interventions were needed.

Fawcett had said it was understandable that many of the people he talked to were desperate for a newborn child, whereas most of the children in need of adoption were older. These people wanted the full experience of parenthood, and they believed that a newborn would be without the issues that a child who had experienced months or years of bad parenting might come with. Didn't these selfless, loving couples deserve the best start with their new baby, just as the baby deserved good, traditional, loving parents?

Together, they would fix the wrongs of their childhoods and build better futures for the next generation of children born to bad mothers. Fawcett had a lofty vocation, in his mind. Over time, more and more evidence would build up demonstrating the benefits of early intervention, helped by the case studies he and his associates were building, one by one. Three already this year! Fawcett had told Stephen Grey they should be proud of the difference they were making. Combined with his ever-growing popularity and influence, Fawcett was going to transform the country, starting in Lancashire, before expanding his work nationally.

Except, rather than continuing Fawcett's early work, providing safe spaces for children in the care system, he had decided to play God, decide which mothers were unfit, and engineer their fate so that they would be ripped apart from their child regardless of the actual facts of their circumstances. Because Fawcett doesn't believe women like that can ever change. His mother never did. Nor did Stephen's.

Fawcett promised Stephen that he would always protect him. He reassured him that he would never break his promises, or let him down. But he had. He had left Stephen wide open to take the blame for his masterplan, and he thought Stephen was pathetic enough, *gullible* enough, to let him. Stephen realises that isn't love, or respect, and it certainly isn't protection. Fawcett has broken his promises, Fawcett is a liar. And he lied about the women, how well they were doing. Stephen Grey has been lied to a lot in his life. When his mother promised things would change, that she would fetch him and bring him home. Stephen loathes liars, and that's why, in the end, when he started talking to Hoppy and Payne, he couldn't stop.

He has told them every detail, and has given them copies of the files that he has for each woman. He doesn't know where Pound is, but has agreed to try and tempt him out, when the time is right. For now, they can't risk alerting Fawcett to their evidence, in case he disappears. Stephen Grey is in witness protection, mainly to ensure he doesn't get cold feet and pre-warn Fawcett. The young man is damaged, has been let down, and he had two panic attacks during his confession. He doesn't want to go to prison, but he does want to be punished. He is confused, traumatised, and very sorry. Payne and Hoppy have promised they will see what they can do to help him longer-term, if he continues to cooperate.

Hoppy takes a sip of tea, rather enjoying his big reveal moment in Farlington Hall. 'With your evidence of the parents all paying Fawcett large sums of money, plus his background interview you found online, which gives clear motive, and the shocking insights you recorded earlier today when he talked about his beliefs, plus Stephen Grey's testimony, Jo's witness statement, the envelope with fingerprints found in Pound's house detailing their next target, as well as the CCTV showing him following Jo over several weeks, we finally have enough to build a case.'

'Finally,' mutters Mila, with a characteristic roll of her eyes.

Ignoring her, or not noticing, rather in his element, Hoppy continues. 'We can get a warrant for his home, office, files, and bank and business accounts now, and that will help um, gloss over, shall we say, some of the information collected in a less official capacity.'

'Oh God,' Wanda says, head in her hands, 'oh God, oh God, oh God. Jo, I'm so sorry I didn't believe you, and Deb, and Kaye – you poor souls. I don't know how this could have happened. How was he doing it – matching the children with the adoptive parents? Playing such a robust system? The parents! They seemed so nice. So honest. They didn't know, did they?'

Hoppy replies, 'Stephen never spoke to the parents, and isn't sure how much they knew, or know. Though our conversation with Stephen leads us to believe that they certainly knew they were paying to be fast-tracked to match with a newborn in the system, and that someone would guarantee that the baby was not returned to the birth mother, by manipulating or influencing the decision makers.'

'They knew,' Jo says through gritted teeth, 'and you should have known too,' she spits at Wanda, who winces.

'Do we think that the woman you saw Fawcett with was another potential client, or adoptive *"mother"*?' asks Kaye.

'Doubt it,' says Mila. 'Surely Fawcett wouldn't countenance a meeting without her husband present.'

'True that,' says Deb.

Fabien scrolls to the photo he got of Fawcett and the woman entering the club earlier that day, and holds it up. 'It's a little blurry,' he says, 'sorry. She was dressed professionally, similar age to him. We thought maybe a girlfriend, or business associate. She didn't stay long. Her name was Julia, I think.'

'Let me see that,' says Wanda, jumping up from her chair, and rushing over to Fabien across the circle. She takes the phone straight out of his hand, and puts it close to her face, adjusting her glasses and frowning. She gasps. 'It *is* Julia. Julia Bainbridge. She's the Director of Children's Social Care.'

FORTY-ONE

Round tables with stiff white table clothes are adorned with elaborate centrepieces. Balloons and flower sculptures fill the corners, with lighting to rival *Britain's Got Talent*. The stage is set with a podium, and tasteful yet nondescript music plays in the background. In one corner is an enormous table cluttered with money can't buy auction prizes. The actual football boot thrown at David Beckham, signed by Alex Ferguson himself. A private tour of the House of Lords followed by dinner and drinks on the terrace with Lord Fabien Knutsworth, no less. Their table at Fawcett's charity ball had been more than guaranteed.

When Wanda had recognised her boss with Fawcett in the photograph on Fabien's phone, they finally understood not only why, but *how*, Fawcett was getting away with it. 'I *knew* she was too hands on, too quick to refuse second chances. Her interest in the women was highly unusual at her level,' Wanda had told them, trying to keep her composure, wondering how she didn't see what was going on right underneath her nose, and why she hadn't fought harder for Jo – continued to believe in her, even when every shred of evidence pointed otherwise.

Mila and Fabien have tried to reassure her that she couldn't have done anything differently. The system was well and truly played by several very devious individuals, and nobody could have possibly known the truth, not until now. The whole Knutsworth family has seen time and time again how diligent, but most of all, how passionate and caring, Wanda is. And now Wanda is going to help put things right.

Fawcett's operation is slick, and with the Director of Children's Social Care obviously playing a role in identifying the "right" babies and birth mothers, and finding ways to fast-track the adoptive parents, someone in Wanda's position could never have known. She only deals with her own cases, she doesn't oversee every application, and back when she was Jo's social worker she only worked with birth families. Now, she only works with potential adopters. With social workers overstretched and bogged down in day-to-day work, Julia had been able to easily cover her tracks under the guise of mucking in. The way Fawcett had the women framed, especially Jo, who was caught red-handed and convicted in court, was impossible to deny or argue against.

As everyone else had comforted Wanda, Jo's face had started to soften. She could hear what they were saying and although she wasn't ready for Wanda to not be at fault, something inside her was shifting. Wanda explained tearfully that she had been so devastated after Jo's conviction, she'd had to change roles as she could no longer believe herself capable of helping the women she was employed to support.

Wanda had said she would do everything she could to ensure the children were reunited with their birth mothers quickly, and with all the settling-in support they all needed. It was then that Jo had started to cry, and Wanda had gone to her. She had allowed her old social worker, her long-time champion, to hold her. She still smelled of patchouli oil. They had hatched the plan there and then, and it had been immediately and miraculously signed off by Payne.

DI Payne is waiting outside the fundraising event in the car with PC Hoppy, until it starts, and the audience is captivated. They need to take Fawcett by surprise; they want to get to him at the exact same time as they get to Julia and the adoptive parents who illegally paid to get what they wanted no matter the human cost, and maybe had even been privy to the details – time will tell. Julia, it has transpired, is a long-standing member of Fawcett's church group and, according to a number of Wanda's colleagues who have been called one by one, has worked tirelessly to get a role in Children's Services, and finally had done so with the help of a number of good words through Fawcett's political network.

So, here they are, all dressed up in black tie and evening gowns, some old, many borrowed, all uncomfortable. Fabien, Mila, Jo, Deb, and Kaye are sitting at the table for eight with Lydia, Susannah, and Susannah's husband, Martin. They all know what is coming, and are looking forward to a very exciting and original evening. Well, Lydia and Susanah are, at any rate. Mila, Fabien, and the three women are a little more nervous. And Martin doesn't like a scene, and tried to get out of attending, but as the Mayor's husband he was never off the hook these days.

'Hello! Hello, old chap!' Gordan says, as he beelines for Fabien. Kaye tries to look neutral. Is he her baby's adoptive father?

Fabien rises to greet him, and kisses his wife's cheeks one by one. Introductions are made, with Jo, Kaye, and Deb being introduced as working with the charity. Lydia detracts attention with Susannah's help by charming the couples as they all shuffle in towards their new aristocratic friends, lapping up the attention they notice they are getting from the other tables around them. Everyone here is wealthy, well-connected, or both, and all are fans of making friends with lords and ladies. It is, they feel, absolutely where they belong in life.

A microphone is tapped, and a disembodied voice welcomes Mr Frederick Fawcett to the stage to formally open the fundraiser before dinner is served. An order of events sits at every place setting between shining silver cutlery: three forks, three knives, a side plate, butter plate, and a napkin the size of a tablecloth. Glistening wine glasses and water glasses finish off each setting. Mila is only glad they plan to start before dinner, as she doesn't think she can stomach what is listed tonight, preferring simple food, usually. The folded white card with gold embossed lettering tells them that following a welcome address by Frederick Fawcett, dinner will be served. After that will be the auction to raise funds for Fawcett's campaign, followed by entertainment and dancing.

But they aren't going to get that far. Fabien texts Hoppy to let him know Fawcett is on the stage, and Mila presses play on her phone. She has linked it to the big screens on the stage, which is not difficult if you know how, and is using a portable speaker with really high volume. As Fawcett opens his mouth to begin, his voice is drowned out by the sound of Jo's, as her face fills the two screens either side of him. 'My name is Jo and this man stole my baby,' her recording begins. Jo's face on screen morphs into Deb's. 'My name is Deb and this man stole my baby,' she says, before her face morphs into Kaye's. 'My name is Kaye and this man stole my baby.'

'What is this?' Fawcett yells. 'Turn it off. I don't know who these women are! I haven't stolen any babies! Preposterous! Is this a joke? Is it the LGBTQ+ lunatics again?'

Fabien and Mila are by the stage, telling the AV guy in no uncertain terms to leave the films playing, and not to touch the plug. Fabien thinks about trying to keep hold of the man, but he is quite burly, so he slips him two fifty-pound notes instead, which does the trick. Lydia and Susannah are by the entrance doors, which they have locked, as it is predicted the adoptive parents may decide to leave early when they realise what is going on. Jo, Deb, and Kaye walk up the steps and stand next to Fawcett on the stage as the recordings continue to flash through their stories, one small revelation at a time.

Someone from Fawcett's team runs up to the stage to help him down, but they are intercepted by Hoppy and Payne, who flash their IDs, and guard the stage. Fawcett is frozen in the centre, the women whose lives he tried to ruin are flanking him. Mila strides up the steps and relieves him of the microphone.

She hits a button on her phone, the screens go black, and a new voice begins. 'Recognise this voice?' Mila asks Fawcett, as the recording starts to play. It is Stephen Grey. 'Frederick Fawcett paid me to instruct a known criminal to frame three women so that their children would be taken from them. This man stole these women's babies.'

Fawcett gasps, and there is a kerfuffle at the back of the grand room, as Gordan and Lucinda, Theodore and Cassandra, and Maximilian and Harriet all try to leave, but are stopped by the team of police officers that Hoppy and Payne have brought along.

'We didn't know! We are victims!' shouts Theodore.

'You can't take my baby back!' wails Cassandra.

And Jo, Deb, and Kaye don't believe for a second that they didn't know, but they still physically feel the pain, the wrench of these parents, who will now have to go through the very thing they caused them to go through. It gives none of the three women any pleasure at all. But they'll do anything to have their babies home in their arms, and that includes allowing themselves to forget the pain the adoptive parents will probably always feel.

Hoppy does the honours, cuffing Fawcett as he reads him his rights, and explains the very long list of crimes that he is being arrested for, much to the shock of the room full of political donors in black tie. The parents are cuffed, as is Julia the Director of Children's Social Care. Mila puts the film of the women back on, but now it is photos of them with their babies when they were born, and had visitation rights. Wanda's voice comes on in the background, singing their praises, and quoting from their files: the progress they had made, the dedication and love they each had for their baby. The audience is spellbound as Fawcett, Julia, and the adoptive parents are led away and Jo, Deb, and Kaye embrace. Mila starts to applaud the three brave women, and soon the audience is doing the same.

The audience rises to its feet, giving the courageous women on stage a standing ovation. The three women hold hands and gesture at Mila and Fabien to join them. They do, and together, they dare to take a small bow. Lydia and Susannah dab away their tears of pride, overwhelmed that Mila has done it again, with a little help from her friends.

FORTY-TWO

It's late March, and the weather is slowly improving. The nights are getting lighter, and it can be quite pleasant to sit outside in the garden at Farlington Hall. Mila and Fabien are playing Uno with Konstantine and Karlie under the last of the day's spring sunshine. They have fleeces on, and blankets over their knees, and Fabien has lit the fire pit. Earlier, they had been to the new swings in the playground with the whole gang: Jo, Deb, and Kaye, and their three beautiful babies.

With Wanda's help and assurances, Jo had quickly been reunited with baby Sarah, Kaye with Bobby, and Deb with Jacob. The babies soon adapted to being back in their mother's arms, but the women were each assigned a counsellor and specialist support from their own social worker to ensure the babies settled in, and to limit any long-term emotional issues caused by the strain and upheaval. Rob eventually gave up trying to make contact with Jo, and it seems life is pretty normal and uneventful, which is just what she has always dreamed of.

Fawcett denies everything, and so a trial date has been set. He still believes he in invincible, and he is trying to throw poor

Stephen Grey under a bus. The only flaw in this plan is that Stephen Grey managed to lure a boastful text message out of Pound, giving away his location. He is now in a Spanish police cell waiting to be extradited. And Pound is willing to testify to the fact that Stephen Grey *was* working for Fawcett, and knew next to nothing about the details of their plans, in exchange for a more lenient sentence.

Stephen Grey had been very surprised that Pound even knew about Fawcett, as he was sure he had been as good as his word and not once mentioned Fawcett to Pound, but after a little chat with Hoppy, Pound was convinced he had been directly involved with Fawcett on a number of occasions.

Pound refuted Grey's claim that he was going to overdose Jo. He claimed that despite Grey's text message, he had planned to let Jo go as soon as he could, and would never have killed her – he was just biding his time until it was safe to do so without repercussions. 'I gave her my chocolate Hobnobs, didn't I? I was nice to her,' he had argued, unconvincingly. But he agreed to help nail Fawcett if they'd drop the conspiracy to murder charge against him. There wasn't much they could do about the drugs running and abduction, so he was still going to go away for quite some time.

The fly on the wall documentary had not gone quite as Lydia had planned, but it had been repackaged as a true crime documentary, and aired to critical acclaim, with a focus on the Last Chance Cooperative, and how the Knutsworth family had used their resources and estate to help solve these heinous crimes and reunite these mothers with their beautiful babies. With some persuasion, Chris-Whatsit had edited out much of the scene in which Lydia is brandishing a rifle and Susannah a poker, so, for now, their reputations remain intact, and the family is very much in favour. Even Gareth Davies from the

Farlington Gazette has covered the recent events with a positive spin. They've also earned a healthy amount in royalties, which they've put towards the upkeep of the hall – and helping the three women to find their feet.

'Uno!' shouts Konstantine, who has won again.

'Damn you!' says Fabien, lifting him up, and tickling him while he squirms and squeals.

'He always wins, it's not fair,' Karlie pouts, coming in for a cuddle with her aunty Mila, who gives her a squeeze.

'We're doing okay, aren't we?' says Fabien, smiling at Mila.

Mila returns the smile. 'Oh, I think we are doing more than okay.'

'Fabien! Mila!' shouts Elodie, as she and Anna run towards them up the driveway, Wanda trying to keep up with a fast walk behind them.

'Gosh, I thought their meeting was hours ago,' says Fabien, waving at his sister as she reaches them, Anna at her side, both out of breath. While they pant for a moment, collapsing into the spare chairs, Wanda makes it over to the table. Wanda is the new Director of Children's Social Care, yet still insists on being Elodie and Anna's personal social worker so that she can oversee their adoption application. She started with them on their journey, and she can't give up on them until they become the family they dream of being.

'We've been approved, and we have a match!' Elodie yells, holding tight to Anna's hand.

'Two little boys, brothers, two and three. And they're perfect,' says Anna. 'Where's Lydia? We couldn't wait to tell all of you! We meant to wait until everyone was here.'

'I'm sorry, I couldn't keep it in!' says Elodie.

'That's so wonderful!' Fabien says.

'It's perfect,' Mila says, as they all embrace each other and

Wanda. They break apart to see Lydia coming down the entrance steps from the hall towards the table where they sit, eager to find out what the commotion is about.

'Oh, Mummy!' shouts Elodie. 'Just wait until you hear our news! We're going to have our family!'

22 July 2025

Happy first birthday, Sarah! Today has been perfect, just like you. Earlier, I took a photograph of you with your favourite teddy, the one with the yellow bow tie, surrounded by all your presents. Granny and Grandad had huge proud smiles – things are so different now. The girls and their kids were here too, a gorgeous mess of my favourite people on the carpet, screwed up wrapping paper and ribbon everywhere. I bought the bear for you when you were born and he was ten times the size of you. I dreamt of the day you'd be here with me and that daft, enormous cuddly toy. Now you're half his size and these days go so fast, and I keep on writing to you so I don't forget a single moment. I'm going to frame that photo, just like all the others, and one day we'll run out of wall space and I'll get us a bigger house, just you, me, and our big bear with the yellow bow tie.

THE END

ALSO BY LISA NICHOLAS

Sister, Liar, Suspect, Sleuth

When Mila's sister is murdered, her life is shattered.
Framed for the crime, with her homeland at war and her young niece
and nephew missing, Mila flees to an English village. But her presence
stirs prejudice, gossip and hidden tensions...

BUY NOW

ACKNOWLEDGEMENTS

Thank you to everyone in the amazing team at Bloodhound Books. And most special thanks to Betsy Revley for taking a chance on me and my stories, Rachel Tryer for bringing the magical editorial combination of rigorous attention to detail and genuine care for my characters and their crazy antics, to Tara Lyons for always making sure everything comes together perfectly, and to Hannah Deuce and Lexi Curtis for their hard work in bringing my books into the world through their marketing prowess. I feel very lucky to be part of the Bloodhound gang.

And to my lovely friend Rebecca Robinson – thank you for taking the time to sensitivity-check my ideas around how to write about adoption. I have tried to be considerate of the complexities and powerful emotions involved while writing about some highly unusual events in the plot.

Huge thanks to my writing pals! Kirstie Pelling and Danielle Owen-Jones – thanks for being my cheerleaders and for all the sage advice. Thanks to my Lancaster University Creative Writing MA gang – Claire Gray, Suzi Nelson, Lara Hurley, Geoff Cox, and Phil Murray for all your feedback and encouragement.

A heartfelt thanks to my wonderful family. To Mum and Dad for reading my work and telling me it's brilliant, whatever state it is at the time, and for always believing in me. Thank you Cade and Ellie for being the best step-kids anyone could hope for. And finally, the biggest, most loving thank you of all to Steve for everything. It is only with your support and love that I get to live out my writing dreams.

ABOUT THE AUTHOR

Lisa Nicholas lives with her husband Steve and two big, daft dogs in a rural hamlet in Lancashire. Other than curling up in front of the fire with a good book, she enjoys long walks, yoga, and travelling to warmer climates.

A NOTE FROM THE PUBLISHER

Thank you for reading this book. If you enjoyed it please do consider leaving a review on Amazon to help others find it too.

We hate typos. All of our books have been rigorously edited and proofread, but sometimes mistakes do slip through. If you have spotted a typo, please do let us know and we can get it amended within hours.

info@bloodhoundbooks.com